Gobah & the Killer Healers

———

The Rainbow's End

Bob G. Kisiki

Published by Cook Communication
6086 Dunes Drive
Sanford, NC 27332

ISBN 978-0-557-08027-4

www.author-me.com

Not affiliated with Cook Communication Ministries

Table of Contents

Gobah and the Giant Killers

Gobah & the Killer Healers

Bob G. Kisiki

ONE

KIDNAPPED

Gobah and Marla were inseparable. Gobah was fourteen, and Marla was two years younger, but as it is said that girls grow much faster than boys, many people thought the two children twins. The belief was even helped more by the keen resemblance the children bore to their father, Mzee Wadua. Mzee Wadua was very proud and fond of his two children, for they were his only biological children, not counting Sama, the boy his wife came with in the womb, when they married. Sama was now Gobah's senior. He lived with his aunt in Buwenge.

Mzee Wadua's family lived in Idudi, a village covering three giant hills in Butembe County. Butembe is very well known for its hills, many of which carry horrifying stories on their backs. The three hills on which Idudi lies, however, are harmless ones, and people had always lived there in unprecedented harmony and tranquillity. It was only when you left the valley on the western side of Idudi that you ascended one of the most deadly of the Butembe hills. It smoked on the top, like a constant bush fire was always going, and it was said that no one who ventured to go up and see what caused the smoke ever returned. Some people with modern and others with Christian tendencies denied these stories, but not even they had volunteered to go up and verify what the cause of the fireless smoke could be.

Our story, however, is not about Idudi, but about Gobah and his sister Marla. These two children loved each other so much, where Marla was, Gobah was, too, and if one saw Gobah approach, one just had to wait awhile, and Marla, too would approach. And then people would say, 'How are you, the twins of Mzee Wadua?' and the supposed twins would beam at each other, beam at the Idudi people, and answer that they were fine, thank you. They were the darlings of the three hills, because not a person who lived in Idudi did not know the Wadua family, especially this pair of miraculous children, Gobah and Marla.

Marla was a particularly gorgeous child. At twelve, she had already started attracting peeping eyes and whispered remarks, yet she was only in Primary Seven. And who could blame anybody? She had these big eyes that were like two miniature mature moons, and a smile that made people crazy with love for her. Many Butembe people believe that a great woman must have big behinds, and if anyone had big behinds, Marla did. So what feature of beauty was lacking in this girl?

Which could be why Gobah was so fond of his sister that he did not want her out of his sight. They loved taking distant walks together during their holidays, going as far as the valley below their hill, and sometimes beyond.

They were taking one such walk one day, when the sun went down on them. They were very far away from home, and Marla started to panic. 'We'll be fine, Marla dear,' her brother comforted her.

'I know. I just don't trust the dark, that's all. Times are changing, Gobah.'

They hastened their steps back toward home. They had not gone very far from where they turned back toward home when car headlamps hit them on their backs, and on the road ahead of them. Taking his sister's hand, Gobah drew her away and they stepped off the road. The car slowed down, however, and stopped by their side. A young lady was at the wheel, and another woman, more advanced in age, occupied the co-driver's seat.

'Are you going far dear twins?' the elderly lady said with a king-size smile.

'Yes, thank you,' Marla said, as she disengaged her hand from Gobah's grip. Gobah, however, was hesitant. A red light flicked on in his mind.

'No, Marla, come-,' he was saying, but the back door was already opened, and Marla was stepping inside.

'Marla! Marla! Come out!' Gobah screamed, alerting the two ladies to his being more informed than they had suspected. Acting fast, the old lady opened her bag, removed a small bottle, pressed a lever on it, and sprayed some sort of perfume all over Marla's face, as the young woman pulled away at top speed.

'Stoooop! Stop them! Thieves! They've stolen my sister! Maaarla!' all Gobah got in response was a cloud of dust, and echoes to his voice. The darkness around the hills had intensified.

Gobah practically ran all the way back home, a distance of over five kilometres. He ran, and did not know that he ran. He ran so much, when he got home; somehow, he just collapsed before his bewildered parents and passed out.

Picture, then, the panic and confusion that followed, when Mzee Wadua and his wife received this sight. First, they had been anxious about their children. It was already dark and they were still out. They had always told Gobah not to stay out late with his sister, but the children loved each other so much, anything that let them be together, alone, they would do, with little care. Now what had happened? Where was Marla?

That was the big question: where was Marla?

They called out Gobah's name. No response. They shook him like an inanimate thing. No reaction. They poured cold water on him, and he revived, but he could say nothing intelligible, except an absurdly rhapsodic repetition of Marla's name. He would call Marla, laugh without mirth, cry, and keep on calling Marla, becoming more frantic by the minute. Time was running out.

Mrs Wadua was ecstatic, to say the very least. She was just holding back, but her entire system wanted to scream, to call out to Marla. So when she saw her husband's panic also reach to the skin, she gave in. She let out a wail that brought in not just the neighbours, but also other Idudi residents, to find out what had befallen the Wadua family.

There was a big crowd in Mzee Wadua's compound. Some people came with torches, some with clubs, while others came in with whatever they were eating still in their hands. Everybody was talking at the top of his or her voice, asking the nearest person what had gone wrong. Was someone dead? Was it a robbery? There was a small rumour beginning to sneak around, that Mzee wadua had beaten his wife. Else, why was she crying?

The men of the hill pushed their way through the clusters of women and children, and got the true story from Mzee Wadua himself: his girl Marla, the beautiful Marla of the hill, was missing!

The search party was formed in a flash. Dividing themselves out into groups to cover the entire hill, old and young men, plus a few daring women set out to look for Marla. Marla, the favourite of beholders on the hill. They had to help the Wadua family in their time of great need.

By the time the search party left, Gobah was in a high fever. The delirium had subsided, but he had developed such a temperature, Mrs Wadua's crying now took on a new facet. She was convinced that she was losing her two children the same day.

'Somebody help run to Nurse's house,' Mrs Wadua pleaded to the few people who still lingered about. This Nurse was actually not a nurse. She was an elderly woman who had once worked in a hospital, far away in Buwenge, for well over twenty years, and had now retired. No one knew for certain what her work had been, but it sure hadn't been a professional job. Some suspected (and whispered, of course), that she had been a cook, while some said she used to clean patients'

4

wounds before real doctors could dress and treat them. Whatever she had done, however, had lent her some knowledge on essential drugs, and how to dispense them, and to inject the injectibles. Now she was the nurse of the village, and that's how she had got her name, Nurse, from the villagers. Nurse.

Someone did run to Nurse's house. She had just returned from treating a man who had been bitten by a snake, when the young boy entered her compound, looking like he had just encountered a leopard.

'Nurse, Mrs Wadua's son… she wants you,' the boy panted.

'Mrs Wadua's son, she wants me? Make some bit of sense, child!'

'Her son is ill. Please rush over.'

In a tick,' she said, dashing into the house post-haste.

'What is he- but you wouldn't know,' Nurse mused.

'What?'

'His disease.'

'Complicated. His sister was maybe stolen, he came home running, and then the fever grabbed him,' the boy explained, piecing together what he'd heard the crowd say.

Nurse knew what to take. Take a bottle of PPF, some sedatives and tranquilisers. And maybe quinine.

When she got to the Wadua home, they had already done their part. They had put water in a *kalai*, an aluminium basin, and it was boiling on the fire. A smaller pan lay by the side, scrubbed to a glitter.

'Where's the boy?' Nurse asked, her frame erect, hands akimbo and eyes opened to full capacity.

'Inside,' everybody around chorused.

Bring him here… no, I'll go in. Somebody please bring in the water.'

The water and the pan were taken in by the same boy who had gone to collect Nurse. Once in the room, she dropped the syringe and needle into the water for a while, then pulled PPF into the syringe, and emptied it into Gobah's bum. She repeated the process for a second shot. 'This is a high fever,' she explained, as if to justify the second shot. People had always accused her of doing anything to fatten her bill at the end of the day. They likened her to a coffin maker, who was never happy when people were alive and well.

After the injections, Nurse left Mrs Wadua with three packs of quinine tablets, just in case there was another emergency, and they didn't know where she had gone.

Two search parties were back by the time Nurse left the Wadua compound. There was no news of Marla. Slowly by slowly, the other people returned, the last group turning in towards ten o'clock in the night. This group reported some people as having heard a child scream about his sister being stolen, but since no such thing had ever happened in their neighbourhood, they had ignored it as a case of children out playing in the night.

The answer was out, then. Marla had been kidnapped!

TWO

DEAD MEAT

By the next day, Gobah was fully revived, and he managed to give his parents the full account of what had happened. His parents in turn gave it to the villagers who returned that day, to find out if there had been any new developments since the previous night.

'That is yet another kidnap,' one man said.

'How? Nothing like it has happened here before?' another said.

'Not on this hill, but it's been happening,' the first man said. 'The other week they took a big girl from her mother's house. Right from her mother's house, and during the day.'

'How?' a woman wanted to know.

'They had no firewood in the home. The mother asked the girl to pick dry maize cobs, to use to make a fire, as the mother chopped *dodo* for sauce… are you sure you didn't hear this story?'

'Where did this all happen?'

'Huh huh, you tell us!'

'It happened last week, on the hill just after the one after ours. Mambya. Yes, on Mambya hill. Anyhow, the girl was picking old cobs when she was picked. The mother heard her scream, and when she ran over, a man was disappearing in the coffee shamba with a bundle struggling in a sack. The girl has not been discovered, as we talk.'

'Eh, people, now won't we send our girls to do anything away from home?

'Not just girls, by the way. These people take even boys, and I hear sometimes even adult men and women.'

'Take them where?'

'Who knows?'

'Mzee Wadua, you have to report this to the Local Council, and maybe announce on radio.'

'But the LCs were here last night,' Mrs Wadua said through her tears.

'That's not enough, Mama,' a woman said. 'Officially, you have to report, then they can maybe involve the Police.'

Messages were sent to all Local Council levels, up to LC III, and someone was sent to the police at Idudi Trading Centre.

Hardly an hour had elapsed, when the man who had ridden to the police returned. 'They want Gobah and Mzee Wadua.'

'Now for what?'

'Statement.'

Gobah was still weak, and emotionally low. But police is police, and what is more, the family was on the receiving end. Collecting some funds, the villagers got two motor cyclists to take the duo to the police post, where they spent close to a full day giving information about Marla's disappearance, as the police kept calling it.

'But the child didn't disappear,' Mzee Wadua protested. 'She was kidnapped.'

'So where's she now?' an irritated policewoman had barked at him. The old man shook his head sideways and opened his palms in an 'I-don't-know' gesture.

'So why go on so about kidnap, instead of disappearance?'

Mzee Wadua was silent.

At the end of the day, the police had done absolutely nothing besides repeatedly asking Gobah and Mzee Wadua questions. At sundown, they sent them home, with a promise to do their best to help. 'If we need more information fro you, we'll call you again,' the OC had said. Mzee Wadua had a mind to tell the blasted OC not to bother them any more, but he was already tired. Very tired.

On the third day, radio announcements were dispatched, and more feelers of varying natures thrown around beyond the hills, for information regarding Marla.

No information came regarding Marla.

Gobah was devastated. One, he did not heal completely. Every day that dawned brought a new angle to the complications in his health. The temperature fluctuations continued, but now they had been joined by a constant dull headache, followed by unexplainable constipation. It was a strain to Mzee Wadua who, in addition to the initial treatment costs Nurse had taken, had to spend daily to ward off these ills.

Gobah was wasting away in this one week. He was not eating, and he lived in a kind of zombie-like state. He refused to talk to anyone. Even when he was talked to, he responded with a nod, a shake of the head, a wave. He used no words. His parents were very worried, but had nothing to do for the boy.

It was Saturday, a week after Marla had been kidnapped. The police had never come up with any report, neither had anything come of the radio announcements, seeking rewardable information about Marla.

Everybody was painfully but slowly coming to terms with the fact that Marla was gone, probably dead, and there was nothing they could do to alter the fact. Mzee Wadua was a beaten man, and Mrs Wadua lamented and thought about nothing else. As for Gobah, he was beyond what words could describe.

Then that Saturday the Waduas got a strange visitor. It was early in the morning, so nobody can tell the story straight, but Mzee and Mrs Wadua were convinced it was the sound of a big motorcycle. It stopped in the yard, and was there for hardly three full minutes. Then there was a frantic knock on the door. Almost instantaneously, the motorcycle roared off, and there was silence.

Mzee Wadua opened the door. Even before the door was fully open, a mad stench pushed into the house and filled it, shoving Mzee Wadua reeling back. After he regained his mien, Mzee Wadua stepped out. In the middle of the yard was a wet-looking sack of something.

He called to his wife. When Mrs Wadua saw what was in the yard, and was hit by the stench, she needed no telling. The alarm issued from her throat without bidding. She screamed, wailed, alarmed.

In only a matter of minutes, the Wadua compound was swarming with people holding their noses. To many, it was clear what the sack bore. A few brave young men approached the sack, handkerchiefs tied to their noses. The women stood at a distance, and little children were held away. They should not see whatever was in the sack. It was bad for their innocence.

The sack was untied. The dripping, stinking thing was the breast-less, handless and feetless body of Marla. Her private parts, too, were missing.

Mrs Wadua fainted.

It was a mean hour. It was not horrifying, the way you would feel walking through the city the morning after a heavy battle, bodies littered all over the streets and in alleys. It was not grieving; no, not the way it feels to lose someone you love dearly, like a mother or a sibling. It wasn't even scaring, like the feeling we get when gunmen are in our next door neighbour's house, and they have just shot dead someone. The mood that reigned in the Wadua compound that morning was indescribable. It included people who would rather they had died in Marla's stead; people who burned to lay hands on whoever was responsible for this; people who believed with all their hearts that this should have happened anywhere else – anywhere, but in the Waduas' home; people who were just lost, knowing that what had hit Marla could hit again, and should not hit again. All manner of people. It was a mean hour.

As Nurse was collected to attend to Mrs Wadua, and another group of women attended to Gobah, whose friend it was lay in that sack, stinking, mutilated, a number of young men were dispatched to take the news to the organs of the law. You, go to LC1; you to Two and Three, since they're neighbours. You two, go to Police. You, take radio announcements to Idudi Trading Centre. Inform all relatives, friends and in-laws.

Gobah was in utter shock. It was the noise outside that had woken him, and he came out, still struggling to push his hands through his sleeves. He abandoned the shirt, and then he just went... not dead, not... wacko, he just ceased to communicate his presence of mind. He did not weep, he did not speak, he just sat at the door-step and let things happen to him; around him. The women who went to him were therefore trying to elicit some sort of human response, but to no success, at all.

Not all of Gobah's senses were numbed, however. He could see, he could hear, he could smell. Only touch and feeling were dead, temporarily. So as people talked about what had caused Marla's terrible death, he heard them. He heard them talk about child-thieves. He heard them talk about witchcraft, and big houses, factories and

11

other things that need sacrificing for. He heard them say that it must have been the likes of such who had been behind the death of his friend and sister. But even when these things registered in his mind, he did not internalise well enough what he wanted or had to do about it. He did not, yet.

The police and LCs arrived almost at the same time. The police were so armed, you had to wonder if they expected the mutilated and rotten body of Little Marla to riot and cause havoc. They rounded up a few people, took them aside and asked them a fresh torrent of pointless and futile questions, at the end of which they granted permission for Marla's body to be buried. It was then that the body was taken inside the house, rolled up in proper burial clothes, put in a coffin and burial rites arranged for the Late Anna Marla.

THREE

A VOW TO THE DEAD

Mrs Wadua revived that day, shortly before Marla was laid to rest. Gobah, however, persisted in the zombie-state for three days, not talking, not weeping, not sharing any emotion. He ate and drank, however, when given what to eat and drink. On the fourth day, tears started to stream from his eyes. They run endlessly, yet not a sound escaped from him, except when he spoke, for he indeed began to speak, that very day. He said he felt very bad about the realisation that Marla was beyond reach. He had hoped that one day she would be found alive, but all his hopes had come to smoke.

'We can't undo it, son,' Mrs Wadua cuddled her son, like if she let him go, he would disappear and re-appear a week later, mutilated and rotten. 'When we act this way, we only let down her love.'

'I know, Mummy… I know. It's you who might not know.'

His tears had not ceased to flow, and now his mother, too, recommenced her crying, and they did not talk to each other again that day.

In his heart, however, Gobah was making a resolve. Vital information had played in his mind, and he had all along been churning it, turning it over and over in his head. Now it was clear to him what he must do. But to do it, he needed a new type of knowledge. Not just information, but knowledge. Technical knowledge. Knowledge about a system. About a category. About a culture. He had to have that knowledge immediately.

Nurse was said to be the most knowledgeable people in the area, after the men in the age bracket of Mzee Wadua. Gobah could have

13

talked to his father but these were not things to discuss with family. No, he would involve them at a much later hour, when and if need arose. Nurse would do for now.

She was just licking mashed beans off her fingers after lunch when he found her, in the shelter that had been erected at the back of the house. He beckoned to her. Because of the state he had been in, nobody denied him anything he wanted, even their attention. So Nurse laid aside the plate she had eating from, and got up to go to Gobah.

When Nurse started walking to him, Gobah walked away, so she could follow him. She was hesitating when a look behind from Gobah told her he intended that they talk away from the crowd.

'Are you feeling well, my son?' Nurse asked when Gobah ushered her into his room.

'In a way, yes. I need to learn some new things.' His sombreness disturbed her. Yet she thought she detected a certain eagerness and excitement behind the sombre appearance.

'About what?' she asked, like she discussed a business deal with a fellow adult.

Gobah moved closer to her and laid a feeble hand on Nurse's shoulder. 'I need to find out about witchcraft. And about sacrifices, and the people who offer them, and what they must offer, and why, and-'

'Wait, son,' Nurse cut him short. 'Why do you need this information?'

'I need it. There are things that must first make sense to me, before I know my bearings in this whole episode.'

'You sound different, son. You sound like I have never heard you sound before.'

'That's far from the point. I need-'

14

'Okay, okay, okay! But what have all those tings got to do with-'

'With Marla's death?' he laughed a short puff of laughter, which refused to affect his facial features. 'You must think that I'm the dumbest child in these hills, Nurse.' She was about to protest, but he waved her into silence, as if he was the adult, and she, a child. 'You tell me, Nurse, why my sister's body was the way it was, with the arms, legs, breasts and... with all those parts missing. Tell me why those women took her away, and why some stranger returned her so early, and could not stay to offer an explanation. If you can explain all those mysteries without touching on witchcraft, and human sacrifice, and child-theft, I'll let you be, and let Marla's death be.'

The elderly woman was netted. She had no way out of this. Maybe she could buy time, and consult with fellow adults before she could commit herself.

'I'll tell you.'

'Will? When? You tell me NOW!' Gobah was getting angry, a thing that took the two of them by storm.

'Gobah my son, I'll sure tell you, but I need to talk to your father.'

'My father? My father?' Gobah's voice was rising at each 'my father'. Nurse tried to silence him, but he got more and more heated up, till there was a knock at the door.

Nurse answered the knock, and told Mzee and Mrs Wadua that nothing was the matter, and she would explain to them later what was going on. The old couple hesitated a while, then retreated, after asking Nurse to involve them, should it be necessary.

'This is ending between you, Nurse, and me. And even after this, you'll tell nobody about it. Please,' Gobah added, his voice breaking with the first approaches of despair.

'Fine. Agreed.' Nurse surrendered.

'So now tell me.'

'I hope you can control yourself, my son.' Nurse began, putting a tender arm behind Gobah, and patting him gently as she told him his story.'

'I can, and I will.'

'Good boy. I'll first tell you a short story, before I answer your questions. It must have been in my Primary Five. I was quite a big girl. I was returning from school, playing on the road with my friends as we moved towards home. There was a man on our village, whom all parents mentioned to subdue their children into silent discipline. The man was called Kabonero. It was said that if you got into Kabonero's hands, he would eat you. These stories, however, were told to really young kids. By the time I was in P.3, I had seen behind their threats, and Kabonero was actually my friend.

'Kabonero had a large motorcycle. It was a BSA, though in the village it was called something like *Byesse*. The sound from this motorcycle was thunderous, which could have added to the scare Kabonero gave to infants in the village.

It was this same motorcycle Kabonero was riding that evening, as we played on the road. He came from behind us and stopped. I ran to him and asked him to take me home. He readily accepted, and even fished a doughnut from somewhere in his bag and gave it to me. This I ate with one hand, as I wrapped the other hand around Kabonero, as we rode away.

Now Kabonero's home was a few houses away from my parents' yet when we approached home, he just increases the speed! He accelerated so hard, I started to scream. To my horror, Kabonero barked at me, ordering me to shut up, else he would kill me, then take me to his house, dead. I yelled even louder. By then, we were passing home. Mustering all the courage I could, I let myself fall off the monstrous machine, and dropped in the grass by the path. It hurt a lot, but I was glad to be off that beast's motorcycle. He did not stop, and for a long time, he was neither seen nor heard of in the village.

And that was not all. Hardly a week later, a girl disappeared from our school, and her body was found in a bush the next day, with the head and the genitals missing. It was then that I first knew about these things.

By way of response, Gobah sighed and unwound Nurse's hand from behind his back, then propped himself on his elbows, looking at Nurse as she proceeded with her narration.

'It is believed that every time rich folks build big houses – really big ones, or construct factories, or buy monstrous vehicles – you know, like the coaches we see, trailers, etc – they have to sacrifice for them. Nobody can verify these claims.'

'But why?'

'Why what; why can't they verify-'

'No, no, no! Why sacrifice?'

'They say if they don't sacrifice to these things, they will sacrifice on their own, anyway, killing the rich people themselves, or their families.'

Nobody wants their people dead! 'Is all this true?'

'Like I said earlier, I can't tell.' Nurse leaned back, her look pensive. She told Gobah to move farther up the bed on which they were seated, to avoid the sun rays which hit them directly, through the open window. Outside, the chatter of the mourners was growing, as more and more people collected in the shelter behind the house. 'You see, son, we heard before of cases of cars which were not sacrificed for, and before they had been driven for a month, they had killed a person. One man is said to have run over his one-year-old daughter as he reversed out of the garage.'

'But anybody could do that? It's called an accident.'

'So would anyone say, yet they attributed it to sacrifice. As for houses, it's said that they could fall down and kill up to a whole family.'

'Damn!' Gobah swore silently, but there still was that look that tried to add all this up. Just when he thought he had a case, all this coincidental sounding stuff came in. Exactly what was the truth? There had to be some truth, because Marla's body bespoke some form of truth regarding this world of ritual sacrifice.

'Well, these people, therefore, always look for people to sacrifice, to stop their wealth from sacrificing their own families.'

'And does it always have to be little girls?'

'That's the bit I was coming to. It's not the rich people only who sacrifice. Some people may desire to become rich and successful, some desire to acquire high positions of responsibility. All these people go to medicine men, who ask them for undefiled, perfect human beings to sacrifice. Now you'll agree that on average, there are more perfect children than adults. As for why it's always girls, I don't know.'

'So?'

'So they go to those medicine men, who ask them to provide humans. These people then hire other people to kidnap the victims, as Marla was kidnapped. If they're successful in the kidnap, they are paid very highly, and the clients take the whole person, or curved-out parts of the person, to the medicine men, who then use the parts to concoct charms. Sometimes they ask for the liver, the heart, hands, whatever. A queer practice it is, my son. I'm sorry!'

Gobah was shaking with heavy sobs. Nurse moved closer to him and held him with both hands, enveloping him into a kind of eternal embrace. When he calmed down a bit, she helped him up and together, they returned to the shelter behind the house.

The sun was climbing high in the sky.

FOUR

RECRUITMENT AND FAILURE

If you went to Idudi and asked for one Christian family, you would be lost if you were not taken to the Wadua family. Mzee Wadua and his wife were ardent followers of Christ, and they had instilled the love of God into their two children. Every day broke with prayers, with Mzee Wadua rising early and rousing the rest of his household with the music of praise of God, whose mercies are new every morning. The entire family would then gather in the living room, each with a Bible. Mzee Wadua always made one or the other of his family to take a prescribed reading, at the end of which he would conduct a short discussion on the significance of the day's portion of scripture. Finally, he would deliver a short sermon, which would then be followed by prayer. In the night, the family gathered again after supper and prayed together, sang themselves into yawning, until one by one, they would stumble into their beds, and pass out.

They were gathered again, this specific night, and instead of four, they were only three. Marla was not with them. Nobody said a thing about her absence, yet her absence dominated their presence. Everyone's mind was engorged with Marla's absence. The hesitation in starting prayers was because, it seemed to all, they had to wait for another arrival, yet they all knew there was no other expected arrival, because Marla was no longer a part of the family.

The portion of scripture that night was from Mark 14: 17-26. Mzee Wadua, sounding very distant and strained, preached about what has to be, having to be. Some things may be hard to take, but they have to be, that the purposes of God might be fulfilled. Judas had been predetermined to betray Jesus, which is why Jesus knew it beforehand. It had to be, that God's purpose could be fulfilled.

When the sermon ended, a long silence reigned, in which Mrs. Wadua dubbed at her eyes, Gobah looked down – so nobody could tell what he went through – and Mzee Wadua wished people would not continue doing things which re-poke into his old wounds. He needed quick healing, if he was to pull through with this.

Prayers were brief that night. After the weakest, broken-voiced 'amen' at the end of the grace, Mzee Wadua suggested that in the morning, Gobah be sent to Buwenge to collect Sama, Gobah's half-brother who lived with his aunt. Sama had come to Marla's funeral, but had left a fortnight ago, when most people started leaving. Now the family was left on its own, and Mzee Wadua just realized that they needed extra people around, and they could start with Sama.

Gobah could not sleep that night. His father's sermon disturbed him. The night's portion of Scripture disturbed him. Fine, Jesus had to die, in order that God's purposes could be fulfilled. But did He have to be betrayed? If He had died without being betrayed, would He not have been a saviour, nonetheless? Plus, was Judas not really guilty of betrayal, treachery and accessory to Jesus' death, predestination or not? Surely whoever caused the death of another deserved to die, too? And not just die physically, but die eternally. Go to hell.

These are very heathen thoughts, Gobah told himself. He tried to chide himself for harbouring such morbid ideas, but try as he did, he failed. He knew that revenge was bad. He knew that he was not supposed to judge others, if he too was to survive judgement. He knew about praying for those who wronged us. He knew all those things. But he also knew that whoever was behind Marla's death had, at the very least, to be taken to a court of law. That way, he would not be guilty of vengeance, would he?

For, he told himself, look at it this way. We all die, someday. But did it have to be now, when she was most needed? Nurse had said that those rich people kill others to save their own families. Is that fair? What about the families of the victims? Then his mind went to the people who were paid to kidnap the innocent girls. Were they not like Judas? They gave innocent lives to killers, for the sake of money. Why wouldn't they give in their own people? Oh well, he knew the answer. Nobody wanted their family members dead. It was the very reason he was failing to sleep, because Marla, his fiend and sister was dead.

Gobah did not stay awake the whole night. He fell asleep towards 4:00am and, surprisingly, slept soundly, without the bad dreams he had been having in the past two weeks. He awoke to his father's singing and went to attend the second three-people prayer session.

Again Marla was not with them.

'When do you leave for Buwenge?' his mother asked after prayers.

'Right away,' he answered with over-emphasised finality. His parents exchanged looks.

'Explain to your aunt that Sama is needed, and will not be back there for a long time, yet,' Mzee Wadua said, as he gave Gobah the transport fare.

Gobah was pleased with this development. He was bound to benefit from Sama's presence at home. Who knows, he might come in handy.

Sama and their aunt were at home when Gobah arrived. Aunt Naudo was at first scared, thinking that more terrible things had befallen her sister's family. But on second thoughts, she told herself that if anything went wrong, Gobah would not be the person to send. All was well, she could even see from the boy's relaxed countenance.

Aunt Naudo lived alone, in her husband's house. Her husband had moved out, when they had a grand fight one month after their wedding, way back in 1985. Without touching a single piece of property, he had walked out of the home, and went to work and live in S. Africa. Aunt Naudo was pregnant when her man deserted her, and at the advice of their mother's friend (their mother died when they were only little girls), she had aborted. Their mother's friend had insisted that there was no way she could look after a child single-handed with no job to earn a shilling from.

Sama had gone to live with their aunt when he noticed that there was an impenetrable bond between Gobah and Marla. He had very much wanted to be Gobah's friend, but he found Marla a big obstacle. However, Gobah was obsessed with his sister, and all Sama could do was go away with their mother's sister, when she visited them one day. He was eight years old when he left Idudi.

Aunt Naudo agreed to the arrangement to have Sama go, and Sama, after some convincing, agreed to return to Idudi with his half brother. In his mind, Sama knew he still loved Gobah, and if he searched carefully, he could see traces of relief – absurd relief – at the fact that now he was going to live with the Waduas and Marla would not be there.

They talked on the bus as they travelled back to Idudi. They talked, oblivious of the people around them, because Gobah wanted to utilize this time to woo Sama into this cause. He wanted the two of them to join forces and follow up Marla's killers.

'But this is sheer madness, Gobah, Sama protested.

It's not. We can get to the end of this, brother. Marla can't just die like that and… and I look on.

There was a short, thought-filled silence. Sama was telling himself that you see, it is him Gobah, with his sister. Sama had nothing to do with it. Besides, if they got into this chase after the Devil himself, he would never have enough time with Gobah. There was no way he was going to consent to this proposal. Gobah, on the other hand, was regretting his not using the unified 'we', and opting for the selfish 'I'. It had cut the only band that he could have hoped to cling on to have Sama's support.

'Sama, no danger will come to us. We shall be careful.' He was practically pleading. The woman who shared the seat with them marvelled at how daring this young boy could be, suggesting that they go after witch doctors!

'It's not danger I'm fleeing from, Gobah, if that's what you think. It's the prospect of running after nobody, which in the long run may then draw danger on our trail. Then we'll be the hunted, not the hunters.' He turned his head and looked out the window, refusing to see the desperate plea in his brother's eyes.

'Oh Sama. Let's give it a try!'

'No, brother.'

Gobah involuntarily sighed in unmistakable exasperation. His head bowed, he murmured that Sama give it more thought for sometime, and if he thought better of the proposition, he, Gobah, would be waiting.

The bus hummed on undeterred.

They arrived home past sundown, but Gobah would not sit down. Hardly had he talked to his parents, when he zoomed off, without offering an explanation. He had to see Ida.

Ida was Marla's schoolmate and friend. She lived with her parents on the same hill as the Waduas. She was Marla's age mate but, it had to be admitted, she was more mentally mature. Gobah always teased Marla about this difference, telling her that if she was pampered less, she too would have ceased to be a big baby. Marla would then tell Gobah to stop spoiling her, and then call her a big baby.

Ida listened to Gobah's request without interruption. In the end, she just told him in simple but very serious terms that she could not bare herself to death, period. Nothing Gobah could do would return Marla's life, and to go after those killers would be to offer them more meat. Sorry, no.

Thus defeated, Gobah lumbered back home, a defeated fighter. Yet deep inside of him, he was resolved to follow his purpose to the end. If nobody else came along, fine. He would go it alone, so God help him.

.

FIVE

A CHANCE ENCOUNTER

The craze to do Marla this one last turn did not lose its hold on Gobah. On the contrary, it kept growing like a tumour in his mind, denying him rest, denying him concentration. Yet he so desperately needed someone to do it with. Deep down, he knew that to go it alone was dangerous, all the same.

He had talked to Sama and Ida again, and again, each of them had refused to cooperate. He was sure heading to a dead end.

One day, he resolved to talk to his mother. Most probably she was going to declare him insane, and start watching him, and post guards over his life but well, as he heard old folks say, by the time you choose to confide in a lunatic, you have run out of sane people to talk to. He went to his mother.

'Ahaaa! It's good you brought yourself to me,' his mother said in welcome. She was in the kitchen, chopping down *dodo* greens on a flat surface, made purposely for rolling chapatti dough on.

'Now what?' Gobah asked his mother playfully.

'I want to send you to the market. Go and change, and come back here.' Gobah had no choice but to obey. He went into the house and checked in his wardrobe. It was a wall-built wardrobe, with a curtain for a door shutter. He selected his favourite maroon shirt, then remembered that it was the one he wore the day Marla was kidnapped. He dropped it back, refusing to hang it back in its original place. In its stead, he picked a sky blue short-sleeved shirt, and an over-sized pair of army-green shorts. This was a good enough market outfit, he decided.

'Gobah, are your clothes fighting, or what?' his mother called out from the kitchen. Their relationship had always been good, but the death of Marla had made it even more cordial and free.

'I'm coming!' he screamed back in his unbroken voice. Kicking off his slippers, he pulled on a dirty pair of sneakers, and then ran over to his mother.

'You never tire of those shorts, Gobah. They make you look like –' she couldn't finish, the idea of Gobah soiling his shorts tickled her so.

'Say it, I'm used to it. You've said it before. But if I know there's no *pupu* in my shorts, what do I care?' He too was laughing.

'Nothing. Now go to – no, let me give you this.' She undid the string that held her *Gomace*, and unstrapped a bank note she had tied onto it, and handed it to Gobah. Buy tomatoes of 500/=; coco-yams of 200/= and steel wire. My pans are looking like those of an old woman.'

'Is their owner young?'

'If you think her old, go find a young mother. Where is your brother, by the way?'

'Don't know, and don't - ...er... I don't know.'

He had intended to add that he didn't care, but ever since his mother had said that she had noticed a cold treatment pass between him and Sama, he was careful what he did and said. He walked out of the kitchen.

The evening sun had already lost its heat, though it was still very bright. It cast a long shadow in front of Gobah as he walked, forcing him to hasten his step. It was only a kilometre to the market, but he knew that from this bright light to dusk was only a matter of a moment. Besides, he still intended to talk to his mother.

The market was built on a wide square overlooking the railway line. It was made up of small make-shift structures, of poles supporting a scanty thatch, in which traders sat, selling all manner of wares. On ordinary days, there was basically only foodstuffs and the usual essential household essentials, but this being market day, a lot of other items were on sale. There were animals, clothes, pots, silverware, chinaware, shoes and bags, bicycle parts and plenty of other things.

At the end of the market ground, a throng surrounded a man who was yelling over a megaphone. Gobah was used to those men. They sold herbal drugs, which they claimed cured practically all ailments and conditions, from the simple flu to AIDS. One simple root would cure backache, impotence, infertility, hernia, typhoid, malaria, and even go an extra mile. It could cause your spouse to love you more, or if you had no spouse at all, it could win you one. It caused Gobah untold wonderment that the same root would be used to acquire love, but the herbalists also said the root would help you get rid of your enemies.

Gobah bought the items he needed, and was just leaving when the throng around the medicine man shouted, and scampered in fright. Gobah stopped. Instinct told him to go over and check. He went, clutching his goods tightly over his chest.

The medicine man was a little unique. In addition to selling herbal medicine, he was also a charmer. He had with him a suitcase full of snakes, and was pulling out one after the other, and doing very amazing things with them. He would put a snake's head in his mouth, and say they were kissing; then push one inside his coat. Once in a while he would let a snake take a leisurely crawl over his shoulders. It was one such that had fallen off to the ground and rushed for the crowd, when they made the noise that had attracted Gobah.

After the snake antics, the man turned to talking drugs. 'There's not a problem I cannot solve,' he cried. 'If there's someone bent on terminating your life, I can reverse that, and do to that foe anything you prescribe. If someone takes your wife or your man, I am the solution. If you want your business to succeed, or to open one, come to me. And if your house has been stagnant for an abnormally long spell, who knows, it might need one little thing only I can give you. Try me.'

Then he turned to selling his roots and rolled clay, and an astounding sale did he make of it.

When Gobah walked away, it was dark, but his spirit was alight. He was elated. Perhaps not really *that* elated, but he was satisfied with his findings. And he was also determined not to rest until he had reached his dream's end. He needed not even talk to his mother or anyone else now, he decided.

SIX

A VISIT TO THE SHRINE

As Gobah walked back home from the market that night, he was awed by the things he had seen and heard. A group of people walked ahead of him, chattering away about the day's market experience. Gobah hastened his step, to catch up with the group of mostly women, so he could share their company. There is security in numbers, you know. But also, he though he could steer the conversation to something he was interested in.

He did not have to bother, for hardly did he catch up with them, when one woman struck up the topic of the snakes. 'Whenever I go to listen to that man,' she was saying, 'the snakes come in my direction. There was belly-borne laughter as the group remembered the scampering of the medicine man's audience, when the snake rolled off his shoulders.

'Oh, I had to run,' another woman said. 'What do you do if it enters your undergarments?'

'It could even bite. I can picture you having to explain to your man what you were doing looking at a medicine man.'

'Know what, your co-wife will automatically conclude that you were buying a love portion.'

A gigantic thunderous burst of laughter, then a woman says, 'But do these things really work? Those roots and rolled clay, do they cure all those incredible diseases they talk about?'

'Who can tell? Some people come and testify that they bought from such and such a market, and now their problems are gone.'

Gobah's ears pricked up.

'Those are their people, brought in to boost the sales with such fake testimonies. They are paid to do that.'

'But some of them are people we know on this village.'

'So? Didn't you hear the story about Marla, Mzee Wadua's daughter? The woman who took her away knew her and her brother. Your knowing anybody doesn't stop them from being dubious.'

Gobah was now like a dog that had smelt roasting meat. Could it be possible that the people responsible for his sister's death were known to his family? Yes, he recalled the woman calling them 'dear twins'. Only people on this hill called Gobah and Marla twins. Besides, how did whoever it was know that Gobah and Marla would be out walking that late? It was very unlikely that they were just taking a leisurely evening drive when the idea struck them to kidnap an innocent child.

'Me, I want to know one thing,' another woman was saying. 'Where do these men come from? They seem to go to every market, but nobody knows them for sure.'

'Who says? This one, for instance, works for Nsinze. Do you know Nsinze?'

'The is-it-High Priest of Nsinze Spiritual Hill?'

'Exactly. Nsinze never leaves his shrine, I am told. So as he conducts business at headquarters, he has his boys who traverse the whole region, doing what this man at the market was doing.'

'Where is Nsinze?'

This question was welcomed by all heads turning to look at the new voice in their midst. It had not been heard before, and nobody had noticed this person walk among them.

'Why, it's you my child, Gobah! How's Mzee Wadua?'

'He's alright.'

'And mother?'

'She too is well. Where is Nsinze found?'

Even in the half dark of twilight, the women cast questioning glances at each other.

'Nsinze is about ten to fifteen miles from here,' one woman decided to explain. 'It's a great hill where the seat of the great spirit of Nsinze is found.'

'And that's where this man's boss is?' Gobah asked.

'Yes, child.'

Gobah fell silent. He had known enough. To ask more would be to arouse unnecessary interest and curiosity. As his mother always said, curiosity killed the cat. It was not good. Anything that killed one was not good.

When Gobah's questions ceased, the women, too, ceased to chatter. It was as if they were ruminating over the child's special interest in spiritual things. Soon, they began to branch off into tiny footpaths leading to their homes, and goodnights and farewells were the only talk from then on.

Gobah's plan matured in the one week that remained of his holiday. In two days, he would be going back to school. He had to act fast.

Mzee Wadua's ancestral home was in Busesa, in Iganga. Nsinze, too, was in Iganga. It was long since Gobah had visited his father's people. So when he confronted his father asking for money and permission to go and see his granny before school opened, he had a case in his favour. Mzee Wadua loved and trusted his son. He gave him the money.

'Would you like Sama to come along?' Mrs Wadua asked Gobah, in a bid to get the boys to get closer again.

'If he so wishes.' In his heart of hearts, though, Gobah did not want to involve Sama in his business any more.

'I don't want to travel now,' Sama said decidedly. Gobah could have shouted Alleluia at the refusal.

The following day saw Gobah set off for Nsinze. His original plan had been to go to Busesa first, then link up to Nsinze, but he thought better about it. You never know, the grandparents might hold onto him longer than was healthy for him and his business.

The Idudi bus dropped him in Iganga town, where he boarded a taxi to Nsinze. His advisers had told him to ask the conductor to leave him at the mosque at Nsinze. From there, any person he asked, even a child, would direct him to the great shrine of Nsinze.

The taxi dropped him at the mosque. The place was devoid of people, and he was at a loss what to do. Should he move right or left? Or should he wait till someone came by? He decided to walk in the direction the taxi had followed. A few houses littered the place, but many of them were locked up. People were certainly still out in the fields, farming.

He had walked about 400 metres, when he met a young girl, about five years his junior. In the usual tradition of people seeking directions, he greeted the girl with exaggerated humility, and then asked her for directions to the shrine.

'Oh, the shrine!' The girl looked at Gobah awkwardly, wondering what a boy his age could be going to the shrine for. She knew only big men with cars, and big, married or working women, went to the shrine. Not children, moreover decent-looking children like this boy.

'Just walk back slight-… maybe I should take you. Let's go back,' Gobah turned, and they went back. They walked in silence, the girl still wondering to herself about this boy's mission; and Gobah beginning to fret about his mission. Just about 100 metres down the road, they turned into a well-tended path. After sometime, Gobah spoke.

'I'm sorry I derailed you from wherever you were going.'

'No,' replied the girl. 'I was only taking a walk. I'm here on holiday, and my aunt can't let me go to the *shamba* with them. So I simply loiter about and see the place. But I've been here before, so I know the place well. Now do you see the wooden steeple up there?'

'Yes.'

'That's the shrine. You'll turn off at the next left, and then you'll walk straight into the shrine. I must stop here.'

'Why?' Gobah found himself asking.

'No, it's nothing to do with the shrine, the girl reassured him, a bemused grin on her face. 'I have been there, as I've told you, so I want to go elsewhere.' She still wore the smile.

'What sort of place is it? Sorry to hold you longer.'

'Oh, I'm fine. It's… it's a busy place.' As if to prove her right, a heavy Mark II came from the direction of the shrine. It was driven by an equally heavy woman, with another woman in the passenger seat. Gobah's mind went back to the past.

'Yes, as I was saying,' the girl proceeded, 'it's a very busy place. Nsinze hardly ever sleeps. He has patients all day and night long.'

'Patients?'

'Well, people who come with problems... problems of all sorts. Do you have a problem?'

'Not really. Yes, I may say I have a problem, but I'm not going to consult with Nsinze.'

'So why are you going there?' the girl was apprehensive.

'To study how Nsinze works. Where do you come from?'

'Me?' she laughed a bit. We live in Kampala. My dad works in Kampala. He is a teacher. There are many people from Busoga teaching in Kampala schools.'

'So I hear. Well, I'm going to take a risk. I'll tell you about me, but only because you've been of help to me. Do you mind that?'

'By no means, dear. No way.' Of a sudden, the girl was enthusiastic.

'I come from Idudi. Recently, my sister was kidnapped, and a number of days later, a stranger brought her body home, early in the morning. Nobody saw him. We only heard the sound of a motorcycle, and a knock at our door. Then the motorcycle raced away. When we opened the door, there was the stinking, disintegrating body of my sister, with parts missing.'

'I must go away, I'm sorry,' the girl said, turning away hurriedly.

'No, please wait,' Gobah cried, running after the girl. 'I'm safe. You're safe with me.' He checked himself, remembering that Marla was in his company when she was kidnapped. He would not tell the girl that bit. The girl stopped.

'Look, if we must talk,' the girl said rather too seriously, 'it must only be at my aunt's place.'

'Fine.'

As they walked to the girl's aunt's home, Gobah told her the rest of the story, plus his decision to probe into the workshop of witchcraft and human sacrifice, and how he desired to find out who was behind his sister's death.

'Sounds very dangerous,' the girl said.

'Agreed, but Marla's worth it.'

'Was that your sister's name?'

'It is.' Gobah put emphasis on the 'is', as if to stress that Marla still lived, at least in his mind.

'It's a very sweet name.'

'She was a sweet girl, my sister.'

'I'm sorry… But why did you come this far?'

'I don't know. I knew of no other people dealing in these gory things.'

'I wish I could be of help. Unfortunately, I go back to Kampala day after tomorrow.'

'I'll see how I manage, thanks.'

'I have a cousin who could help. My aunt's son. He is in his S.6 vacation, and is helping Auntie on the farm. He could be of help.'

'That will be great. If I have a friend nearby here, things will be more convenient for me, by far.'

'Zanah is a good boy. He'll be willing to help. So you'll be at home, till Zanah returns. He normally returns home before Auntie. Auntie has to supervise the workers before coming home. Sometimes we have to take her lunch to the farm.'

'Is it a big farm?'

'By village standards, yes. It's a dairy farm, but she also grows maize, cowpeas and bananas. She has a big *shamba* of *matooke*.'

They got to the girl's aunt's home. It was a big house, with servants' quarters to the eastern side. As the girl had said, by village standards, this was a marvel of a house.

'Is your aunt married?' Gobah asked, as the girl brought a bench to the shed.

'Nope. She got her two children while at university. She went to Nairobi University, and her two sons are both Kenyan. Their dad had wanted to marry Auntie, but she preferred to return to her home country. And then the man could not come back here with her. As soon as she returned here (Zana was then an infant, and Ben, his big brother, was two), the man married a Kikuyu woman. That woman said the next time she saw the Muganda woman, she would kill her, before killing their man.'

'You're Baganda?'

'No, but to many Kenyans, all Ugandans are Baganda. Anyhow, since then, Auntie chose to be on her own. Now Ben is doing his final year at Makerere University, in Commerce. Zana did Physics, Chemistry and Mathematics.'

'That one is going to be an engineer,' Gobah offered.

'If they let him.'

Zana found them still at it, talking Auntie and Ben and Zana and Kampala and Rose, who the girl was.

Rose did the due introductions. As she had said earlier, Zana was an amiable person, with a perennial smile on his face. He said he was glad to meet Gobah. 'But what are you doing here?' he put to him.

Rose embarked on telling him about Gobah's mission, and how they would like him to offer whichever help he could.

'Now what sort of help can I ever offer you?'

'Any. For instance, I want to go to that shrine to find out if they are genuine. I have only today and tomorrow.'

'Don't even bother. They're far from genuine. Alright, their drugs do work, sometimes. But this rot about spirits is all a hoax.'

'Sure?' Gobah was incredulous.

'I can take you there. Nsinze knows me, by the way. I studied with his son at O' Level. Actually the boy died in our S.4 vacation. Can we go over this evening?'

But Gobah was getting fretty again.

'Oh, you'll be fine. I told you there's nothing there. We'll do this. You have a problem. We want him to tell us what it is. The rest will follow naturally.'

The shrine was a large round-shaped, grass-thatched hut, with a long steeple on its tip. The inside was divided into two. The clients sat in the outer half, facing the door. All shoes were left at the door. No electronic watches, phones or any such device were allowed in the shrine. No one sat on anything else but the bark cloth already spread in the shrine.

Nsinze and two of his assistants sat in the inner section of the hut. Before they cross into this inner part, however, they engage their visitors in a long chat, during which they picked clues of the problems which have brought them to see Nsinze.

Gobah and Zana had already gone through this ritual, and sat expectant, as four other clients awaited their turn to be interviewed. Nsinze was now talking to an elderly half-Ugandan, half-Asian man, and his two assistants were chatting with a young woman who had driven in shortly after Gobah and Zana had arrived. This woman drove a Land Rover Freelander. Gobah wondered what sort of problems could face such a woman. At school, they usually engaged in car-talk, and the Freelander ranked among every boy's dream cars.

Finally, all interviews were done, and Nsinze and his men went inside. Suddenly, something like an explosion went off, sending shivers into all clients, except Zana. Darkness now reigned in the hut. Rattling sounds crept and crawled all over the hut, rising in intensity as new sounds started. It was a ghostly moan, coming from the thatch-top. Then Nsinze's spirits arrived.

'Stand up all of you,' a shrill, hollow voice ordered. Everybody stood up.

'Are you standing up? Now sit down.'

Everybody sat down.

'Are you seated? Now stand up.'

'Are you standing? Now sit down.

The sequence went on for sometime. Stealthily, so he could not alarm him, Zana drew Gobah's attention to himself, and then stayed down, even when he was supposed to stand. Gobah was tempted to follow suit, but he feared.

When the stand-sit sequence was done, a new voice came in… a deep, guttural voice that calmly and gently greeted the 'grandchildren'.

'When you come here,' the male spirit said, 'you are naked. We know all about you, in and out. Boy with academic problems, your step-mother! Your step-mother! Your step-moootheeer!' the rising intensity and pitch of the voice was scaring, and with the last 'mother', the rattling sounds and the deep moan came in again. Gobah could have peed on his legs. 'Ooooh! My grandchild with an enemy on your back; she wants your man and your life. Your man and your life. Blood! Blooood!'

Again the rattles and the moan.

In that order, the voice went through all the problems, mentioning jealousies, murder intent, academic trouble, travel and business. Plus a lot of love-related woes.

Then came the prescriptions. Gobah was supposed to bring, in addition to fifty thousand shillings, a pure white cock and a pitch black hen. Come back when you're ready.

When they finally got out of what Gobah considered a demonic shrine, he was relieved. Relieved to be out of the spiritual and physical filth, and the heat, but also relieved to know that no real big danger lay ahead for him in his pursuits. This was certainly going to be easier than he had bargained. Thank God.

SEVEN

A STRANGE DISAPPEARANCE

Gobah was back home on the appointed day.

Every person lies to someone some time or other, though this is not to justify lying as moral. Gobah hated to have to lie, but by the time the first question about Busesa came, he had the full story out. He had left everybody well, thanks, and yes, he had had the grandest time down there. Every person had gone out of their way to make life comfortable for him, and there was no doubt when he broke off for the following holiday, he would be back in Busesa. To qualify his story as genuine, he had got from his friends in Nsinze lots of stuff to bring back home, including fruit, groundnuts, maize and some money. A typical returnee from the ancestral home of his father.

Gobah had big plans, though. That same evening, he started preparing for his return to school. He packed his school box, fried his groundnuts, bought all the basic essentials and got his parents to give him pocket money for his upkeep at school. He was all set to report to school the following day.

Sama was persuaded into escorting his brother to school, a ten-mile journey from Idudi. It was Mzee Wadua's practice to rent a car to return his children to school, and even if Marla was not around any more, the usual pick-up was hired, and Sama and Gobah were seen off. Mzee Wadua and his wife never took children back to school. They said it was a bad practice, which retarded the mental development and the confidence of a child, as they grew to expect everything to be done for them.

40

Sama was back home before midday. He had helped his brother with all clearances and to take his luggage to the hostel. When he saw that Gobah was settled, he got onto the pick-up and they drove back to Idudi.

It was an hour after Sama had left for home. In total, Gobah had sixty thousand shillings in cash, in addition to the bank draft that was his school dues. He took the draft to the school bursar and then returned to the dormitory. There, he changed into his ordinary work clothes – what the kids called civilian clothes – put all his 60,000/= in different pockets, put his identity card in the shirt pocket and walked out of the dormitory.

The school was surrounded by a perimeter fence, except for the road that led to the staff quarters, and into the school farm. The staff quarters were strictly out of bounds to students, but if a student was seen in the company of a teacher, walking to or from the quarters, that was a different issue altogether. So when Gobah walked with the Geography teacher, talking textbooks and reasons for a not-very-great performance the previous term, nobody bothered to think beyond what they saw. They walked to the extreme end of the blocks of houses where the Geography teacher lived. There, they stood for over ten minutes, discussing the new term, at the end of which discussion the teacher excused himself and Gobah walked away, stealthily taking the path to the farm, then breaking into a Pheidipides sort of sprint.

The school farm was bordered by villagers' homesteads and beyond that, other farms, and homes, and about five miles away, a small township where one could get the quickest means to Jinja town. Jinja was at least fifty kilometres away by taxi, a one-hour journey. If one was so unfortunate as to use a bus, one could spend up to two hours or longer, depending on how often the bus stopped to pick and drop passengers, which was inevitably often.

Gobah crawled through bushes and thickets, dodging homes and gardens where he could be seen or identified. The sun was quickly gliding down the western sky, leaving an orange-spotted blanket across the horizon. Gobah knew that once the sun set, getting a taxi

41

to Jinja would be close to impossible. He, therefore, did as much running as he possibly could. At one point, he nearly ran into a squatting couple in a bush, by the side of the road to the township. It was a man and a woman; the man's hands round the woman's neck, their mouths touching. When Gobah nearly crushed into them, they were scared, but after the boy (possibly running away from a cruel step-mother, they thought) had changed routes, the kissing couple now sat on the grass and proceeded with their naughtiness.

Gobah found the last taxi beginning to fill. When he boarded, there were still three vacant seats, which seemed to him to have a repellent in them. The driver and his conductor were outside, yelling out to every prospective traveller to fill the car.

Jinja! Itanda! Wakalenge! Itanda! Budondo! Only two more people; Jinja! Itanda! Budondo! Wakalenge!

Gobah was frantic. If his disappearance was discovered at school, it was not altogether impossible that they could look for him, and who knows, fate could easily lead a person to this damned place. He would be ruined.

A woman boarded the taxi, just as a man disembarked, tired of waiting. Possibly he had been the first to board, or he was just one of those people who wait in a hurry. Whatever the case, Gobah did not think very kindly of him. Other people began to get fidgety, and more people could have cancelled their journeys, had God not brought in a family of three (man wife and son) to fill up the vacant seats. The taxi was ready to move.

It was school policy to conduct a roll call on the evening of reporting back for the new term, just to know which students were back, and which were still at home. It was this roll call which revealed that Gobah and his sister Marla were missing. Gobah had already told a few of his friends about Marla's death, so they passed this information on to the teacher in charge. As for Gobah, his absence at the roll call was hard to explain. He had certainly been seen around.

He had even cleared with the proper authorities. He couldn't be in the dormitory, because all dorms were checked, then locked up before roll call was conducted.

'Sir, we saw him walk to Mr Nyende's house,' one boy said. Mr Nyende taught Geography at O-Level. A message was sent to Mr Nyende, who responded with an I-don't-know chit. He had walked to the quarters with the boy, yes, discussing the boy's class performance. But he could not say where the boy went after they parted.

The issue was reported to the administration. At the main gate, no one had been seen getting out. All vehicles were searched before they went through the gate. That meant that no student had escaped through the gate. Gobah was either in one of the staff houses and would get out at bedtime, or something sinister was brewing.

The Dormitory Captain of Gobah's dorm was told to be on the alert, so that if the boy came in during the night, they report the issue immediately. That night, Gobah did not report back. In the morning, the administration decided to take official measures. First, a representative was sent to the boy's home to find out if they knew where he could have gone. Now that was the other trouble; the pandemonium which was caused by the news of Gobah's disappearance. To an elderly couple which had recently lost one of their two children – and lost her to kidnap – this news was nothing short of a disaster. Mrs Wadua wept, and Mzee Wadua wanted to kill someone. He insisted that the next time he dealt with someone from that damned school, it should be as they hand back his son – for good. Life was certainly more precious than all the school learning there was in the universe.

Back at school, the news from Idudi threw them into big confusion and panic. Where, O God, had the boy disappeared to? The case was reported to the Police, but even as they took this step, nobody expected anything to come of it. The Police had always been known to act only after they were sure that they would not be effective anymore, like after a death, or after stolen property was returned. Then they would come in, take the returned property away, scribbling down statements from the property owners and their neighbours, and then refusing to release the property until the owners redeemed it with cash… sort of buying your own property. That was the Police, nobody could change them.

Meantime, hell was reigning in Idudi. Mzee Wadua refused to be comforted, keeping a panga by his side, ready to chop anybody to slices who said anything about his only surviving child, Gobah. When the neighbours brought Nurse to sedate him, he dared her to touch him, and they would see who would need medical treatment thereafter.

On her part, Mrs Wadua had wept herself hoarse. She lay on a mat in the living room, hiccupping endlessly, looking like anything could happen. The Idudi villagers were bothered. What had become of this family? First, nobody could accuse the Waduas of being bad people. Not a person on all the three hills of Idudi had as much as picked a quarrel with this family. Besides, they were as Christian as anyone knew Christians to be. So just what was the matter?

The women tried to talk Mrs Wadua into relenting from her state, but with no positive results. 'You'll cause more trouble, acting like this,' they argued.

'It's a bad omen, lying in the sitting room, in this manner.'

'Just like weeping for the living. We have no proof that the child is dead.'

Mrs Wadua's tears flowed afresh. The women were beaten.

That day ended, and the next, and a week elapsed, and Gobah was not back. Not at home, not at school. And no decomposing body was brought in by any stranger, too.

EIGHT

LOCAL TECHNOLOGY

It had all been worked out well. Zana had openly explained Gobah's case to his mother, who was willing to help the two boys out if for no other reason, at least to get those wicked activities stopped. Having such operations in an area bore its costs, and Zana's mother was ready to do all in her ability to contribute to the death of the shrine in Nsinze.

As Gobah went back to Idudi, Zana bought the hen and cock. Money was not his problem; it was always available. He had also bought a sound system, comprising four micro-chip bugs; two mikes, a wireless pocket Hi-tech amplifier and a rechargeable battery. The equipment had been tried out. Zana bugged his room, and then started testing the equipment at varying distances: 100m, OK. 500m, OK. A kilometre… At a kilometre, he could receive his mother's activities alright, but not as clearly as at half a kilometre. So they had decided that for the sake of clarity, they would use the house of a friend about 600 metres from the shrine. All was set, then.

Gobah arrived at Nsinze after ten o'clock that night. He was worn-out, and after he had eaten and freshened up, he fell asleep, till the following day.

Zana roused his friend when breakfast was served. Gobah had slept soundly, and when the light of day blinded his unaccustomed sight in the room, he was embarrassed.

'I can't believe I slept this much,' he said sheepishly.

'Oh, it's really understandable. From your account of the past two days, you couldn't expect less,' his friend reassured him.

Gobah pulled himself out of the sheets and walked into the WC. Zana could hear the sound of the toilet as Gobah emptied his bladder, then flushed the water. He brushed his teeth, and then took an abnormally quick bath. Presently, he was leading the way to the breakfast table.

It was a plain breakfast, of coffee and cream, toast bread, sliced yams, an egg each and water melon. Gobah loved water melon, a fact he established as soon as he learnt that Zana's mother grew them on the farm.

They ate in relative silence, because the mother was still in the house. Towards the end of breakfast, however, she walked out of her bedroom, dressed for the day. She had purchases to make for the farm, and was driving to Kawanda in Buganda. She would be back in the evening.

'Did you sleep well?' she asked Gobah.

'Like a corpse,' he said. They all laughed heartily.

'Great. Now I must leave you in your brother's hands. Everything's been attended to, and good luck. But take care, it's a dangerous undertaking.'

'Thank you madam,' Gobah said.

'We'll be fine, Mum; there's nothing serious there. They are quacks.'

'The more reason they'll be ruthless in defending their secrets. This is not to discourage, though. Just take great care, Zana.'

'We will, Mum, thank you very much.'

'Thanks Madam, and good day,' Gobah added.

'Good day. And Zana, should you need anything else, feel free to get it. Only be sure to account for it all; OK?'

'OK mother.' Zana knew his mother trusted him, and he would be the last person to abuse that trust.

The two boys heard the Land Rover drive out of the garage and away. Breakfast was done, and Zana suggested that they rest a bit, before launching into their work. They had the whole day to them, so there was no cause for worry.

'Though I would think that instead of just idling about, you could let me see the sound gear.' Gobah was anxious, and would appreciate anything to keep his mind off the possibility of danger. He had not taken for granted Zana's mother's words. Those adults saw deeper than young people could.

'No sweat,' Zana dashed into his bedroom, from where he returned with a box the size of an average portable stereo. This was all the equipment. He laid it on the study table where Gobah sat skimming through Zana's Physics texts.

'This is the amplifier, here. It has in-built power storage, so you charge it through this inlet,' Zana explained. 'You activate it with this button–.' He cut himself short, preferring to explain everything when the equipment was all turned on. He got one of the micro-chips and pinned it behind a curtain, then stuck a mike onto Gobah's collar. The other mike he stuck onto his shirt. He then got out a small Sony recorder, into which he put a tiny cassette. The recorder he took to another part of the house, and then he instructed Gobah to stay in the house and do as he pleased. He walked out of the house and went to buy a cluster of ripe bananas. When he returned, it was time for the lesson.

Every movement, every sigh, every bit of activity Gobah had engaged in, however slight, had been recorded on the cassette, as was every sound Zana had produced, from his steps as he walked, the rustle of his clothes, the dialogue with the girl who sold bananas.

'Is my boss satisfied?'

'Except in one area. How will we plant mikes on Nsinze and his people?'

'No need to. Absolutely no need. The chips alone are good enough. I put mikes on us for my own sake, to see how much of the low and soft sounds could be picked... and I'm very satisfied.'

'Fine with me, then. Thanks man.' Gobah walked over to his friend, brother and mentor and pumped his hand like a true comrade would.

They set out for the shrine at two o'clock that afternoon. Because they had the two birds, they each carried a large straw bag, each containing one of the birds. The sound equipment was in Zana's bag.

They passed by the friend's house. It was to be the control centre. The friend had moved out, for he had business to attend to in Iganga for two days. He left the keys with Zana. The equipment was set, when the two young men walked out of the house.

At the shrine, there was busy activity, as usual. Nsinze himself was in the inner chamber, so he had to come out when his assistants announced that the two young people with academic trouble had returned.

'I'll be over in a moment,' the priest's voice boomed. And in a moment, he indeed came out. He was in his regalia, which made Zana wish the equipment had visual attributes as well. Anyhow, they would do the best they could. Acting afraid and submissive, they handed over the cock and hen, which Nsinze handed to one of his assistants. The other clients (three of them) looked on, hoping that they too would one day be at payment stage, which actually heralded the end of one's troubles.

As all this was happening, Zana was scrutinising the doorway to the inner chamber. He had seen a particular spot which was conducive, and was already fingering the chip on a background of dark, glued cardboard. It was too small to be seen except at very close quarters, and by one who had prior knowledge of its existence. In this hut with its darkness and dark mud walls, it was next to impossible that anyone should see it.

Gobah had already counted out the prescribed money and handed it over to Nsinze. This, the Priest kept himself, as he went to the inner chamber to collect the talisman. It was a little pillow-like object sewn in black cloth, with something hard as granite inside.

'Sew this onto your uniform shorts. Inside. Do I make myself clear?' Nsinze boomed.

'Yes.'

'You'll see the results before long.'

'Our gratitude to the Grannies.'

Gobah laughed to himself at this irony from Zana. The fact that they were fooling a man – indeed an established system –feared and revered by many, brought such relief and joy to the two young hearts. They felt like they could accomplish anything now.

When Nsinze dismissed them, one of the young men supported himself by the wall as he got up. It was a thing anybody would do, after being immobile on the floor for some time.

They nearly flew to the Control Centre, to play back the tape and listen to the whole discourse. They burst into the house with deep enthusiasm, and rewound the tape. Everything was there. They hugged each other in self-congratulation.

'Can't we listen to them live, Zana?'

'We could, but not on this recorder. When we have to listen to a live broadcast, we have to bring in bigger and stronger equipment.' I have to bring a big radio and connect it to this system.

They went home for a rest, and were back in the night, with a big radio.

49

NINE

A HEAD FOR A HOUSE, BREASTS FOR A CAREER

The equipment was set. Gobah and Zana waited, their anxiety mounting by the minute. Zana had brought with him a packet of biscuits and two half litre packs of instant milk, but none of them could touch a thing. Time dragged like a bride in a forced marriage, but the shrine had only the usual chit-chat between Nsinze and his assistants – instructions about seating of guests, mixing of herbs, when and where not to speak. They made rude and even crude remarks about some of their clients, to which they reacted with malignant, lewd laughter, like hyenas fighting over carrion flesh.

'Nothing will come of this, Zana.' Gobah stretched and yawned.

'Too soon to give up. There may yet be a guest.' He put down the small amplifier and began searching for a cassette in his jacket pocket, when there was the sound of a vehicle passing by their Control Centre, heading towards the shrine.

The two young men reacted like they were suddenly electrified. Zana was back at the equipment desk, his hands adjusting buttons and meters. Gobah crouched by Zana's side, his every muscle tout like a competitor in a 100m dash at the start line. The system had already started picking the approaching vehicle. It stopped, doors banged – two doors, which meant more than one person getting out. Customary and routine welcomes and greetings… the guests ushered into the shrine… the attendants issuing the usual instructions. Total obedience while in there. No telling lies, as the spirits know even unspoken facts. Nobody goes beyond the outer chamber – only Nsinze and his assistants can face the spirits. Etcetera.

A big bang, low, then rising moans, and Nsinze's voice advancing from within his chambers, coming to meet his clients.

'Welcome, grandchildren!'

'Our respects,' two masculine voices responded.

'I see trouble printed on your faces. The High Ones will solve whatever it is, worry not.'

'We're confident they will,' one of the men said. 'It's why we came.'

'You don't come from close by, I can see,' Nsinze groped for clues now. He knew that people who came from close by would not have come in this late.

'No, but still… we should have come earlier, if that's what you mean. We're from Kampala.' It was the same man talking. Maybe he was the bolder of the two, or he had the upper hand in the essence of the visit.

'This is my brother, recently graduated with an honours degree in Commerce. Brilliant man, by every inch, but you know our country. Somehow, he did not get the kind of degree he wanted.'

'I know how it is, my children. This is Uganda.' He was poking for more details. He needed all this information.

'The problem is, with all the degrees floating around in Commerce, one cannot get a good job.'

'Yet you have your eyes on a specific position, you see.' It was a shot in the dark, but Nsinze had come to know the trend. And judging from the bewilderment on his guests' faces, he could see he was right.

'How do you know?' It was the Commerce graduate who spoke this time.

Nsinze laughed a throaty, disdainful laugh, the lead hyena at the rotting feast. 'You don't know where you have come, I can see. This is Nsinze's shrine.' He wanted to make another guess, but the thought of destroying what he had so far achieved was too much for him to undertake.

'Well, then,' the big brother proceeded, 'we do not want to give other people a chance. We want to move ahead of them.'

This was all the pointer Nsinze required.

'When did you lodge in the application?' he asked, and his clients' eyes grew big again.

'Last week,' the big brother said.

'Hah!' It was a puff of a laugh. 'Last week had seven days, as all weeks do.'

Nsinze was not in control.

'Mzee, it was on Tuesday… Tuesday last week,' the graduate hastened to answer.

'Well, well! We must act before you go back for the interviews. When are they again?'

The consternation this time was not only on the faces, but also in the voices, as they chorused without prompting. 'Friday next week.'

'Fine.'

It was just that one word, but in it Nsinze put all the confidence, all the finality of someone who knew that in no time at all, he was going to make big money. He had just shifted back to his chamber when a car pulled up into his compound. An attendant went to meet the lone woman who got out of the car, and to interview her. The system was so well organised, Nsinze was not going to be brought out for small steps, as the High Ones would be out any time.

The moaning commenced, rattles traversed the roof, a trillion bees buzzed in the hut, and the spirits spoke. To the two men, everything here was awesome. The High Ones already knew the full story, they needed no telling. They were already talking prescriptions.

'There's this man with four degrees. He has a brother in the firm. He has no doubt that the job is his. But we are the High Ones. We know no human relations.' *Rattles, horns, moans. A shrill laugh.*

'The job is yours. For it, there will come here a pair of untouched breasts. Fast! With the breasts here, we'll do the business and name the price.' *Shrieks, bells and agonising moans.*

'I see need out there. Bring the news. Bring the news right in. Bring the news.'

The two men didn't know which news, till one of Nsinze's assistants entered with a huge woman whom he ushered beside the career brothers, and then went into the inner chambers briefly. A loud bang and furious rattling sent him scuttling out of the chamber, and a new voice was in the roof, laughing. It was feminine.

'You really believe you can tell me anything? Fool! I know the house. Daughter, I know the house. I saw the threatened bloodshed. Blood for blood. Blood for blood, I said. Blood for blood!' the final time was a lamentation, a forecast of a terrible death.

'There must be a head, else there will be deaths. A head for deaths. Quickly. A head, off an undefiled child. Boys are dirty. Boys are dirty. The price after the head!'

And the divination was over.

'Run, Gobah. No, you can't drive.' Zana was frantic. 'We meet at the Mosque. Run there. Now!' he disengaged his sound equipment, and was out of the house in a flash.

It was all Gobah could do to desist from screaming in triumph. To him, the battle was not only on, it was won. God bless Zana.

When Gobah reached the Mosque, Zana was waiting in his mother's Pick-up. Two cars had passed him on the path from the shrine, a white Hyundai and a maroon Mazda. Amazing, the sort of people who visited Nsinze.

'Did you notice which car had the two men?'

'Doesn't matter whom we follow, Gobah. Any will do as well.'

The chase began. While they were still in the village, it was easy. First, nobody would suspect a thing. But also, Zana could easily keep track of his culprits.

It was only a 20 minute drive to Iganga town, and there the two cars parted roads. The woman turned towards Mbale, the men towards Kampala. It was easy to tell who went where, because the men had told Nsinze where they came from. Zana chose to follow the woman. Kampala had a lot of complications, ranging from distance, to heavy traffic, to more sophisticated people. The woman would be easier prey.

She was an accomplished driver though, this woman. She was fast, and she knew the turns and twists on the road. Zana, however, knew his skill, too. They tore past Nakalama, towards Tororo. Traffic speed was high in the night. This was good for Zana. In heavy traffic, it would have been hard for him to keep track of the Mazda.

A rugged dirt road turned off the Iganga-Tororo highway, a few kilometres from Busitema Agricultural Institute. It was a less used road, as Zana could see from the grass growing on its sides as he followed the bouncing Mazda on it. At one point, the apparently suspicious woman stopped a bit, testing intent. She knew that wrong people would also stop, involuntarily. When Zana just drove on, she moved on, but a little faster. Zana decided to maintain constant speed, as long as he could still see her lights ahead of him.

'You're absurdly quiet,' he said to Gobah.

'Tension.'

'You're tense? Why?'

'The kill. I could easily pounce on them as they do it.'

'Not soon. Tonight is only a reconnoitre mission, but we can't be sure when the real hunt will be on.'

'All the same.'

It was now drizzling a bit, but this did not deter Zana's progress. The road was lined by lantana camara thickets, the type of shrub that was the favourite of tsetse flies. It also made the road seem a trifle darker, therefore more dangerous, apparently.

The woman turned into a compound by the road. It couldn't have been her house, for it had mud walls, with a craggy roof. A few rickety poles supported a meagre roof to make what must have been the kitchen. A few stunted banana plants created darkness around the homestead, and there was barely anything else to talk about.

The woman was certainly not a stranger here, for hardly had she turned off the lights after parking the car, when two men emerged from the house, a hurricane lamp in the hands of the older man, who must have been the owner of the home.

'Welcome, Hajat,' the man with the lantern said.

'Thank you. Are we sitting out here?'

'We may have to. There are ears inside. My wife returned today, with her sister. And the children are still awake.'

It was hard to imagine how the entire mentioned population could fit into that hovel.

Meanwhile, Zana had driven on, without causing any alarm. Luckily, a path turned off the dirt road about sixty metres ahead, and onto this he turned. Acting swiftly, he turned off the engine, locked the car and he and Gobah raced backwards towards the home. The plan was that they go to separate sides of the house, lest the voices be inclined on one side. But as luck would have it, the party was outside. Stealthily, the boys tip-toed to less than ten metres of the small cluster and listened, their hearts pounding in the excitement of the game.

'You must act quickly, though,' the woman was saying.

'We missed the-' Gobah began, but Zana waved him into silence.

'Hajat, this may be easier than you think,' the older man said. It was the man who had got out with the lantern, which had now been returned to the house. 'My wife's sister is only ten, and I doubt that anybody has touched her.'

'Oh, you don't know girls of today,' Hajat laughed. 'But surely you don't want to use…'

'What are you saying?' the man said. 'This is business, and you just said the faster the better… A head for lives, you said, not so?'

'Yes.'

'He'll do it, tomorrow,' the man said, pointing at the second man. 'We know how. A visit to the well down there, the rest will be easy.'

'A well's a public place,' Hajat protested.

'She doesn't get there. The path to the well runs through my garden, where Kalenge here will be waiting,' he said, before turning to the said Kalenge and adding, 'Noon. In the heat of noon no one is out. You will wait in the charcoal pit. Fine?'

'Very OK with me,' Kalenge affirmed.

'Good,' a satisfied Hajat said. 'I'll be at the site the whole day tomorrow.'

'Do we bring the head there?' Kalenge wanted to know the magnitude of his task.

The woman jumped with the fright of the suggestion. 'Bring the head? Where?'

'At the site, Hajat,' the older man said casually.

'You're mad, the two of you. And why the head?'

'What do you want with the whole girl? We will need her body for burial, in a day or two.' It was the condemned girl's brother-in-law who spoke.

'But no head is coming to the site. Do this. At seven sharp, I'll be at home-'

'We can't come all the way to Iganga, you know that, Hajat,' the older man said.

'I see no difference between Nakalama and Iganga. It's a difference of only... is it five miles?'

'All right, we shall be there.'

Back to the Pick-up, Gobah was crying. He wept so uncontrollably, Zana didn't know what to do for him. He put his hand on the boy's back, and let the tears flow down, till he was calm.

'Gobah, we shall soon catch these monsters.' Gobah only nodded. 'I know how it must feel.'

'Zana, can't we save this girl?' Now this was the last thing Zana had expected.

'How?'

'We... we look up that charcoal pit and... and we save her.'

'Too dangerous, Gobah. Besides, we need the evidence.'

'We shall be as guilty, Zana. We're already accomplices to that murder. At least let's alert her before she can get to the well, Zana. We must.'

'Gobah, it's very hard.' Zana was in deep thought, then he said, almost to himself, 'Fine, we shall give it a try.' Then to Gobah, he said, 'We'll do the best we can. Let's get home and talk about it.'

Gobah wept silently all the way back home. He did not only weep for Marla, but for this innocent ten-year-old girl, too. Deep inside, he knew they would not save her. And yes, Zana was right. To confront those beasts was to step into a lion's mouth, with your eyes open. God help the poor girl.

TEN

A BLOODY ENCOUNTER

It was a hot morning. It was the sort of heat that sometimes precedes rain in the tropics. A thin path wound its way downhill, separating a banana shamba from a rather lush bush, with occasional thickets of lantana camara here and there. The spear grass in which the thickets grew was also tall, creating a viable environment for anyone or anything that could have wanted to hide in it.

The slope became very steep at a point, almost too steep for anything but well-grooved shoes. Below this slope was a large pit, like a dried-out mini-lake. Grass grew in patches of this pit, but the rest of it was bare and red, like an anthill. Bordering this giant pit, by the path, was a large mvule tree. A man stood by this tree, hidden from anyone who did not know that he was there.

The man by the tree was a thick-set fellow with a blunt head, on which grew a grove of dirty, unkempt hair. The beard, too, was unruly. His rat-like eyes were fixed on the path winding its way downward, towards the well, past the tree under which he stood. However, if one studied this man carefully, one would notice two things: Whenever the wind rustled the spear grass around him, the rat-eyes would shift and widen in fearsome apprehension. And two, every now and then, his right hand kept reaching inside his dirty coat, and touching something that was concealed there.

At the extreme end of the large pit crouched the two young men, Zana and Gobah. They had arrived much earlier than Kalenge, the man who was supposed to carry out the kidnap and, God forbid, the murder. Gobah had at first refused to come down the pit, imploring

Zana to let him go back to the car, three kilometres down the road, where they had left it parked. He was visibly terrified. Every now and then gigantic shivers would creep up his spine, shaking him like shafts of electric currents being run up his brain. With time, he even started whimpering.

'Gobah my goodness, you'll get us into trouble,' his colleague pleaded.

'I'm sorry, Zana. I just can't control myself.'

'Try.'

'I will… I will, Zana. O God above!'

His whimpering subsided, but the shivering intensified. It was so powerful; his hands could hardly hold each other. Zana made up his mind to let him go away. He was more of a liability at this point, and would possibly get the two of them into grave danger.

'Gobah,' he said to his young friend, 'sneak from here and go gather yourself. I'll find you in the car.'

'Is it OK with… will you be safe?' Gobah's voice lacked conviction in his concern for Zana's safety.

'I will. I know how to take care of me.'

'I can hardly bring myself to stand up. See you, Zana. Take care…'

Gobah was still dragging himself to his feet, when voices were heard coming down from up the hill. They were certainly girls' voices. Gobah hit the ground again. This was the moment. Crawling like a guerrilla, Zana moved towards the tree where the thick-set man hid. The camera they had carried with them was in his pocket.

'They will see the grass move, Zana,' Gobah whispered, his entire system brimming with red-hot adrenaline.

'Shut up, you!' He crawled more rapidly.

60

The two girls were now in sight. One was taller than the other, and carried a 20-litre jerrycan in her hand. The second girl, of about twelve or so years, had a smaller jerrycan, and trudged in front of the elder one.

The man behind the tree saw the two girls come down the path. Godammit, his target was not with them. But what the hell, this little thing in front could do as well. He could take her, instead. On second thoughts, however, he decided that he could wait. Girls in this area were sharp, a girl her size and age could be capable of lots of experiences. So rather than alarm them, he chose to hide and let them pass. Acting swiftly, he dived in the bush behind the tree, a stone's throw from where Zana lay, his small camera poised.

The two girls had barely disappeared down the bush path, when another girl came down, running. Her bare feet came a-slap a-slap a-slapping the hard beaten path, a jerrycan in her hand. She obviously was trying to catch up with the two ahead of her.

The man heard the little girl's advance and peeked up. He jumped out of his cover, darting to under the tree. His left hand drew a dirty piece of cloth from his trouser pocket, and then he threw himself right in front of the little girl. She could hardly stop herself, as she steered herself right into his arms, an ear-piercing shriek ensuing from her throat at the same time. The man quickly gagged her with the dirty rag, rendering her incapable of screaming. Her frail hands clawed about her, instinct bidding her save her life. Down the path, the two girls she had been chasing after had heard her, and were also shouting in some sort of response.

The man knew he had no time. He pulled the little girl under the tree, where he laid her on the ground. He put her hands together and stepped on them with one firm foot, while the other foot held down the legs by the ankles. Still, the terrified girl fought on, writhing violently… until the knife the man pulled out of his coat descended on her throat, slicing deep, breaking flesh and gullet. Blood gushed out, and the man cut once more, before jumping aside to let the blood ooze out. He then picked up the head and, heading for the banana plantation, disappeared.

Zana was terrified, but he would take two more shots. Mustering his courage and strength, he went up to where the decapitated body lay. The hands were clasped together, like each had tried to get the other to help in the desperate struggle. The blood was still flowing out…

Zana's head was reeling. He sprinted back to where he had left Gobah. Caution had deserted him now. He was in a crisis.

'Gobah,' he yelled out loud. 'Gobah, come out quick!' No Gobah. He ran faster, to where his colleague lay, panting for breath, his face contorted, drooling with saliva and mucus and tears.

'Gobah man, get up! We have no time.' Seeing no response, he lifted up the collapsed boy and ascended the hill, hoping that nobody found them. They would certainly be the first suspects.

Gobah did not regain his strength till after he had been laid in the pick-up, and Zana was racing back to his mother's house. He was himself in ugly shape, but he also knew that if he let such factors materialise in his mind, this whole thing was a total flop. No, even if it meant taking over the whole scheme from Gobah, what he had just witnessed was enough to cause him to risk anything, to see these monsters apprehended.

'Zana, I want water,' Gobah's voice came weakly.

'Not now. You can't.'

'Please Zan-'

'No!'

Gobah attempted to sit up, failed, and slumped back onto the seat. The pick-up raced towards their home.

Gobah's temperature refused to go down. Zana had run for drugs at the drug shop down the road, soon after they arrived home. He had helped his friend swallow four chloroquine tablets, plus two tiny pills the shop attendant had said would cause him to sleep almost instantly. He had slept alright, but his temperature remained high.

Zana rang up his mother. She was in Iganga, for a Local Farmers' workshop.

By the time Zana's mother arrived, Gobah was delirious. He was screaming about blood, and soldiers, and Marla being butchered. He was also hitting at anything his frail fists could reach. He was rushed to Iganga Hospital, where cerebral malaria was diagnosed. He was admitted late that afternoon.

ELEVEN

RISK AT THE SHRINE

Gobah was bed-ridden for three days - days during which not much could be accomplished. Zana told his mother about their horrendous experience, and she insisted that they should have instead helped save the girl. However, now that they had not, they had to report to the Police. Zana was, however, opposed to this. 'If we involve the Police at this point, we forfeit greater accomplishments in our pursuit, mother,' he argued.

'And if you delay,' his mother said, 'this whole thing might come to nothing.'

'No.'

'And what makes you so sure? This is Uganda, my child.'

'It may be, but even in Uganda, the empirical evidence of still pictures and recorded voices might not be easy to deny.'

'Listen, Zana. Those people are right now at Nsinze's shrine, getting whatever rubbish they want. How are you to trace them after they have disappeared?'

'Mummy, the Police will find a way. We will give them the proof, and tell the public that we have. Then the public will expect the Police to find and crush these monsters.'

'Oh, Zana, pity the parents of this girl. They-'

'They have already lost her. If we rush this thing, other parents whose children are alive today may also lose them, soon. No, mother, until we have got the person causing all this, we'll not be solving any problem.'

Thus the issue was resolved, as Zana awaited the recovery of his comrade. He checked on him daily at the hospital, till he was discharged on the third day.

'Can you work now, Kido?' they were driving back home from the hospital. It was evening, and the atmosphere was enthralled in a crimson shawl, like a shroud over a slain combatant. The traffic was rather heavy, but it could move without halting at any point.

'If it means dying in the process,' Gobah said, 'I'll die. But I'll have to do it now. TODAY.' His mind was flooded with memories of what they had witnessed only days ago. 'Where do we start now?'

'Right now nothing can move until we catch up with the shrine. We must know what Nsinze is up to.'

'So?' Gobah cast a quizzical look at his mentor and friend.

'Someone must go over to the shrine.'

'You're mad. We have no cause-'

'We do. We must-'

'No, Zana… we got what took us there. They don't expect us back.'

'Gobah, even things given by God need follow-up. You have to keep praying to keep them. If it means cooking up another problem, you shall.'

Gobah was silent for a while. The scene of the murder of the little girl replayed in his mind. The shriek. The blood. Then that eerie gurgle of blood coming out of the decapitated trunk…

'Fine. I will go.'

It was late evening. Bloody clouds decorated the western sky with a mutilated pattern, like scattered pieces of flesh. A morbid silence pervaded the atmosphere, save for the silent static on Zana's equipment. It was close to thirty minutes since Gobah had set out for the shrine. He had said to decide on what to say when he got there, depending on the prevailing environment. If Nsinze suspected anything, there was no telling what they could do to Gobah. These were a ruthless lot, by every measure.

A cracking sound came onto the radio's reception. Zana jumped to attention. The time was up. He put the head phones on and waited, every second seeming like ten hours.

'…body get in. We'll get him to come over,' a voice was saying. There were sounds of voices of people whispering as they moved into the shrine. Zana could make out the footsteps. He wondered if Gobah was one of them. After a while, silence reigned. It was now clear that they were in the awful shrine, awaiting Nsinze's entry. Then he heard lone footsteps approaching the shrine, where Gobah evidently was, with the mike chip.

'He'll be here presently. Let's have those who have been here before on one side… this way, please, and those who haven't, stay that side… Good. No, no, no, young man, stay there. Very good.'

Then silence.

The next thing Zana heard were the rattles and shrieks which announced the commencement of the divination. How had Nsinze got in unannounced? Had he already been in that wicked shrine of his?

'*He he he he he heeeee! Hi hi hi hi hiiiii! Ho ho ho ho hoooo!' Traaa Treee Traaa Ta tat a ktraaaaaa…* A shrill-voiced 'spirit' was addressing the clients.

'All stand – quick!'

There was shuffling as the clients stood up.

'All sit!'

They hit the floor.

'All stand. Standing? Sit. Sitting? Stand. Standing? Sit.'

Zana smiled, in spite of himself. If these things monitored the people, how come they could not see if they stood or sat, and had to ask? And why couldn't they realise that someone was there with ill intentions?

'Blood in this place,' he heard the 'spirit' say. 'There is blood! There is blooood!' *Tra-tra-traaa traaaa!* The rattles seemed to move around the hut that was the shrine. Zana recalled the first time they had been to the shrine together with Gobah. Though he suspected deception behind the noises, he had actually got scared. There was something wickedly chilly about the whole experience. It could be just possible that Nsinze mixed reality with deception. It could just be possible.

'On your bellies, all of you… face down!' a new voice said. No rattles accompanied it. Rapid steps approached the hut, entered and went beyond the place where the mike was. They receded, evidently entering the inner chamber. Nsinze had come. Immediately, the prescriptions started.

'Where there was no virility, I see sons. Masculine sons. I see sons… sons… soooons!' Rattles, and a rumble as of a distant but giant peel of thunder. And deep sighs from the crowd in the hut.

'Thanks for the bird. We saw the bird. We got the bird. Daughter, you have the house. I see a mansion. A mansion. A mansiooon!' louder rattling and very shrill shrieks, accompanied by raucous laughter.

Zana's heart beat faster. Could that be the woman for whom murder had been committed only days ago? He wanted proof. He wished Gobah could send him a sign… some sound to signal recognition…

The machine went dead.

It happened to fast, nobody knew how. The divinations and prescriptions were still going on, everybody stiff with awesome fear and anticipation. Then the young boy who had been seated by the edge of the fresh group sprang up and headed for the door. Taken unawares, the settled clients scrambled up and scattered all over. Nsinze's voice snapped shut, and then there was hyper-activity outside. The shrine attendants had already known that something was amiss. They shot after the youth, giving wild and desperate chase, but he outran them. When all the dust had settled, with everybody only speculating as to what exactly had happened, Gobah was out of the hut and away from the vicinity. None of the people could identify the boy who had sprung out from the shrine.

Nsinze was incensed. He was unsettled, too. His spirits came back to take the rest of the clients through more drills, as he rushed out to contend with his assistants. Somebody was up to something. A hunt had to be mounted. They could all smell a rat.

Meanwhile, Gobah ran straight to the Control Centre, or CC, as they had started calling it. He was out of breath when he got there.

'I saw her! I saw her, Zana! The woman of the head!'

'I understand,' Zana said. 'I suspected as much. Get seated and cool down.'

'We must act fast, Zana.'

'Cool down, man. If we panic, we'll lose it all. We must plan this now, else all's lost.'

'No time-'

'Shut up. We must plan. First: Why did you run away?'

'What do you mean?' Gobah was perplexed at Zana's turn of conduct.

'Now that you have broken our contact with them, what do you expect us to do?'

'We... I could... Look, I am sorry.'

'Fine, you are sorry. So?'

Gobah was silent and crestfallen. He had brought the hunt to a stupid and premature end. By rushing out of the hut like that, and snapping off the mike, he had actually cut the whole thing short, and rendered all their efforts futile. He wanted to cry. He wanted to kill himself. How terribly tragic!

'Gobah?'

'Wait! Wait!'

'I am waiting, man.'

'I have an idea. There was the couple I was seated next to. The man whispered to the woman he was with, possibly his wife, about failure to get the girl they had wanted.'

'So?'

'No vehicle has passed so far, on the way from the shrine.'

'And?'

'If we act fast, they could find the girl.'

'I still don't see how that's going to help us. Even if that couple gets Nsinze's men to get them a girl, we have no way of linking up with the shrine. After what you've done, there's going to be security at that wicked place.'

'You don't know yet, Zana. It'll work out. Let me explain.'

The plan was agreeable. Zana's anger at Gobah's foolish action thawed rapidly like put in hot water. They discussed the possible modalities involved, and were eventually ready to move to the next step.

Zana stayed at the CC, with the Local Council officials and the Police. He had convinced his mother to contact the LC Chairman for them, since nobody would believe a couple of boys on an issue like that. She had finally consented to talk to the Chairman, who had contacted his defence secretary, who in turn involved the Police. Now all waited at the CC, listening intently on the equipment the boys had set up.

'Do you have the pictures you've talked about here?' one of the policemen asked, taking down notes.

'They are at my mother's house. I'll pass them to you after we're done with this.'

'And you'll have to take us to the place where the girl was living – straightaway,' the other officer said. He was a serious-looking man, with pointed whiskers and blood-shot eyes.

'Anything, Officer,' Zana said. His mind was on where his compatriot had gone, into the zone of death.

'Chairman, we're surprised that you've never got concerned about this Nsimbe man-'

'Nsinze, Officer, Nsinze,' Zana corrected.

'Whatever.' It was the whiskered man. 'These people should have been nabbed by now!'

'It was not easy to suspect anything, Officer. One needed to go over to know anything concrete.'

'We shall find out, after we're through with this.'

They talked into the night, with nothing coming onto the monitors. The LC men were just suggesting putting off the hunt till the next day when a sharp scream tore the night silence on the equipment. Everybody tuned their senses.

TWELVE

ANOTHER KIDNAP

True to Gobah's word, the girl-seeking couple had indeed talked to Nsinze's men. The assistants had, after lots of haggling and pressing, agreed to find the said girl. It would be no sweat, they had said. The fact that no child had ever disappeared around the village would make it easy. Yes, in a day or two, the couple would have their child… for a handsome fee of five hundred thousand shillings.

Now as the sun ran swiftly towards the western sky, two men prowled the shrine environs, wary of going far, lest they should fail to carry their booty if anybody gave chase. They were sure to find a stray child soon enough.

They walked from one path to another, seeming to go nowhere in particular. By a stroke of luck, not many people walked the paths this particular evening. For if they had, it would have been obvious that the two men penduluming all the village paths were up to no good. That would surely deny them their succulent success.

Gobah was scared rigid. He knew by now how ruthless these people were. Should they decide to scrape off whatever parts they wanted on site, he was finished. So every time he saw the two familiar men pass by his hideout, the old debate would resume in his now close-to-numb mind. Go out now. No, don't. Now! Later! No, just beat it, man. Leave! No, go to them now. Now, go!… no, never! And it was getting late. The sun had set, and the men now passed him, headed towards the mosque. One of them, a squat man in dark jeans and a

72

Sportsman topee, kept glancing furtively hence and thence, like one who walked the streets of a deserted war-ridden city. He walked in front. The second man was – or seemed – more confident and brave. He was a lanky man, with legs that hardly bent when he walked. They made Gobah think about meningitis. He had been told that meningitis made a victim's limbs go stiff. But also, it was known that when it came to running, such people were usually racers. The type who did tens of kilometres non-stop. The men disappeared down the path.

Meanwhile, the men were getting restless. Had they been wrong about these environs? It was already getting dark, and their mission was flopping. They had moved up and down practically every path in the vicinity, to no profit. Now they were headed straight for the shrine, if nothing happened. At the mosque, they had found two girls. One was much bigger than their target age, but the second was just about the right age. If they had got her, they would be in business. But what could they have done about the other one? Attempting to grab the little girl would have been a most stupid move.

'Wait!' the lanky man grabbed the squat man's hand.

'What?'

'It's over. Shh! Don't move.'

'Where?' the squat man's eyes now darted madly, scanning the environment rapidly. Then he too saw.

The girl they saw could have been anything between fourteen and sixteen. That was their range. Even if she reached seventeen, the difference would not be dangerous. This was their girl. She was dressed in a long flowing dress, with a fancy scarf on her head, tied at the back and the ends hanging at the front, covering the breasts. Most certainly a town-bred girl, probably from Jinja or Kampala. Iganga was too rural to breed such exotic girls. The Jinja or Kampala girl was sure not to be pure, but who cared? Who was going to do a clinical test to see if the wench's membrane still existed?

73

The girl was moving in their direction, walking at a leisurely pace. Either she hadn't seen the two men advance, or if she did, she did not care. These were safe grounds to prowl upon, early in the evening. The men were now about three metres ahead of her. Either something itched around her waist, or she was adjusting the tight band around her panties, but her left hand lingered around there awhile, then it fell back. The men were just abreast now. One parted from the other and passed on the girl's left side. The lanky man stayed on her right. When both grabbed her, there was no chance of escape.

The long scream was followed by angry threats from gruff but clearly different voices.

'Shut up, you.'

'If you make any other noise, we kill you right here.'

'We go no. Move!'

'The bastards!' said one of the policemen; the one who had promised the LC Chairman trouble after this fight.

'They're making him walk.'

'Yeah,' agreed his comrade. 'That way it doesn't look dubious. Everybody will suspect two men they find carrying a boy between-'

'Girl. He's a girl now,' Zana corrected.

There was nervous laughter.

'Girl, sorry,' the Policeman agreed. 'We should go out now, gentlemen,' the LC Defence man suggested.

'No way.' It was Zana's firm refusal again. He had his entire plan laid out, and nobody was about to disrupt it with rash suggestions.

The walking could have taken about ten or so minutes, but to the waiting group, it seemed like forever and a day. Anxiety gnawed at the Chairman, impatience at the Defence Secretary, bitterness at the Law and Order men, and vengeance at Zana. He could not wait to have a chance to see all the beasts involved in these ghastly activities nabbed, and set for punishment. In his mind, there was no interlude for remand, hearing, possible conviction and eventual imprisonment or whatever other punitive measure. To him it was arrest and these 'whatever other punitive measures' that he refused to admit to himself that were what he desired most for people who killed innocent little girls. Old King Hamurabi was right: a life for a life.

'Where do we keep her?' they heard one voice whisper on the monitor.

'Shouldn't we show her to Mzee?' the other voice said. The 'girl's' voice came through, too - was whimpering softly. Gobah was certainly a great actor. So far so good... good, if the reigning tension was not borne in mind.

'His time will come. Right now we keep the bitch, till after our bosses return.'

'You're certainly out of your mind, Ngobi,' one man said. That was one name. It entered the Police records.

'Keeping her even till only tomorrow is but glaring foolishness. We cut off her things now, tonight.'

'Now that is real clinical insanity, Sir.'

The name, you fool. The name, one of the Policemen was thinking to himself. Everyone crowded around the little set like they actually watched a live telecast of the kidnap on it.

'What about the body, Sir?' the first man proceeded. 'We cut off the... the... her things, and the breasts, and dig out the liver and heart, and what do we do with the-'

At the mention of the 'things' and breast, the little CC group winced and grimaced, but when the liver and heart were mentioned, the LC Chairman could take it no longer. 'Gentlemen,' he said, 'if we don't go over there now, we're making a grievous blunder. The boy might be in danger.'

'No, Chairman,' Zana protested. 'Once they discover that he's not female, he loses no 'things', no breasts and no-'

'You don't know what you're saying,' the hot-bloodied Policeman said. 'When they discover his sex, there will be no dilly-dallying. They will kill him. He has already seen them, and their hideout, and he would tell on them.'

'Quite so,' agreed the second Policeman. 'We should set out now.'

'And do what?' the LC Defence man asked, his every security instinct stimulated.

'Arrest them, search the place, get them to tell us where all the other crooks are!'

'And?'

'Damn you, Mr Defence man!' the tough Police Officer barked, to the shock of everybody else. 'The rest will come later. We're killing time.'

Their debate was cut into by a sharp scream, this time not of a girl's voice. It was the real Gobah now. Now it was a scream of pain.

The party moved out. They carried their equipment with them, with ropes, manacles, batons, two AK 47 rifles and a club the Defence man carried.

They practically raced all the way to the shrine. Zana's youthful and vengeance-seeking legs carried him at the front all through; the older men following. The LC Chairman lumbered from behind.

Towards the shrine, they stopped. They had to talk. There were only two major buildings: the shrine and Nsinze's main house. Both had to be covered. The grass-thatched kitchen may not have been a problem. Zana suggested that each major building be covered by an armed person, with civilian support. And so it was. Both buildings were covered, then the fire-spitting Policeman announced: 'Everybody in there get the hell out. Quick!'

THIRTEEN

PUNISHMENT FOR A MEAN LIE

The squat Sportsman-topeed man was impatient with his lanky colleague. They had to do the curving out of the parts now, or the entire exercise lost meaning. He had moved with his knife, in case he had had to use it out during the hunt. He now pulled out this knife and ordered his lanky colleague to hold up the girl's dress.

Gobah's heart was by then pounding like the throb of a self-reloading machine gun. He now knew that he did not have much longer to live. The whole scheme was coming to smoke. Poor Zana! Part of his mind told him to outrightly call out to his friend. Then another part, the saner one, told him that shouting would just scare the assailants away. That would sure be the end of it all. He risked silence.

The lanky man (called Ngobi) grabbed Gobah by the hands and pulled a scarf from his pocket. He bound the girl's hands behind, then found a handkerchief which he gagged Gobah's mouth with. It could not work, so he gave it up. First shock: the girl wore shorts under her dress.

'Pull down the shorts, Ngobi,' the rougher man barked, blood on his mind now. Ngobi pulled the shorts off. Beneath the shorts were undies, with a disturbing protrusion at the sacred region.

'What's this, Mister?' Ngobi asked, looking up at his colleague-turned boss. 'What's this we have got here?'

'What's what we have got where?'

78

Ngobi touched the protrusion. Male genitals, unless he was, as his colleague had suggested earlier, sick in the head.

'Our girl here is male. She is a boy!'

'Don't be silly.' The squat man bent over and pulled off Gobah's underwear, only to see tangible male genitals. Both men sprang back in shock.

If Gobah's entire system had not filled up with adrenaline, he might have found this experience very amusing. However, his sixth sense told him the fun would not last much longer. A look at the topeed man confirmed his fears. A snarl of utmost hatred and anger covered the man's head like a Death's head. Gobah's heart sank.

'You boy,' the angry man said gruffly, 'just what do you think you're up to?'

'Who do you think you're fooling?' put in Ngobi.

'Keep off, Ngobi. I must handle this alone.'

'Why-'

'Keep silent! Now boy, can you explain this?'

Gobah tried to talk, but some canvas membrane covered his voice. He coughed and tried again. No voice. It was like the feeling one has in a dream, when one wants to scream but cannot.

'You'll pay dearly for this, idiot. Grab – no. No need.'

The so far nameless man advanced towards Gobah, and before Ngobi knew what was what, the boy was screaming, blood flowing, half his scrotum and one testicle lying on the floor of the room that was at the same time used as the lobby for the shrine visitors.

Nsinze was in the house when the scream went off. He was startled. Jumping off his bed, he pulled on his trousers and practically ran out to the shrine.

'What's going on here?' he asked, his breath coming in gasps.

The nameless man jeered and turned towards the wall. Ngobi wore a deathly grimace on his face. A figure in a dress lay on the floor, as good as dead.

'Ngobi, I asked you people a question, the least I want in response is an immediate answer.' Nsinze's fangs were out. Ngobi gestured towards the topeed man with his head, words eluding him.

'Kirevu, what's this?' Nsinze was now menacing.

'What can't you see? A boy in a dress.'

'Better give me a full answer, or you will both lie here beside this thing on the shrine floor.' Neither of them had ever heard this kind of tone ensue from Nsinze, nor had they seen him look that way. It was Ngobi who offered the first explanation.

'Kirevu castrated him.'

A deep, dangerous silence reigned for an uncomfortable moment.

'Kirevu?'

'He fooled us. Some of your clients asked us to get them a girl. The couple seeking to kill their business rival. We went out for a girl, and found this… this idiot. He was dressed like a girl. Only to get here and discover he was male.'

Nsinze was suppressing a sardonic smile, but managed to ask, 'Did you have to castrate him? And do you… I mean, since when did you have to find sacrifice items for the clients?' He was frothing by now.

The silence which followed was unbearable. Then in a sudden swoop, the old man grabbed the knife which was still in Kirevu's hand and stabbed him in the shoulder with it. The thick man grimaced, whined, and withdrew to the far end of the room. The blood was flowing vigorously. Ngobi collapsed onto his haunches.

'Ngobi?' the voice was now steely. The lanky man jumped, his eyes bulging. 'Ngobi, do you people know why this boy was dressed like a girl? Do you know why he made it easy for you to kidnap him? Do you even... Oh my God!' the old man fell silent, his breathing coming more difficult. It was then that Ngobi recalled the incident of the little boy who had sprinted out of the shrine only the day before. He groaned.

'What's it?' Nsinze asked.

'Please send for a light,' Ngobi managed a croak.

'For what?'

'I want to look at this boy.'

Nsinze pulled a torch out of his trouser pocket. He handed it to Ngobi, who flashed it in the boy's face.

'Oh God!' his groan was desperate. 'It's the boy who was here yesterday.'

'Everybody in there get out: Quick!'

The voice from outside raped everybody's mind to alertness. Even the bleeding Kirevu jumped and huddled close to the old man who only moments ago had stabbed him. They listened.

'Ngobi and your friends, if we have to force open the doors and get you-'

'They know you!' Nsinze said. 'Get out and talk to them.'

Ngobi stayed put. The old man kicked him hard, whispering commands that Ngobi get out. Ngobi did not move a muscle.

There was the sound of a gun being cocked. Nsinze moved to the door of the shrine. He peeped outside.

'They're armed – at least one bastard is. Come on out.'

'They will find me in here,' Kirevu growled. 'Pass me my knife.'

'I'll instead finish you off myself, before they take me,' the old killer-healer said between gritted teeth. Kirevu followed Ngobi outside, and Nsinze followed them.

'Hands up, all of you!' the tough Policeman said, covering the three men with his gun. 'Who's in the other house?'

'My family,' Nsinze said.

'Are you Nsinze?' the LC Chairman asked.

'He is,' Zana answered, to the consternation of the three culprits. 'Where is the boy?' he addressed the question to Ngobi.

'In there.'

Zana rushed in. It took him only a moment, and he was back, screaming. He threw his torch at Nsinze's head, tearing the old man's eye. 'You beast!'

'Go easy, young man,' the tough Policeman said. 'You're not the Law. What's up?'

'They cut off his balls!'

FOURTEEN

WHO KILLED GOBAH'S SISTER?

Nsinze, Ngobi and Kirevu were arrested, together with three other assistants to Nsinze's murderous activities. They were all taken to Iganga Central Police Station for questioning.

Inspector Kamya, the tough Policeman, walked into the Questioning Room, known among the officers as QR, a few minutes after ten o'clock the following morning. His colleague, ASP Luboira, had gone to Jinja to help in another couple of arrests. The group from the shrine had revealed that the woman who had been behind the Tororo murder was in Jinja, and she might have a few other vital names to name.

Inspector Kamya sat atop his desk, notepad in hand, two other Policemen standing by the doorway. He summoned Nsinze to him.

The old man who stepped forward was tall, heavy in build, but with age beginning to show in his movement. He was beginning to grey, and his skin stretched uncomfortably over his face and hands. He had been in the murder business rather long.

'So you're the boss behind all these atrocities, eh?'

'I am a healer, Officer,' he said amazingly calmly.

'Not a killer?'

'Healer. I deal in traditional medicines.'

'Aha! And the human sacrifices you demand?'

'I never ask anyone to kill a person. They can look for dead people and cut out what I ask them to bring.'

'Do you see a dunce when you look at me?' Inspector Kamya's voice was chilly. The old man was silent, but rather defiant.

'Mzee Nsinze, I'll not pester you over what you do not want to say. We have all the time in the world, with you. Just tell me this. How did you manage to fool everybody?' he was now chatty.

'How do you mean?' the old man's defiance had been melted by the conversational attitude the Inspector had adopted.

'Those spirits. The spirit voices.'

'Technology.'

'Oh, no doubt in response to Museveni's call for modernisation, eh?'

They both afforded light but tight laughter.

'What was your technology like, Mzee?'

'Wiring. We had a kind of studio in my house, where various people used different voices, which were delivered in the shrine over speakers in the roof.'

'Wow! And the rattles that move across the roof?'

'Same thing, Inspector. We did it the way disco lights are done. The electric current would travel around a plastic tube in which the rattling sounds are, causing the impression of rattles moving across the roof. That goes for all the other sounds, too.'

'Fascinating, Mzee. Very fascinating!'

'I don't know,' Nsinze's voice was flat.

'Fine. Call me one of your attendants. The one with the wound.'

The interrogations lasted five hours, without a break. When Inspector Kamya told Kirevu that Gobah was recovering at Mulago Hospital in Kampala, the killer man said he wished the goon had died. 'But it's never too late,' he mused. 'Never too late.' He, however, also revealed very useful information for the law. It was from him that Inspector Kamya learnt that the woman who was behind the murder Gobah and Zana witnessed and recorded was also linked to the people who had asked for the genitals, breasts, liver and heart of a young girl – the things for which Gobah had lost his manhood, because he could not avail them to the suppliers.

The search for that woman yielded more than the expected results. In addition to her, the LC III Chairman of Idudi, Gobah's home village, was arrested. It was for him that Marla, Gobah's sister, had been kidnapped and beheaded.

'Why did you do this? You're a public figure!' ASP Luboira asked him at Iganga CPS.

'I am sorry. I couldn't do it myself – I didn't do it myself.' He was weeping.

'That's not the point. You paid for it, so we see no difference.'

'Please don't torment me. I am repentant.'

'The boy whose sister you killed has been rendered absolutely useless, for life. He will never know what it is to be a real man. His parents are old beyond repair. What use is your repentance, then?' ASP Kamya's voice carried tears in it. It made Zana, who had come in with the new arrestees, weep, too.

'Nobody knew that you were involved in this murder. Why did you stop the Police at Idudi from at least pretending to work? It caused a few people to suspect, you know.'

'It would have come out much earlier,' the Chairman said.

'Which makes no difference. It's now out and it's going to make it worse for you all. That is where the big difference lies, my dear sir.'

'I am sorry.'

A deeper probe had to be done at Idudi, to unearth the entire racket of kidnappers there. If those women had called Gobah and Marla 'the twins', which was a common reference to the brother and sister, it was clear that they were familiar with the life of the village. They had to know more.

The team that set for Idudi comprised ASP Luboira, Zana, the arrested LC III Chairman of Idudi, the Head-for-a-House woman, and two Police Constables. They boarded a Police-registered Toyota Hilux Pick-up. Inspector Kamya stood outside the Investigation Chamber, his hands across the chest. A faded beret rested on one side of his head, giving him a perplexed appearance, like he considered giving up on the rate of crime in the district. He had been in the force for over twenty years, and he had never known people to be as lawless as they were now. Surely the end of the world was nigh.

The Hilux Pick-Up slowly backed out of the Police yard, turning onto the tarmac beyond. To go to Jinja, it turned right, and Inspector Kamya heard the gears climb to running speed, until he could not hear the tiger-car's whine any more. In the distance, a workers' siren wailed, announcing lunch time.

The Police Officer turned and went in to glean more information, if more was left.

BOB G. KISIKI

MUKONO,

2000

The Rainbow's End

Bob G. Kisiki

*I contemplate the horizon
and its sun-crest,
and I have seen rainbows at
the water-hole,
but I have never tried to
touch the objects.
That way lies
disappointment, that way
madness.
There is nothing wrong with
ambition….What is wrong is
to try and capture that
ambition. For too often it
melts as you do, and slips
through gaps between your
fingers.
(Robert Serumaga, A Play).*

THIS STORY IS DEDICATED TO A
YEAR, THE YEAR 1999 WHEN:
I WAS DELIVERED FROM LABOR, TO
WORK; FROM ROUTINES, TO LIFE;
AND I GOT A JEWEL IN MY LIFE:
SUSAN.
IT IS ALSO DEDICATED TO THE
MEMORY OF A TEACHER AND
MENTOR, R-O,
AND TO A TEACHER, FRIEND AND
SUPERIOR:

AUSTIN BUKENYA.

(BK)

ONE

LEMAH was far from her usual self. If you failed to notice this from her unusually curt manner in dealing with her work-mates in the News Room, you would detect it in the way she all the time kept to herself, keeping out of the way of everybody else. One would be tempted to think that if she could, she would have hidden from herself, even. Finally, she decided to escape into the privacy of her office. This was not 100% privacy, but at least she would know how to get along with Mercy, her secretary. At this time, the typists were not in yet, and she could afford to shut herself into her own world until she felt like the usual Lemah again.

In the office, Mercy looked at her Boss-friend and kept their communication to the intimate, "Hello, Lemah". To venture beyond that would be like opening a bitter capsule onto the tongue. Lemah sank onto her seat, drowned into her thoughts and shut the rest of the world off. Her head was thrown back, her eyes half-shut, her arms hanging limp on the sides. She cut the image of a tragic heroine in a Greek drama. In that posture, only a lunatic would dare disturb her…. yet in a way that is what she desired most: something, somebody to cut short her roaming on this wild highway of painful whims. She ached to return to the lanes of Possibility, she knew it, but something… somebody had to snatch her from wherever she wandered. She desired that somebody distracts her, so she could flare at them, and then before her sick mind could sneak away again, she focuses it on the day's work.

When nobody budged into her thoughts, she steered her mind to the innumerable lectures, speeches, magazine articles, propaganda posters and handbills she used to stuff into her mind when she still associated with and believed in the Uganda Women Empowerment Movement. 'All this talk about a woman needs a man in her life is rubbish, real rotting rubbish. What is it about a woman that renders her incomplete until she lets a man mess her life up? Typical chauvinist mentality, that.' Yes, even the women who believed in and supported such theories were chauvinists…Lemah had actually staunchly believed in and subscribed to all this nonsensical preaching, practised what it said even, till she discovered, by personal experience, that it was one thing to be a human being, another to be a woman, and still another to be an individual - male or female.

Things had started to happen to her inside, things that seemed to have come up specially to take her mind off the UWEM teachings. At first she thought that it was the rebel in her that did it, but more and more regularly, she discovered that the rift between her mind and her emotions was growing wider and wider, and deeper by the day. Coupled with her childhood dreams - dreams that had fashioned her life even beyond university level, she let her inner mechanisms lead her on, other than listen to things other people said. She would compare notes, and then make a decision.

From the time she had been a little girl, Lemah had had dreams. Dreams about her education... dreams about her career pursuits... dreams about her marital life. Amazing even to her, she did not model her life on anyone she knew, whether out of real life or from fiction. In her mind, she just saw a grown up Lemah, learned and educated, a successful, powerful woman with an office – spreading far and wide in the dominion of journalism, and in a successful marriage. Only one thing refused to take clear shape in her mind, even when she ceased to look at herself as a girl: just what was a successful marriage? That was difficult to sort out.

At UWEM, they had always talked about a woman having her way. Her way! What was a woman's way? Was that a way that pushed men completely out of the picture-frame? But that was not what the Church preached about marriage. The Church did not preach that a good marriage was based on how a couple make, share and invest their money, or who the owner of the children is, or on who gives up their name and adopts whose. The Church lays no absolute terms about who looks after and caters for whom in a home.

91

The Church preached love; oneness. And submission, one to another. The Church was the only institution where one plus one equalled one. That is what it preached, oneness of husband and wife. No separatedness, no squabbles about material, emotional or status equality. One cannot struggle for equality with oneself, can they? No, Lemah would be an individual, a human being, and then maybe a woman, as a plus. Not that she went totally against the whole Women Empowerment teaching; but she had to let her life lead her on. This is what she was doing.

She had pursued some of her dreams to a satisfactory level, at least. Sailing through her education like a swallow through a windless sky, she had graduated from Makerere University with an Honours degree in Mass Communication. She had also completed a diploma in Human Resource Managerial skills at the Uganda Management Institute. At her own expense, too. No sponsors, no man involved in it, no rubbish. She had not moved about spreading her precious legs to quack and actual potential job donors. As soon as she completed her second Internship, she had an offer from KITANET, first as a Programmes Announcer, then as a news anchor. Even when she told them that she had to do her Human Resource programme first, they did not change their mind. So she had completed the course (which she did as she worked part-time as Programme Announcer at KITANET) and now she was promoted to newsreader. She had every reason to be content, at least for now.

So were there no men at KITANET? Were the people promoting her this rapidly not men? Or had they exploited her sexually before shoving all these favours down her female throat? No dear, she was going through all this purely on merit. She had studied for it, and she proved in her work that her First Class Honours degree had not come out of shady deals with the proverbial sex-oriented tutors at the university. She had proved it during her internship; she still proved it now that she was with them on full time basis......

'Is everything well with you, Ms Nabasa?

'Er…. well, yes, of course, Mr. Ssali,' she promptly lied, Mr Ssali having slipped in without her notice. She could feel the impact of the lie under her skin, so she did not pursue the issue any further. Besides, she knew Mr. Ssali to be a talented mind reader, so to fib around with him always proved futile. 'I just wanted to be sure,' he concluded in his accustomed impalpable manner. 'Now I am!' He proceeded down the corridor to the lifts, possibly going to floor four of the KITANET Complex. Mr. Ssali was one of the three Assistant Directors. He rarely said more than a few courteous words to junior staff on his way up to his office. Yet even that little, it occurred to them, seemed too much for him. Many thought he was creating impressions. Lemah, however, understood. The man was simply a bonafide introvert.

As soon as Mr. Ssali disappeared, Lemah returned to her thoughts. If she had achieved all the other dreams, why not this final one? Why could she not get the boy of her dreams? She found herself at a dangerous crossroads. One signpost read: WATCH IT! LADIES *NEVER* TAKE THE LEAD ROLE IN THIS DRAMA! The other said: LADIES, JUST LIKE MEN, LOVE AND COULD… but the rest of the wording had been eaten away. Was it by Time? By some malicious or cowardly person? By conventionalist despots? And what had it said, by way of completion?….COULD AS WELL PROPOSE TO MEN?….COULD (even, preposterous though it may sound) MARRY MEN? Ho! Picture that! She, Lemah, taking Theo to church, footing all the wedding bills, then finally leading him to her…. rented room? Apartment? Mansion? She was still housed by KITANET, but she had mature plans to purchase a self-contained house in Ntinda, Kampala. She had the money, she had the will. The house was what was not ready….. yet.

KITANET was a most promising enterprise. Thriving. True, all business ran by returnee Asians were booming, but KITANET was a unique case. Besides D'Souza himself, there was not another Goan in what one could call a key position of management. Instead, there were names like Ssali, Kitonsa, Okirya and Kaliisa. This Kaliisa was the controversial middle-aged man whom everybody called young, not because he looked it, but because he acted it. But maybe that was not too bad. What really killed people in the Health Department where he was Head, and indeed others in other departments, was his impetuous nature of command. It was even said that if he had been alien, maybe it would have been better. Better to be treated strangely by a stranger… people used to say. "Look at D'Souza himself," they would add. "He is pure Goan, all the way form Asia, but he never shits or walks on anybody's head."

"Ah –ah, forget his being Goan, even. He is the man on whose shoulders we all rest, including that Kaliisa. This is all his money, but he sometimes makes us feel like we employed him here. He is so meek, that *Muyindi*!"

"But isn't that what any foreign investor should be – meek and amiable? Yes, they have the money, but we own where they can plant it so it can germinate quickly, grow on viable soil, in a good climate and bear quick fruit. Most important, we know ourselves and our community. If they do what I hear some other *Manubais* do, what do you expect? If you spit in people's faces and call them shit names, tell me, what do you expect? Their business will either remain stunted, or totally die from lack of sunlight and water in the soil. We have seen these things before, man!"

Manubai was the common name given to returnee Asians who ran business on the Ugandan market, and *Muyindi* referred to any Asian, whether he owned a Casino, a Supermarket, a Video shack or a dustbin. You see, they were everywhere, even in the pauper circles.

"And now this goon Kaliisa, just because he hails from is it Rwanda or Burundi or wherever, he thinks he dropped from Heaven on high. Let him wait!"

"Huh! Wait for what? Doesn't he own us all? What under the sun could happen to him?"

"You ask that? You can as well ask what the child warthog asked his mother."

"That what?"

"It asked why the mother's teeth spent all their time outside the mouth. Said the mother: 'child, when you're of age, you'll know. One day you may have to answer the same question from your child. Just you give it time.' See?"

Thus they would go on and on, about Kaliisa's despotism and conceit. But not everybody. One day Lemah had heard two men discuss Kaliisa so, and she had wondered yet again why gossip was always attributed to women. She wished she had not quit writing for *The Free Woman*, the official magazine of UWEM. But now that that was a thing of the past; she resolved to tell them off point blank.

"I may not be an expert in nationality analysis," she had said, "but I doubt if all the Rwandese behave the same."

"So? Are you suggesting that he is Ugandan, or Asian like D'Souza himself?" The man who asked her this was really bitter with Kaliisa.

"That is not what I am saying, and I am sure you did not hear me say it. But Kaliisa is an individual. He has a unique personality, as does each one of us, depending on wherever we came from-"

"See, she contradicts herself," put in the other man indignantly.

"Not the country of origin, of course. That's not what I mean!" Lemah's serene nature was beginning to wane. "If that is what I meant, then it would be Uganda to blame, not Rwanda. You know as well as I do that Kaliisa does not have the slightest idea what Rwanda as a country is like. He was born here; he grew up here. He works here."

"So?" asked the first man, in his characteristic angry, cynical manner.

"So let's not blame his country of origin for his character. It is his home, the schools he went to and his social history to blame!"

"But why are you so bothered? Theo is not a Munyarwanda, and you know it as well as we all do. Why are you defending them?"

There it was again! The entire KITANET staff knew about her and Theo, and always grabbed every opportunity to either tease or even insult her about it. This time it was the latter, and she knew it was because the lousy man did not want to take her point. Pity! She should have answered back on that, but she preferred not to. That would be to act on the recommendations of UWEM. She was Lemah, and Lemah was an individual, a human being, not an organisation's mouthpiece. One day these men would learn their lesson.

Theo had been a legend at KITANET while he worked there. He had at first served as Entertainment Presenter, but he later rose to head the same department, and by the time he quit, he was Controller of Programmes. This was one of the chief posts in the establishment. With time, however, the adventurer in him had launched him forward, and he started a personal FM radio station in town. What with his gentle character and Asian-like business acumen, his radio station was booming, much to the pride of D'Souza. Rightly or not, D'Souza always said that Theo acquired all that expertise while he worked at KITANET, so the glory was to be equally shared out. Whether this was true or not did not matter. What mattered was that D'Souza fully accepted and welcomed Theo's move, and instead of sabotaging, he actually helped Theo out whenever there was need for him to.

Who would not? Theo was a sweet young man. Everybody agreed to this, even Lemah, who only saw and worked with him for the first month of her internship at KITANET. When he quit the place, it was clear that she was affected. And so was he. No wonder then, that he found every excuse to come around, every so often.

It had happened this way. Theo saw this new Intern and believed her to be the best thing the Lord had put on planet earth. Lemah saw this young C.O.P and thought, O God! What a model! Where are such boys manufactured? Yet none of them talked. It was clear as Noontime to both what each thought of and felt about the other, but that was all. Taking the faith step and bringing the affair out in the open was a thing none of them was prepared to do. To Theo, Lemah was too good to be driven away from one's world by such a silly and rash step as proposing to her. He loved her too much to drive her away so. And for Lemah, nothing was to make this Arch-Type lose confidence and trust in her. At least it was not going to be so foolish a thing as her indicating to him that she as much as thought him that good. No way. He would think her too forward, and what would that do for her? No, she was capable of better than creating such an impression, at least for now….

But that "for now" was stretching beyond what she could bear. There was no more doubt now, it was clear that Theo knew she adored him, as she knew beyond all types of doubt that she trod on his heart in and beyond his presence. And the KITANET staff, too, saw all these things.

So now, seated in her office, head thrown back, arms hanging limp, eyes half closed, she tried to figure out how all this was going to come to an end. She knew how, finally. They both had to grow up. They had to stop acting fools. The song her mother (God Rest Her Soul) used to play whenever her father (God Rest His Poor soul!) was away, came back to her mind:

Reach out and fetch me;

Stretch your loving arms

I am cold; I am lonely;

Reach out and take me

In your warm embrace!!

Yes, that is exactly what she wanted Theo to do. But Theo and her were acting fools, and that could be detrimental. A wise girl would make it easy....different....determinate...and so would she.

TWO

IT was rumoured that a new rebel group was in the offing. The leader was an army deserter. Some Major so and so – the names did not count a lot. Whether a war was led by Kebba or Iraguha or Lucifer himself, what counted was that it was being fought, that it affected everybody, soldiers and civilians alike, one way or another. What really counted was the fact that somebody thought that something was wrong – genuinely or not – and that they thought fighting the best solution to the problem. That is what mattered, ultimately. And it mattered unfairly.

It had started with news from all corners of the country that armed thugs were breaking into banks, automated teller machine kiosks, bars and any place where there was an armed guard, and making off with the guns, cash and other supplies. The Police formed a special unit to deal with what the Government preferred to call thuggery, but it sooner became evident that the ordinary Police was not equipped to handle the gangsters.

At a crisis meeting at the Head of Police's residence, a joint force comprising the different security organisations had been formed, with the mandate to shoot to kill, disable or arrest whoever was involved in armed thuggery.

The reaction from the public was chaotic. While some said the new force would cause some repose for the residents, others said the Government had taken to using draconian methods, to fight supposed opponents of the system.

KITANET decided that they were not going to sit back and rely on rumours. That was not journalism. Worse, that was not *their* journalism. That was not them. They would go out there for the information, live. Dr. Kitonsa, the Current Affairs Head of Department, had been assigned to talk to Lemah to go after this news. Deep inside of her Lemah knew she wanted to. She was actually excited at the prospect, but…. what if she got caught up in it? Theo!

"Look, Lemah," Dr. Kitonsa said, when he read fear and doubt in her eyes. "It is not everyday that they ask somebody in your position to do such tasks. When it happens – and it has, now – it is blunt proof that they think you superb."

"I will go, Doctor. I will go…. I *will* go."

"Yes, and I will select for you a suitable technician and the best cameraman you may require." Dr. Kitonsa believed in Lemah's genius, and wanted it developed.

"Will it come to that, Doctor?"

"KITANET is a T.V service, not a newspaper, love." He smiled reassuringly at her, then walked away. Lemah was resolute. She would go. She had dreamed; this was the time to put the realisation of the dream to the test. Theo was at stake, but this, at the same time, could be the turning point she had been waiting for. Lord, she would go.

But what was wrong with this country? Before people could know what to conclude from this now famous northern insurgency, other things were cropping up. It was morbid enough, just watching those shots KITANET had screened about the Gulu war. People with bleeding faces, their noses, lips and ears having been chopped off by the rebels! School children stranded with no home to return to; for it was from the very bushes they hid in that the people said to have burnt down their homes are supposed to have come. Passenger vehicles – buses, lorries and taxis - were burnt beyond recognition! Was this a way to express disagreement with a wrong committed? Was anybody too young to have heard of the old adage about two wrongs not making a right?

And UTANEWS, the national broadcaster, because they had the disadvantage of not being capable of screening these ugly scenes for the nation to see, could afford to hoodwink society by toning down the gravity of the war! Now this too was coming up!

100

The formation of guerrilla forces to show discontent was not new to the country. After the era of military coup de tats, guerrilla warfare became the fad. When a soldier was involved in one scandal or another, he fled to the next country and formed a guerrilla force. When one ethnic group felt they were not fairly treated by the camp whose hand was in the cooking pot, they mobilised their youth to join the army and, at the right time, defect and start a war. In the past, a dissatisfied section of the army would organise a coup, now they planned an escape and poof, went to the bush to wage war against the regime. Isn't that the way the current administration had taken power – by force of arms, from the bushes of the Central Region?

To Lemah, this meant two things, each of which pulled in a different direction. It meant improving on her career operations, now that this was even much nearer than the Northern one; but it also meant pouring temporary ice over her dealings with Theo. She only prayed that she would not have to regret anything she did – or failed to do.

THREE

WHEN Lemah first came to KITANET, she was awed by the activity there. The letter the Head of Department of Mass Communication at the University had given her was supposed to be handed to the Head of Department, Current Affairs. The Secretary at the Receptionist's table asked Lemah to "kindly please wait here, as Dr. Kitonsa is still attending a Board meeting".

So Lemah sat down on a cushioned bench, in an air–conditioned waiting room, awe-struck at what she saw. Nobody seemed a part of the other people in the establishment, yet everybody seemed a part of this "I am–not–part-of-anybody-else" set-up. The adjoining room had a collection of computers, at which glue-lipped typists fingered, each apparently unaware of the presence of the rest. Thank God the computer age is here, so much would have been the noise from mechanical typewriters!

Farther down the corridor were other offices, which Lemah was later to move in and out of as she worked. After the Receptionist's, was the library, a spacious room in which were stacked archival visual cassettes, books, film reels and other like resources. Next to the library, one came to another corridor, along which the various producers' offices were ranged, together with the News Readers' offices. Each door had the occupant's name and office tag, and a colour passport-size photograph, stuck on it. All door bells were red, fixed next to the knobs. This was order in reality!

On the opposite side of the Receptionist's and library corridor was the canteen and cafeteria, the studio, and the Department of Entertainment. Lemah was later to learn that these were put together because they all had either noise or bustle as part of their normal running routine, at one time or the other. Up on the first floor were the Sports, Health, Current Affairs, Art, Economics and the Children's departments. The Main Store, clinic, film unit and Engineers' departments were on Floor Two, and the administrators sat on the top floor. These comprised the Accounts Section, the Commercial Division, the Legal Office and the Directors. The Controller of Programmes and D'Souza himself had their offices on a separate adjoining building a few metres off, nobody knew for what purpose or reason.

That was KITANET. But that was only the physical KITANET. The true KITANET that went beyond the physical was an enigma; a phenomenon not many comprehended fully. What, for instance, was behind that degree of success? What magic did D'Souza use to make his entire staff – junior, intermediate and senior – work as though each of them was the sole proprietor of KITANET? How did people even get enrolled to work in such a legend of a place? It all was mysterious.

Not so to Lemah, though. When she finally joined this place, her mind was not set on how it ran, how successful or not it was, or anything that trivial. For her it was how she could achieve the success in journalism that she had craved all her life. So whatever it cost her, she would do her best to do her best, so she could attain the best – be the very best.

This feeling in her had been augmented the day she sat for half an hour waiting for the Current Affairs Head of Department, to be allowed to do her Internship with them. When she saw all these people work that much; that hard, she resolved to work so hard, that even to such people, she would stand out as very hardworking. When Dr. Kitonsa finally showed up, he had asked her why she wanted to work with them. "We don't pay you on Internship, you'll notice," he teased her. And her apt response was: "If that was what I sought, Sir, I would have gone to the oil fields of Bunyoro. I came here to be a journalist, the thing I have wanted to be since I was a child. The thing I feel I was born to do."

That earned her the first Internship, and the second and, ultimately, the job.

Her first job, however, was not as demanding as she would have wanted it to be. She looked at the set-up in the studio – the giant and small cameras, the news desk equipment, the super-sensitive monitors, the modern tele-prompters – all was very fascinating and, to a degree, intimidating. She wanted to try out almost everything at the same time. Her entire body system ached to have an opportunity to have something to do with this technology, to change things in the world of journalism.

The very first day was a dull one for her. Everybody treated her like she had never been trained as a journalist. They offered to do every conceivable thing for her, except the actual announcing of the programme. They did not let her be a part of the hyper-activity there was as machines were swung from one programme desk to another, cameras shifting, others changing direction, buttons going up and down on the Control Room Computer panel board: That is what she called work. Not standing aside as people made a difference, then you step in, wear a synthetic smile, while boiling within at the sheer boredom of it all, and say something as dumb as "And now viewers, KITANET has the pleasure to treat you to another edition of …Dumb! Dumb! Dumb!" How DUMB!

With time, though, she got used to it. She would offer, for example, to be one of the costume mistresses to the news readers, especially when it was Connie, a small, almost child-like woman who used to read the news at 8 o'clock, 10p.m and midnight before the station closed down. Connie had never outgrown her panicking before appearing on screen, so the wardrobe mistresses always had to be handy, with hankies, towels, powders, sometimes even with things as ridiculous as perfumes. "But viewers will not smell this, Lydia!" Connie would gasp in panicky bewilderment. "Yes, but it will do you good. It will calm your nerves when its scent gets into your system". And it would, as sure as God is different from Satan. As soon as the cameras were turned on and she knew she was on screen, Connie would assume this kind of confidence that left her aides bewildered, instead. She had a most powerful voice, an almost native-English accent and a smile that cried out to the viewers to be noticed and appreciated. Lemah enjoyed it all, and wished she too would read news, some day.

One day Connie failed to turn up for the midnight telecast of the close down news. Everybody got into a huge panic, wondering what was to happen. It was only five minutes to 12 midnight. Looking at the frustration of the moment, Lemah offered to do it. The other people were not sure whether it would be all right for her to do it, but she went ahead and did it, in spite of the doubts and outright protests form some people. Putting all her appeal into her eyes and voice, she marched up to the Chief News Producer, told him it would all turn out fine, and without waiting to hear his opinion; she walked to the News Desk. Everybody was perplexed, but it was too late. It struck 12:00 midnight. In the confusion, they forgot to put the back-drop with the KITANET News logo, but trust Lemah; she knew how to go about that. She told viewers that owing to a crisis at the station, they could not get into the regular news room, and so with the change of news reader had come a change of news room. Her colleagues could almost hear the shocked reactions of the viewers out there in the nation! The monitor was on and working, the teleprompter was turned on, and the news reading was underway.

Fate, however, is the biggest bully there is, the world over. Hardly had Lemah read the second news item to completion when the micro–receiver in her right ear buzzed, then communicated an urgent message from Control Room. At first she thought they were pulling her leg to test her ground, but on second (and very quick) thought, she acted accordingly.

***Dear viewers,
there is a crisis in
Chechnya that we trust
is of interest to all of us,
so we will pause here as
we watch it happen, live,
courtesy of CNN
International.***

When she looked down at the monitor, she nearly fainted at the gruesome sight! Chunks and pieces of human flesh flew in all directions. There was wild screaming, and shell after shell landed on a series of semi–detached buildings, and a number of shanties in the vicinity. People who tried to escape were being showered with death stings from a gunship. It was hell! In the midst of this, a CNN reporter's face appeared on screen, and immediately Lemah was told: "Proceed with your news" from Control Room. And all equipment was re-focused upon her.

She fought the revulsion and the tears that stung her eyes, told her viewers: "That, dear viewers, is the world people live in out there", and continued from where she had stopped.

When she entered her house that night, she had a quick shower, swallowed a sedative and went to bed. The world she had come to work in was a troubled and troubling one. But she, Lemah, would live and work in it… she would.

The following day she was summoned to the office of one of the Executive Directors. Her heart sank. They had learnt about last night, and she had just burnt her entire career at KITANET; thrown away the opportunity to work with and among the very best in the industry. Why had she acted so foolhardy? She should have listened to the others' voices – they were voices of wisdom. Now it was too late. O Folly!

She did not use the lift. What was a lift for in a four-storey building? This was shear snobbery! She would walk upstairs. After all, whoever rushed to their damnation!

When she pressed the doorbell, a voice came from the receiver on the door, asking her by name to please walk in. Mr. Prosper Nywai was behind his desk, his bifocals in his left hand, an envelope in the other. His face was blank, which was all the proof to Lemah that the envelope was addressed to her, and that it bore tear–inducing news.

Either Mr Nywai saw her fright and acted on it, or he was just a man of no facial expressions, she did not know. But he handed the envelope to her, waved her out of the office, and said over the door receiver again, "Good day, Ms Nabasa!"

She did not return to her seat in the Secretaries' Office. She walked Zombie–like into the Ladies, her entire system shaking with self–induced defeat, and tore the envelope open. And God of all mercy, she could hardly believe it. The letter read in part:

Dear Ms Nabasa,

The emergency Management meeting that sat this morning was reliably informed of your act of self-motivation and initiative that saved the station great embarrassment last night.

Be informed that this sharpness of mind is a vital pre-requisite for every good newsreader; someone who can handle emergencies and crises like you did. We commend this degree of responsibility, and have unanimously agreed to put you in a position where your full potential can be exploited.

By copy of this letter, we hereby promote you to the office of Newsreader. Please accept our sincere thanks for your initiative, and congratulations on your new office. (She had been promoted to News Reader! Wow!) We pledge every support to enable you grow into an even better journalist.

Lemah's excitement was beyond description. She was never the same, henceforth. She went, as instructed in the letter, and reported to the News Director and Head of Department. She was given the keys to an office, and asked to pick from among the typists someone she would have for a secretary. Mercy Lubega was the lucky one, and together they went out that evening to have a Fanta each in celebration.

.

FOUR

THE day after Lemah had been asked to go out news-smelling in the new guerrilla-infested areas of Bulemezi, things started to happen.

The Uganda Police had a small detach in a little out–village called Katemu, with slightly above ten police women and men. It was never easy to tell how well or poorly armed these people were, but word went round after these things had happened that they had been sufficiently armed.

It had happened this way: It was a Sunday, and everybody was in this light and reposeful mood, before launching into a new week of serious activity. Police officers lounged in the yard of their small post, taking in the air of the dying day. Animated chatter and laughter filled the air. Away in the distance, the whine of a car was heard. The car was evidently moving very fast. Before anybody knew what was what, a Range Rover pulled up into the Police yard. Even before it had fully stopped, all its doors save for the driver's were swung open and heavily armed men and a woman jumped out. They all wore civilian clothes, although they were evidently not civilian. Now nobody could prove this afterwards, but it was said that the O.C was the first to volunteer to surrender to them, giving in his gun, his uniform and his identification papers....*for he had heard enough stories about the methods these people used.* When he surrendered, all his subordinates followed suit, except one young man who refused to take his uniform off. The woman in the rebels' crew opened fire, killing the young man instantly, and gravely wounding the O.C. She then undressed the dead man, leaving him stark naked, threw the O.C into the car and they drove off, shooting in the air as they went along. When the news came out, the O.C was undergoing intense treatment in hospital. Two bullets were lodged in his body – one in the hipbone and the other in his chest. The rebels had driven him to hospital, then they made off to nobody knew where.

Lemah heard these things and called Dr. Kitonsa. "Look", she said, "I just have to leave immediately, Doctor.'

'Right, right, love. But this is not the sort of thing anyone should be going into with that degree of excite-'

'Doctor Kitonsa, this is not the girl Lemah talking. This is a professional journalist attending to her duties. I am out to get news for KITANET.'

Five minutes later, Dr. Kitonsa drove up with Ali, one of the technicians, and a camera man she had not seen before. Dr. Kitonsa introduced them. "This is Dick, our new cameraman. Dick, you're going out with Ms Nabasa here. Lemah, you'll not regret my choices. Gentlemen, all the best.'

"The pleasure is mine, to have to go out with-"

"Not *that* going out, Dick. I wouldn't fix *that* for anybody, not with Lemah, at that. You are going to have your damn heads split for you on a battle front."

"Guerrilla warfare of this type has no front, anyway," Lemah laughed sardonically, albeit nervously.

Lemah and her two-man crew got to the area just in time to attend a short meeting with the local chiefs, the Local Defence Unit (LDU) of the area and two UPDF officers. The Uganda People's Defence Forces had come in as soon as they got news of the raid, but up to that time, nothing had been salvaged, yet. They, however, knew no fear. According to one of the officers, this was not a group to cause panic in a force of their nature. Actually, they were not going to endanger the local populace by fighting these dissidents. They were just going to use a ubiquitous Intelligence Network, and this rebel activity would 'vanish into thin air'.

After that meeting, the two army officers left. Lemah also chose to go and talk to the O.C in hospital. She asked her men to stay behind, and wire her in case anything came up. She got to hospital five minutes after the O.C had breathed his last. Beaten, she turned to go back to the news region, and immediately received a call on her radio call that rebels were said to have attacked another Police post a few miles away. She got into a taxi and told the man to drive at his fastest, ever. "I have a wife and children, madam!" the man said grittily, but all the same swinging the car into a run that caught Lemah a trifle off-guard.

"Is that supposed to mean that husbands and fathers never do what their clients demand of them?"

"Not if their clients' demands are irrational and rash – and suicidal." He sped even the more. Lemah smiled briefly. "Is that supposed-"

"Madam, I am driving." He made it sound like a pilot's SOS to a radar controller, so Lemah shut up.

Even before they got to the scene, they heard gunshots. The man stopped and insisted that he could not commit suicide just like that. She paid him, got into a hasty run and wondered if she would get what she wanted. She first ran to the Local Council chairman's house, where she had left her men, but they were not there. They had left her a note saying that somebody could take her to where they had gone, to try and capture what they could. And true to their word, when the chairman's son got Lemah to the place, they had captured a few useful shots. They had covered the UPDF men exchanging fire with the unseen rebels, and one of the shots had captured one of the UPDF soldiers as he was hit in the arm. Grabbing the camera, she dashed off, leaving the men stunned.

"She will die out there!" Dick cried in impotent fear.

"You're wrong", said the technician. "She is not just a woman, that one. She is Lemah Nabasa."

111

And so she was. When she rejoined them at the chairman's house late that evening, she had a plaster on her temple, but she was fine, all right. She had news. Hot news. She indeed was Lemah Nabasa, the journalist.

FIVE

LEMAH'S news was on KITANET that night. It featured the UPDF/LC/LDU meeting, the death of the O.C of Katewu Police post, the UPDF defensive against the rebels…. And shot by Lemah herself, a rebel retreat, making off with arms, uniforms and other bagged supplies. They first deflated the tyres of the UPDF-registered Santana station wagon they had, then made off with their supplies. The shots had been taken at a distance, from an aerial kind of position, but they made a big difference. Maybe she would have got more, but one of the escaping men had spotted her from a distance, aimed, and before she could dart for safety, he had shot. It would have missed her completely, but Lemah was not the kind of girl to damage hard-earned news on film just to save her life. If they found her corpse with the camera, it would make better news for KITANET. That is how she let the bullet graze her temple, and it lodged itself in a branch behind her. But Lemah was a survivor, so she treated herself, plastered the wound and returned to the world of T.V, the world of journalism. Her world.

The success Lemah was making changed her life in a myriad ways. Her bosses appreciated her much more than ever before, and took every opportunity to show their gratitude and appreciation: even before her not-so-amused colleagues. For all her ambition, however, Lemah was a modest girl. She pleaded with Dr. Kitonsa, for instance, that they desist from citing her as an example of excellence to the other staff. When this came to no good, she chose to maintain a very low profile at the office. She only dealt with people she considered safe enough to deal with – either because they feared her too much to overstep their limits in dealing with her, or because they had a secret admiration for her that awed them into a kind of devotee-like submission. The rest she avoided because either they were too loud, or they had developed ill feelings towards her.

One such person was Musita, a lights man in the News studio. Musita's dislike for Lemah was so intense, he continually repined every time she was in the studio, whether there was cause for it or not. But that did not bother Lemah. As long as she was not asking him to do her personal work, it was all right; he could feel all he desired about her. It is people who ran rather personalised programmes who faced problems with the likes of Musita. Then, the success or otherwise of the programme depended largely on one's relations with the technicians, the cameraman, the sound-men, and maybe the Head of Department. The News Department was different, though.

One of the people whose attitudes towards Lemah were changed by her fame at KITANET was Mr. Kaliisa. Almost from nowhere at all, he started appearing in her axis most of the time. He took particular care to greet her each time she was within earshot; regardless of what time had elapsed since the last time he had greeted her. He did it so often, and so much that even the other staff members in the establishment noticed. Mercy was the first to out-rightly comment on it. "Mr. Kaliisa likes you a lot, Lemah," she intimated. "You're a very lucky lady. He never treats anybody, male or female, with as much partiality as he treats you with lately."

"Really? I have not noticed!" Lemah was the poorest at the games of pretence and lying, and every time she made an abortive attempt at either, she felt her skin glow with the very guilt of it. She felt it now.

"Am I supposed to believe you on that?"

"And if you don't believe me? Mercy, I have told you in as simple a manner as I possibly can, that I have absolutely no time to notice who treats me how. I am more interested in things that make quality differences in my life, period." She knew in her heart of hearts that this, too, did, and to a huge degree, but she was not going to own so. Even Mercy did, and she told Lemah as much in very plain terms.

"If the way Kaliisa or any other person around here treats you, Lemah, does not make a difference in your life, then nothing should."

114

"Really? Maybe. I will be keener. I *will* see."

That dialogue set her thinking. Kaliisa was not a popular person at KITANET. What did the fact that he was gaining big interest in her imply for her reputation among the KITANET community? Besides, she had heard of men who waited till a girl's image changed on the positive plane, then developed interest in her. Was it the girl, then, or the fame, they fell for? That is why she appreciated Theo. Theo had deemed her good enough, even before he saw her at work. He wanted – loved – her as a girl, not as a famous journalist. Theo was a reasonable guy.

Lemah was still pondering over these things when her phone rang. She picked up the receiver rather pensively, and spoke into it.

"Hello, yes, this is Lemah…..yes, yes, can I be of any help?"

When the caller's voice came, it was all she could do, not to drop the receiver. But she was a seasoned girl, so she heard him out. "Miss, don't be alarmed…. That's the breathing of a shocked person. No harm meant," he explained. "I just wish that we fix an appointment, so we can talk it over, face to face. How about that?"

"Mr Kal--"

"Eh! Eh! God, don't mention names. I know it's me you're addressing, so just say what…"

"Yes, SIR, it's you, Mr Kaliisa, I am addressing, and I demand that you know who you're addressing. You're addressing one of your subjects at KITANET, somebody who happens not to be a man, but who came here specifically to work for KITANET, particularly in the field of TV journalism. Anything outside of that I can only consider – C O N S I D E R – outside KITANET. Thank you, and take meticulous care next time!" She hung up.

She was angry. Very, very angry and disappointed that anybody should think her *that* cheap. If he wanted somebody hardworking [the cheek!], why didn't he ask to wed D'Souza himself? He was about the most hardworking being in the entire set–up.

The goon!

The phone rang again.

"Please answer that, Mercy." She was breathing hard, mad with fury. Mercy answered the call, feeling sorry for her friend and boss.

"It's yours. Dr. Kitonsa's secretary.'

Lemah took a deep breath, closed her eyes, and said an almost inaudible "Hello" into the mouthpiece.

"Hello Lemah, you sound horrible! I heard Mercy tell you it was I calling. Is that the reason you're- "

"NO, dear, no! You could never be a cause of distress to me, never at all. How's your day, dear?" She was obviously finding it close to impossible to act sane and calm. She could feel it under her skin.

"Fine, thank you. Well, Lemah I am sorry. Now …. Doctor has asked me to fix an appointment with you so he can talk to you about….er….so he can talk to you."

"About?"

There was a lengthy pause, then from the other end came a timid, uncertain voice, claiming that it did not know what the meeting was about.

"Tell him 4 p.m. this evening. And thanks, dear. Good day…..bye."

There she stayed, receiver still in her hand, against the ear, eyes fixed straight ahead of her, lips parted in mental indigestion. She was so far away that she did not notice Mercy go out. Mercy did not know how to handle situations like that. And apparently ages later, Lemah still sat thus, and she was still too far away to notice someone else enter her office, stop dead on finding her listening to very important information on the phone. After waiting interminably, and realising that could not have been a real phone call, he proceeded to the front of her desk. It was only then that, shocked into sense, she saw Theo, and let out a treacherous mixture of a sigh and a groan. "You! Er… Theo!" She finally replaced the receiver onto the hook.

"You just cut off whoever it was!" Theo said non-committally.

"Cut off how – oh, this, oh no!" She laughed nervously, studying him for signs to show that he had known that she was not actually using the phone.

"Oh no what?" Theo asked. "When I came in – should be about ten or so minutes ago – huh, now why do you shudder? Yes, I walked into here about ten minutes ago, and you were listening- "

"I wasn't listening to anybody. Maybe….yes, sometimes we listen to voices we cannot recognise…even silent voices…it could even have been mine, or the devil's."

"Philosophy has caught up with you, Lemah! Poor me!… Now, may I sit down somewhere?"

"Oh, but of course….Anytime!" she cried, then realised she was getting too excited, and checked herself. "The reason we have seats in our offices is for guests to sit in; not for decoration."

"Lesson taken. But – oh, well, I understand…I think." He too was calculating.

"But what?"

"Mmm….Nothing, I guess. Nothing!" Maybe it was not nothing, but it was nothing mountainous. He had only wanted to ask her whether any kind of guest could be entertained here, whether official or informal. He was informal, or at least the object of his

117

visit was. "Nothing," he said again, with a mighty sigh, and then shifted in his seat. "How's work?"

Lemah thought something funny was happening.

"Funny; that's how work here is," she said dreamily. "Funny things happen here, sometimes. But somehow we survive!"

"Yeah. And frustration….is it – does what?" Theo had once been a student of Literature, but he had never been good at memorising stuff.

"Sorry! Sorry! Give it up, lad. *Tenderness, frustrated does not wither…*"

"Yes, Madame."

A long pause engorged with discomfort followed. Lemah sat there, letting a zillion calculations on how to handle this situation maturely and wisely flow through her mind. She had earlier on resolved to act simple, to let down her guards a bit, but the exact extent still eluded her. Just see him, here in the flesh, yet so far away. Far! What if he just got up, said "Sorry to have bumped into your office, bye;" and walked away – from her office, from her dreams, from her life! God, let nothing like that happen. Let it not, ever!

Theo was mixed up. He felt like a school boy being wooed by his teacher. Again he had this queer feeling that always made him want to test with his hands whether he actually sat on a chair. Yet he could not, for at such moments, when the seat below him seemed to turn into air, his arms also turned queer. They felt like marble beams. Here was the girl he was palpitating for, the girl he must either get, or stay single for the rest of his miserable life; yet she intimidated him so! If only she knew! If only God could make her feel just one tenth…just a tenth of the love he felt for her! One tenth only, Lord! She would either melt or roast with passion. She sure would. But no, there she sat, like a High Court judge, weighing his inability before she could, in the most murderous language, sentence him to eternal damnation. But no. How could she sentence anybody to anything, without a proper and fair trial? No Theo, you have to state your case. Let it be heard in its fullness. Thereafter, you can anticipate some kind of judgement.

"Lemah," he began unsteadily, yet even that startled Lemah. She had wandered very far. "I don't have to hold you off your work long!"

"Oh, but you know it's alright…..I…."

"Come on, an office is an office, and I know KITANET offices. By the way is Mr. Kaliisa still – why, have I – My God! What's wrong, Lemah?"

"Nothing. It's just that when you mentioned Mr. Kaliisa, I remembered there was work I had to do for him, which I have not yet started on…maybe…work I cannot do for him, under the circumstances." She felt the hot glow in her skin. O God!

"See? So I was…what is your programme like?" Theo asked.

"Now? Today? This year? Or for my life?"

"Today, this week!" Theo glanced at the clock on Lemah's wall. She followed his eyes there, and told herself that should she let it go, she might have to regret it the rest of her earthly life.

'Today, I'm fixed up to five, the rest of the evening I'm free. Though I have to close down at midnight." And in her mind, she was praying that God guides his proposition in the right direction. Just like he was praying that she does not have to push it to another day. He would explode with anxious impatience.

"Lemah, I would like us to talk. I …I want us to talk a few things over. Can we… Oh, have I made you recall another piece of

119

work you have not done for Kaliisa?" He had noticed her wince, and her eyes narrowed in recollection.

"Please do not sprinkle your talk with that name. *Please.* But as for what I have recalled, it is nothing to do with *him.*' She paused, to calm her system. "I just have an appointment with my immediate boss at 4p.m. I hope it will not take till come Jesus.'

"I hope not, too. Or should we--"

"Oh no! I'll explain to him that I have another very important session, with a more important personality." She laughed first, to let him know it was an attempt at a joke... Probably to ease the tension in the air. He, too, however, had taken it for what it was, and actually responded to it with another.

'And add that if you disappoint that more important man, the KITANET sun may just choose to stop wherever it will be at the time, and return to the East."

"East as in Mbale and Tororo, or as in Russia and them other Eastern countries?"

"East, where the Bible says wise people came from." Theo was from Eastern Uganda, and he always made it a point to cite the Bible in only that one respect.

"Well, then, five o'clock."

"Is that to chase me out? No, no, no, don't fight," he said as she opened her mouth to protest. "I was going, all the same. Have to see a few big shots about our station. THE station, I should add."

Lemah could see that Theo was excited. He never joked that way, unless he was feeling tops.

'See you then, dear."

"Check." He too attempted to go casual and soft, but the "dear" at the end of her words was a bit of a big one for him. He could have flown out of his skin with sheer delight. In his mind, he resolved that he was not going to see any dreadful big or tiny shots; he would just cruise back to Kampala, straight to his house, and let his mind take in this whole discourse. Certainly God lived. He was a huge Reality, just like his promises were a reality: Whatever you ask for......you will receive. Theo had prayed, probably as hard as Jesus in the garden of Gethsemane had, during his Passion – and here were the results.

At four O'clock Lemah met Dr. Kitonsa. He led her to an inner room in his office, bade her feel at ease and relax, and then looked at her long and hard. "Please speak, Sir." She was ill at ease.

"Yes, I should. Lemah, you know you are a pretty girl."

O God, not him, too! Not another one! I'll burst!...

"You're successful, too. At least in the way you do your work. Almost the entire K–NET executive knows that, and majority of us are impressed, and grateful."

God Father, let him come to the point!

"Majority, I say. Because, Lemah, some people may not be that impressed. And they are justified, too – in their own way. Mark my words, I don't mean that anybody in particular is creeping up your spine, no. But you can't rule anything out, so far."

God, I am bursting! And Theo! Soon it will be 5 p.m.!

'Have you noticed anything strange in the air of late, for instance?" The question came unannounced.

"How do you mean, Sir?" She was unsteady, uncomfortable, unaware of where all this was leading to.

"Anybody around and about who may have changed in the way they relate with you – in any way whatsoever?"

Oh that!

"What have you noticed, Dr. Kitonsa?"

"Look, Lemah I asked you the same question. Don't throw it back onto my court. You're not on trial here; you're in the office of someone who wants you to have all your time for your duties, and maybe for your private life – away from K – NET."

"Mmmm….Musita, one of the lights men?"

"Besides that one? Lemah, you certainly know that I know that you know who and what I mean, don't you?"

A long pause ensued, which would probably have been much longer had Lemah not thought of her appointment with Theo.

"You mean…do you have…..Mr Kaliisa in mind?"

"Have you noticed anything about him?" The Doctor's tone was poking.

"I…. think so. He ….. how do I put this now – he now sort of behaves funny," she wrestled with the words.

"How, if I may ask?"

"Just, Er…. He…He sort of seems…."

"Please stop this 'sort of' stuff. You're a woman, and you people have feelers that other people lack. You must know these things for sure!" Dr. Kitonsa leaned forward, holding the farthest end of his table emphatically. Lemah flared.

"Doctor, let's get this very straight. Whether you're right or wrong about my knowing this in full, at least I know you're very wrong in thinking that all women are photocopies of one original. You're wrong in that. But speaking for myself, let us always recall that I am Lemah Nabasa, and what I am has nothing to do with all the women, nor do the rest of the women have anything to do with Lemah Nabasa."

"I understand, Ms Nabasa Lemah, though some things just seem incontrovertible to me!" The Doctor looked offended, but he was a most amiable man, so he let the moment pass. There were graver issues at stake, he knew.

"Like I was saying," Lemah proceeded contritely, "Mr. Kaliisa now behaves as if he's just met me…or as if it is a new me he is dealing with."

"Yes?"

"To be frank, Dr. Kitonsa, he actually makes me very *uncomfy*. I am scared, I think. Of him, of… of so many things."

"I understand, Lemah. Now I know this may not be very professional and discreet of me, talking about somebody else to somebody else. But as you can see, I have to."

Lemah sighed. "I understand. And I am grateful for your concern."

"Mr Kaliisa is an obnoxious man. Lubricious, even, sometimes. I should not be taken to be undermining him. I am only…"

"No, Doctor, I actually feel the same way about him. At least about his being lubricious. As for that other word — what was it?"

"Oh, sorry," Dr. Kitonsa said with a superior laugh. "The word obnoxious is no big deal. It simply means offensive. Don't you see it in him?"

"Yes, to unbeatable levels. It's no big wonder the other people around are always repining about the way he handles them, especially the people in Health." Lemah had now gained her ground, and spoke with confidence and trust in her voice and congeniality on her face.

"Though, I must say that's not why we are here. I just want you to be careful, Ms Nabasa. It could affect your work. More than your work, even. It is a slippery world we operate in, my dear. You have to be careful!"

"Thank you, Doctor," Lemah almost whispered. "I appreciate this concern."

"I think we're done. Just take care what you do. I should not seem to be tampering with your essential freedoms or patronising you, but as I have already said, you could lay so much at stake. You're too good to be left to over–indulgent forces. Good day.'

"Good day, Doctor, and thank you once again."

Dr. Kitonsa watched her go out, tut-tutted, put his papers in order and closed the day's work.

SIX

FIRE, rumours, epidemics and a revolution must have a common descent. Why else would they spread in an almost similar manner? One small unit of either is planted in a clean and free environment by some either malicious or unfortunate agent, and before you can tell A from B, it has spread; carrying with it destruction, frustration, sorrow and grief and, in a few cases, relief.

A like thing was beginning to happen in Uganda. Someone had dropped a small piece of live charcoal somewhere in the north, and the minds of disgruntlement, of rebellion, of who-is-who, of counter-rebellion fanned it, set it alight with a ferocious fire, and now a big fire continually razed the northern region. Some people cried in mortal terror, some grumbled in deep-seated discontent, and yet others sang alleluias for a chance to benefit from other people's misfortune.

Even if fire had been a kind of fruit whose seed birds could transfer, it still could not have explained how a streak of fire could have flown all the way from the north, down to the south of the country. For there, another fire started, small at first, but like all such fires, spreading more smoke, heat and soot than could be accounted for. It too, was blazing on the dry leaves of discontent, frustration and opportunism. While those fires were still going, we heard of others lit from afar, then brought onto Ugandan soil, to teach Ugandans lessons they have in fact long learnt from their own and other people's blunders.

Fires were going up wherever there were conditions that called for it. Tongues of fire flew from point to point, lighting ready and willing dry grass where it was. It was a fiery period! And the country's infrastructure was damaged, and people were plastered with blisters and wounds all over – down to their souls; and there were no shelters to protect victims from the long eye of Fire lighters imported from distant Fire Masons and Arsonists.

But at KITANET, not all the fire passed the network by. Lemah had volunteered to go out and fish out more news, but Dr.

125

Kitonsa insisted that she reads whatever news had been brought in by the right people. The right people went out, all right, brought in sometimes fabulous items, sometimes not-very-exciting ones. And all the same Lemah felt that it would not have been the same, had she been allowed out again.

As Lemah was seeking new ways of going out to gather concrete news, the Government was also seeking ways of either neutralising some of the existing bush sparks that were flying about, or blocking the emergence of fresh ones. If they let other fires raze the countryside, there was going to be a danger of having a fiery nation where no one would escape being roasted, boiled or scorched.

That was the philosophy at KITANET, too. Researchers were out fishing fresh views of new actual and potential fires. As soon as they found one, they trimmed it down to consumable news – news that would not stick in the gullet; news that would not slide off the plate and stain the clothes of the consumers.

That is how the Government had poured a tankful of icy water on a spark that rumour said was about to set the whole country onto one huge fire that would leave everybody and everything transformed. It was said to be from an internal fire source, so KITANET went inside and nosed about. When the news came out, with shots of secret interviews, meetings and commissions in places that would make Old Lucifer feel outwitted; with magnified documents, everybody was said to have fallen onto their knees in thanksgiving. No wonder, then, that when only a week thereafter KITANET joined UTANEWS in telecasting a major shake-up in the Cabinet, people shook their heads, and gave up on people!

That was as it was, but the already blazing fires blazed on, fuelled not any more by frustration and discontent, but by sheer inflation of wounded egos, by sentiment and by the money that the peasants in the small corners of the country squeezed out of their already flaccid muscles. Even then, in those near-dry muscles, the fire flickered on, relentlessly, fighting against the gales of curtailment.

SEVEN

YOU have either read or heard the story. It is there in the Bible, somewhere in the Old Testament. The Israelites were fighting to settle down in the Promised Land. It was their God-given right, so no uncircumcised bastard was going to stand in their way, wide-legged and hands akimbo. No, they would first have to use those legs and hands to prove that they were stronger than the will of Jehovah, who had determined that Israel would settle in Canaan. And try to prove this point the Canaanite tribes often tried, but the Israelites were not food to be eaten with peanut sauce. They always won, somehow.

So it was even this time. The Amorites were proving to be a huge rock on the way of the Israelites, and Joshua came in. Plucking all the faith he could muster, he commanded:

Sun, stand still over Gibeon

Moon, stop over Aijalam Valley.

And it was. For a full day! Boy, were the Amorites scared! And the Israelites had their victory, and the people were over-joyed for the miracle.

That joy was sheer kindergarten stuff, compared to the deep-rooted jubilation that the KITANET staff had when the news of the miracle came through. Especially the junior staff in News Room, in the studios, in the library, in all the places below the rank of Head of Department. You can bet even some of the Big-Table officers afforded a secret smile of relief when they got the news of the miracle. First, it had been long over-due, but above all, it came unexpected, like the moon standing still over KITANET. Mr Kaliisa had been fired!

No jokes, no wishful thinking, no unfounded rumour.

Admitted, people get fired, almost everywhere, almost every other month. But this was no ordinary firing, both in terms of who

127

suffered it, and how it had come about. It was a case of the moon standing still over the KITANET workplace.

At 5:00p.m, Theo's Volvo had pulled into the KITANET parking lot. A number of staff members were out there, chatting before they could go their different ways; or seeing off an office visitor, or simply lounging about, pondering over the happenings of the day. When they saw the familiar Volvo pull up, everybody lit up with eager excitement. Many moved over to say hello, some waited where they stood, knowing that Theo was not the man to pass by and go without a word to this one, a joke to that one, and a pat on the other's shoulder. And they knew him well, for he was doing just that, when Lemah emerged from the KITANET complex. Poor girl, she could barely hide the sheer thrill of seeing him; she was all aglow with smiles. Seeming to walk on air, she was gliding towards Theo when Mr Kaliisa leaned out of his office window up on first floor, looking down at the scene of hugs, hand-shakes and beaming faces. This seemed to prick his inside, for it was only when his inside was pricked (which was almost always, anyway), that he used the sort of tone he used now.

"Lemah! Lemah! Come up here for a while, something we have to get out of the way quickly!" Everybody looked up, even Theo and Lemah, their hands locked in silent communion. Mr Kaliisa had disappeared, and the blinds in his window were drawn.

"Go up there and see him," Theo whispered to Lemah, giving her hand a communicative squeeze.

"No way! I am in News Depart- Current Affairs – or whatever they call it, not Health. Besides, it's end of day for me." She was on the brink of tears.

"Go, Lemah!" Theo pleaded. "I know Kaliisa….unless he is a changed man."

"Changed indeed, the-" said Lemah, as she turned to go back into the building.

Just as she was entering through the outer door, she bumped into - or rather, she was bumped into by a charging Kaliisa, storming out like a stabbed boar.

"You! Who the f--- do you imagine you are? How can your boss – YOUR *Boss* – call you and you just ignore him, simply because you're talking to some Heaven-cut boyfriend! Hell's teeth! Do you know who you're dealing with?"

Lemah knew full well who Kaliisa was, as did all the people who stood about, looking on with agape mouths and wide eyes. This was a new phenomenon at KITANET, this blowing each other's heads off, moreover in full public view. Poor Lemah, she just stood there, too stunned to talk or make any move of any kind.

"Madam Nabasa," Kaliisa proceeded, "I asked a question, and it is not as if you don't know that questions seek answers. Or maybe I am too low to be answered by a lady of your calibre?"

"Mr. Kaliisa, you-"

"Finished. Don't Mr. Kaliisa me any more. We shall see. Go back to your boyfriend." Then, raising his voice even the more, he called out to Theo: "Hello colleague, how is your station – THE station, doing?"

Those had been Theo's very words, as he talked to Lemah that afternoon. He had said something about meeting some big shots concerning THE station. How had this Kaliisa come to use them? That was something to think about. He must have been eavesdropping, or something.

After that hypertentious incident, the yard was deserted as if by a decree of the Almighty God. There was no sound from anyone, save for the banging of car doors and the silent, shocked grumble of engines, as the cars stealthily rolled out of the scandalous yard. Kaliisa's was one of the vehicles that moved away, only that he gave his an enraged rev, rocked it into a quick succession of gears as he roared away, the tyres on the tarmac below him screaming in protest.

129

Theo was rooted to the spot, astounded. He had known Kaliisa to be a hard one, but he had never bargained it rose to this altitude! And all out of a small thing. Talk about mustard seed eruptions! He had barely disappeared behind his window blinds after calling out to Lemah, when he appeared again at the door, almost throwing the poor girl over her frame. The brute! Theo looked at her, looking so feeble, so vulnerable. When their eyes met, a heavy sob as of a chided child who has just been let off a penal trap caught her by the throat, choked her, then shook her into violent tears. Theo rushed over to her. He had to use this moment to show how much he cared.

"Lemah, it does not help! It does not *pay*!" he said, pulling her onto his shoulder, and letting his palm softly traverse her silken, long hair. She rocked with sobs, both of hurt and of a kind of joy, at the fact that just when her life reached this turning point, there was someone to hold her by the hand and take her through the mire. Theo was set to be her friend.

*   *   *
*   *

D'Souza was just leaving his office when news came to him of the scandal at the KITANET main building. It was wired to him by Mr Okirya. Liza, his secretary, could judge by the look on the *Muyindi's* face and the tone with which he responded to the call that something was grossly the matter. This was a rare – almost new D'Souza.

Mr. Okirya, if he's still around ....no? When did he....immediately?

....Who else was there....Is anybody still there in the yard...Now I'm sorry, you know I would not do this under normal circumstances. Please drive to Mr. Kaliisa's....Yes, I too have his number, but calling him will not reflect the true urgency of the matter. So do drive over and tell him I MUST

see him….Yes, of course…..yes. Thank you Mr. Okirya…..
I will stay right here and wait for him….Whatever it takes,
yes,….Yes.   Thank You.

"You will not believe the things you hear these days, Liza!
I….O Good God! This is the scandal of scandals!" D'Souza
muttered to himself. He was obviously furious. Liza did not say a
thing in response. Her knowledge of her boss was enough to tell her
that he was not exactly telling her anything, only unloading his mind
of something that could have led to an explosion. She was relieved
when he got out of the office, leaving the door ajar.

She had not been alone long, when the two men walked in,
D'Souza half running, and Kaliisa following with long strides,
bewilderment printed all over his face. "We need space, Liza,"
D'Souza ordered, too impatient for politeness. Liza picked up her
keys and was getting out, when D'Souza handed her her handbag,
and told her she could return the following day.

The relief she felt was cut off as she heard the voices of the
two men begin to rise behind the closed door. Remotely, but alive
enough to be felt, a fear arose in her…God forbid it, she hoped
nothing worse would occur.

"Mr. Kaliisa, this is a disgrace! A big disgrace – on you, on
me, on the entire KITANET!" D'Souza hissed.

"What is, if I may ask?" His calmness got on D'Souza's most
sensitive nerves, causing him to yell out.

"What do you mean *what is*? Are you telling me you've not
heard what you did this evening? Is it news to *you*?"

"Mr D'Souza-"

"Wait! Wait! Now listen….I can take any form of indiscipline,
except the sort that denies my workers their dignity. And my system
is to pay disrespect with disrespect."

131

"So?" Kaliisa moved into a chair and sat down.

"You ask that? Well, when you get out of that chair, it will be to go to your office, put yourself in order and hand over, this very evening. I am waiting".

Mr. Kaliisa was dumb-founded. This was way beyond what he had expected. He had underestimated the usually calm, never enraged *Manubai*. Now here he was, sacking him.

"Look, Boss, that's not what-"

"Waste not your breath. Between now and your handing over KITANET property, I will not attend to anything else. Please act – NOW!"

And so it was. An hour later saw Mr. Kaliisa hand over to D'Souza himself the key to the Health Department office, the key to the staff car and the key to the KITANET residence he had been occupying. D'Souza told him he could keep the house until he was ready to move, but he turned down the offer. He said he could take good care of himself.

So when the news broke out, the entire KITANET staff was afire with excitement. It was then that even people who had all the time seemed indifferent to Mr. Kaliisa; even those who had seemed to like him came out as his enemies. Or so they showed themselves to be. However, it was also true that fear could make one do anything, to create the right impression!

.

*   *   *

*   *

Meanwhile, Theo and Lemah drove straight to the central business district of the town. Driving along Kampala Road, Theo wondered aloud where he could take Lemah. There was Chipper's Ice Cream, but that was too much of a Teens' Club, mostly frequented by university undergraduates learning to get into relationships. The crowd there could be noisy, and that was far from what he wanted for such an evening. Could he try Fido Dido? That would be full of parents taking their little ones out for an evening ice cream. They needed privacy now….Yes! There was this new place on Kyaggwe Road, called Genitors' Café. It was a decent place…..It was said that its high rates precluded any idlers from going there. So only serious-minded people patronised it, and nobody sat longer than it took them to have an ice-cold coke and a croissant or two.

The parking lot was behind the building, on a steep rise. Theo looked for a place where none would park behind him, and put the car there. Drivers in Kampala hardly followed driving etiquette, so one had to take special care, else one would have to sit in one's car, until some drunko stumbled up two or even three hours later, ran right into your car's boot, slumped onto his wheel, and slept, leaving you immobilised.

Theo and Lemah settled at a table in a far corner, where they could see anybody who walked in, and where nobody could sit close enough to eavesdrop on their conversation. Theo was particularly conscious of this, for he was about to go into a time he was not sure was going to be comfortable. Only Lemah should listen to him gamble his way out; she could not scoff at his inadequacy.

They made their orders. Lemah said she could do with African tea and a meat pie. Theo ordered a Krest soda, and said he would call back the waitress later, if need arose. The waitress walked away, casting a last "wish you luck" look at the couple that evidently had not come to merely have an evening snack. She had worked there long enough to know the different types.

133

After a few comments on the day's happenings between them, and Lemah had commented on one or two aspects of the organisation of the café, silence fell between the two lovers like a theatre curtain. It was a thought-packed silence, as evidenced by Theo's frequent sighs and Lemah's endless shifting in her seat and shuffling of her feet.

"You are very quiet," Theo said dryly.

"I have nobody to talk to. I am not in the habit of addressing myself aloud." Lemah's eyes looked straight into Theo's. He gave a nervous chuckle, sipped a bit at his Krest, then sighed again.

"Lemah, I love you," he burst out, of a sudden.

"So do I, Theo!" Their hearts were racing, both were surprised at the turn things had taken. This was not how Theo had planned it. The original plan comprised a long treatise on the qualities he loved in Lemah, and why he thought he loved her, and finally asking her hand in marriage. Now see!

"And I want us to be married," he concluded. Just imagine, a two-line marriage proposal!

Lemah was quiet. This was the moment she had waited for all that long, yet now that it had come, she did not know what to do with it. She did not want to do anything rash or foolhardy. The price could be too dear. When she looked up at Theo, he was watching her. A thin smile gathered on her lips, then disappeared. "Huh, Theo…" she began, then shifted in her seat again. "Okay!'

"Okay what?" Theo leaned forward.

"Okay what you said."

And that is how it happened. When they left the café, Theo drove towards Nakasero Hill. Lemah told him she was not going back to KITANET, but he said he knew that, and drove straight on. He headed towards Sheraton Hotel. When he parked the Volvo, he excused himself and told Lemah he would be back in a tick.

Lemah's heart was doing a *cha cha cha* jig as she waited for Theo. This was the day that the Lord had made for her....for them. God was being kinder to her than she deserved, surely. She wondered what Theo was up to-

"I'm back, my lady!" he said, opening the door. He slid into his seat, buckled the safety belt, leaned back, then sighed – again! 'Lemah," he said without looking away from the infinite distance where his gaze was. "You're good and kind. Thanks for acting mature.'

Lemah's smile overpowered her and she let it bloom. "Thanks too, Theo. I have actually awaited this day for so long myself.'

"I have something for you here." He dipped his hand into his jacket pocket and pulled out a little square casing, and gave it to her. Shaking with impatience, Lemah opened it and got out a gorgeous engagement ring. She slid it onto her finger, and then quickly retrieved it.

"You must put it on yourself," she said as she gave presented her left ring finger to him.

"Till our marriage!" Theo said, as he slid the ring onto her finger. Then they hugged tentatively, and he drove off into the evening traffic, flooding the road ahead of him with the Volvo's strong beams.

EIGHT

A SPARK came flying on the horizon. From a distance, it looked nothing more than a tiny red something floating on the wind. But as it came closer and closer, keen observers and professional experts could see the markings of fire – yet another fire. Tension rose.

This fire was unique. It was the closest not only to the nation's capital, but also to the core who determined the running of the nation. An internal fire, if you prefer. A great stir started to shake things up.

The shake up went beyond the core. Other organs of Government were affected. Deployments and re-deployments were made in the army and police. Tribunals sat by day and sessions raged deep into the night. Whispers and memos criss-crossed. And the fire was beginning to give off stinging smoke.

The public had learnt of the old cliché about smoke and fire, so nobody needed to be told in black and white what exactly was going on. Many who had learnt from the past started reaching out for their passports, investment gusto slackened, and all ears were pricked. Word was on the wind.

And the wind reached KITANET.

Lemah had been doing her research, from the time the spark was seen coming on the horizon. It was said that one Brig. Onzi, Ex-Commander in some previous regime, and now Minister of State for Tourism, was getting restless. He wanted to have more – he wanted to be back to the status of the past. Minister of *state*? And what about his military honours? *They* were lying – he had to reach out for what he knew was his due.

Nobody, however, was going to sit by and watch some past killer reinstate himself to positions where he could do more killing and more robbery. So security operatives were put into running gear, and the chase was on.

136

Lemah was knee–deep into it.

First, Brig. Onzi had started up a small force that he was
using to collect arms from ill-prepared military detachments and
police posts. Same old tricks everybody used. When these arms
accumulated to a fair number, an offensive would be launched. And
a civil war would be born!

Lemah had to act. She had talked to Dr. Kitonsa about going
out news-hunting. It would require some daring, so she asked for the
best men KITANET would provide. A list was provided. Musita's
name was on it!

Musita's dislike for Lemah grew like a cancer. He disliked her
beauty. He disliked her success at her job. He disliked her popularity
at KITANET. He disliked her wide knowledge in journalism. Just
who or what was *she*? So every time he got the opportunity, he got at
her. However slightly he did it, it gave him untold satisfaction.
Whenever the rest of the KITANET community noticed it, that was
score enough for him.

Lemah noticed these things. Her first reaction was to play
blind and deaf. Whatever Musita did, she refused to notice. This,
she discovered, did not deter him. He sure had a goal he was aiming
at. So she changed tactics. She would avoid using him, and just keep
the two of them apart. The few times fate brought them together,
she would find a way of steering her talk in such a direction as would
not involve Musita. Sometimes she succeeded, sometimes she
conceded defeat.

Now he was on her team.

True, Musita was the best lights man KITANET had.
Nobody denied that. But did Lemah really have to take him on? Did
the sort of work she was going to do have room for lighting? This
was dangerous work; nobody would have the time to arrange
elaborate lighting. No, Musita had to go off her list.

The following day, she set off with her men. She travelled in the new Current Affairs Double-cabin Hilux Pick-up, with the equipment at the back. She was stunned – indeed more than stunned - when she got to the field and discovered that Musita was on the team.

"How did you come, *you*?" she flared.

Musita laughed, before pointing at the Pick-up truck.

"Look, sir, this is no laughing matter. And now that you're here, you either choose to behave yourself, or go back to Kampala before temperatures rise." Lemah was inwardly scared. In her heart of hearts, she could sense a battle brewing.

"Yes madam," Musita said off-hand.

"Yes Madam *what* – will you behave well or you need the car to take you back?"

"I'll stay."

"That wasn't one of the options, Sir." She was getting worked up, so she moved farther away from Musita.

"Madam, let's not act like children. Your subordinates might not be impressed." The sarcasm bit deep. Lemah turned, considered him, then got into the car. She had notes to write first.

Outside, the crew were laughing, a big burst of laughter whose origin Lemah could not doubt. Somehow, she told herself that she did not care.

When she was ready, she came down and asked the men to get the equipment ready. Everybody set to fixing their machines. Then none of the batteries could be found. Everybody, except Musita got into a panic.

"Who packed the batteries?" Lemah demanded, moving close to the cameramen?

138

"I did," one of them said.

"And did you put them on the vehicle?"

"Positive." The man sounded genuinely positive.

Then Musita, laughing, said that he now recalled that as he was trying to create room for his screens, he had put the battery rack-sack out, and forgot to put it back. He was sorry.

"Mr Musita, who do you think is going to take that lightly?" Lemah asked, advancing towards Musita. He looked at her, stood up, grinned, and said: "Nobody, of course!"

"So?"

"Well, I needed room for my screens, Madam Nabasa!"

"Mr Musita, I scrapped you off my list even before I told anybody about this project-" "You did not tell me, or anybody else. We normally use lighting screens in these shootings, so I could not see how different this was. Your fault." He swept a victorious look at the other men, grinned satisfactorily, before sitting down on a camera case.

Lemah was boiling within. She knew what this was meant to be. The worst she could do now was fan this fire. That way, she would be playing into Musita's hands. She would not give him that satisfaction.

"We put back the equipment, gentlemen," she said calmly – ever so calmly.

"Madam-" one of the men was saying, but she cut him short.

"We go back to Kampala <u>NOW!</u>" And she got into the car, started the engine and told the driver to get in beside her in the co-driver's seat.

139

They got back to Kampala in dead silence. Not even Musita was talking. He had expected that all Lemah could do was send for the batteries, and work would proceed. She had shocked him. So when they got back to KITANET, he got ready for a summons. This was obviously going to mark the end of his employment at KITANET.

Yet Lemah did not report him. She released them all, thanking them for their time. She also said she was sorry that she had wasted their time and energy. Then she went to her office.

Mercy was out. Lemah felt a sharp pang of frustration. She had wanted to talk to Mercy. She needed someone to talk to. She had to talk to someone. She was about to leave her desk when she noticed that her visitors' pad was open on a plain page. She reached out for it, and when she turned the paper, there was a note for her. She ripped off the staple that bound it and devoured the words:

> *Lemah, tarry not. I have information for you that I can only divulge in the privacy of my house. Waiting for you NOW.*
>
> *Connie.*

NINE

LEMAH found Connie waiting. She wore a mixture of excitement and anxiety on her usually composed face. Lemah suspected trouble. "Anything the matter, dear?"

"It's why I called you, Lemah. I have information for you, Lemah, but somehow I feel like it may have a price. We have to be careful, Lemah."

"What's this all about? Tell me; you kill me with suspense, Connie!"

"First promise me two things: One, that you'll act on this *real* quick, and two, that you'll act on it very discreetly. *Will* you, Lemah?"

"Certainly. Now-"

"Easy. I....Lemah, go easy. Yeah? I have a friend who is close to army circles. He told me there was going to be drama at the airport tonight. I can't give you the deep details, but just know that the drama might be of interest to you, and maybe it could be the story you've been waiting for all your professional career life."

Connie was still talking when Lemah jumped up and said she had to move immediately. She thanked Connie, and then fled away, leaving Connie bewildered. The woman was too deep into her career! She too would have loved to be that zealous, but her boyfriend would never give her the time. He monitored her like the metre of a life support machine. God had to help her.

From Connie's, Lemah raced straight to her house. She only needed her miniature video recorder, one or two cassettes and transport the fare. In less than ten minutes, she was heading for the roadside to take a taxi to town. She could not use private means on such a mission. God just had to help her to get to Entebbe safely and quickly.

The airport was exceptionally busy. The lobby was packed with relations and friends welcoming and seeing off travellers. Lemah was familiar with this, so she did not stop by to watch anything. Only one couple struck her as unique. It was not common that blacks kiss in public, in Uganda. But this couple did, all in the name of "I'll miss your warmth." People!

Lemah pulled an official to the side. She did not give him a chance to be hard. "I am Lemah. I am very harmless, as you will prove if you'll care to search me. But I must go through to the field. I *must*. And only you, Sir, can help me."

"Must you-"

"I must, Sir. Now. So where do I pass? Quick, we don't have time to lose." Deep inside, she did not really think this man would oblige her, but she was amazed when he condescended, and helped her. Pulling her by the hand, he led her through customs corridors, and led her right to the other side up the building. He, however, said he had to plant someone on her to watch her.

"Fine with me," she gasped.

He brought a guard and instructed him to keep her covered.

As soon as the official left, Lemah turned to the guard. "I am a journalist. I have come here for news and nothing else. All I have on me is a camera, a pen and a notebook. Plus, maybe, this money for you. Stay, but don't get into my way." No need, then, to add that the man let Lemah be, and did not see her again, for soon thereafter, the stage was set for the drama.

An Emirates flight was about to take off. Suddenly, two civilian-looking young men ran behind a guarded man about to board the plane. They said something to the escorts, who in turn talked to the big man, who was standing about two metres away. The big man,

142

in response, drew a pistol and as he aimed, a quick *taekwondo* kick swung the gun out of his hand. In the flash of time, there was a burst of fire, and one of the escorts lay dead, his weapon falling away before he could pull the trigger. The big man was put under arrest, and led back to a waiting Land Rover in the airport parking yard.

KITANET had the full news that same night. Brig Ben–Yusuf had been arrested at Entebbe Airport as he was moving out of the country, to go and join others in London, where they were starting a rebel group. Papers found in his case proved this. As a result, a number of high-ranking army officers were under arrest, and others were on the run.

D'Souza himself watched the programme. Experience told him who must have been behind it, but he had to have proof. That was how he did his things. So he called up the Controller of Programmes and asked who had done that coverage, and how, when, plus all the other trivia. The answer was as he had expected: Magical Lemah Nabasa!

D'Souza was glad with Lemah's work. However, he was in a dilemma. He knew she deserved a promotion. He also knew that should not be in a position where she sat in an office all day long, all week long. Yet all managerial posts were office posts. Anyhow, whatever the implications, he had to reward her efforts with a promotion. He would find a way. He called a meeting of the directors. The alternatives were headship of the Current Affairs department, or taking her to Health, where Kaliisa was still not replaced. There was only an acting H.O.D there. At the end of the meeting, though, it was decided that she becomes General Producer of Programmes, as well as Head of Research in the Current Affairs department. Those were principally two jobs in one, a most worthwhile promotion. It gave Lemah more status, more money, yet she remained where her dreams could be pursued without hindrance.

A decision was taken to communicate the promotion to her directly, as an official letter was processed. Dr. Kitonsa was instructed to call her up, which he did.

"You'll do well to keep the current reputation, dear," he said in conclusion. He could hear the excitement in the young woman's voice as she thanked him over and over again.

"You bet I will. Do you doubt my potential to?"

"Nothing is impossible, Lemah! Bye, and good luck."

He hung up.

Meanwhile, Musita was uneasy. Lemah's silence after such a blunder he had made did not portend well for him, he thought. He had to do something about it before she got into high gear.

Mercy was just preparing to leave for work the following morning when Musita accosted her. "I am sorry to cut into your progress, Mercy, but I need your help!" Mercy was surprised. *Musita*, seeking help from *her*! Something must have been the matter.

"Anything I can do for you, I will. What's up?" She knew Musita well, so she made sure that she sounded as official and unaffected as possible.

"Er....it's about Lemah....Ms Nabasa." He looked over his shoulder, and into the road that led down to the rest of the junior staff quarters. He then moved close. "I got her angry yesterday. I would like you to talk to her for me."

Mercy had heard about it from Lemah herself. She had passed by Mercy's on her way back home, just to have someone to off-load her excitement to. So big was the evening's success.

Mercy decided that she was not going to pamper Musita. Lemah had said that she would do nothing to him; after all it was by his malice that she had returned to Kampala on time for this miracle news event. But Mercy could not tell Musita this. He had to suffer this discomfort. "Right now I have little time on me. Please see me later in the day. I promise to talk to her, but see me later in the day," she said as she locked her door and moved up the road. Musita followed her.

"Mercy, later in the day may prove too late. Can't-

"Mr Musita, I will help you. But later."

They parted.

Mercy felt a tinge of joy at the battle she was fighting for her Boss-friend. She was thus still congratulating herself when Connie ran up to her.

"Mercy, it's good I found you. Tell Lemah that I'm in big trouble. I'll give you the details later when I see you and I'm settled enough. Bye." She ran off again.

Mercy stayed rooted on the spot. Trouble about what? Why did she want Lemah informed? How could she be of help? Where was Connie running to?

When the questions piled to an unmanageable number, Mercy got back to her senses and walked to the office. Lemah was already in, busy with files and cassettes.

"Hi Mercy, you look flustered. Anything the matter?"

"Connie. She-"

Lemah was up in a second. "She what? Is she in trouble?"

"Do you know something then, Lemah? You use her very words. She said she's in big trouble, but gave no details. She ran away and left me there, standing."

And that is exactly how Lemah, too, left Mercy. In the office, standing.

Lemah did not remember to buckle up the seat belt of her official car, a Hyundai Accent. She drove to Connie's. The door was locked, but she could hear the radio on. She knocked. Nothing. She hammered the door, still to no avail. She shouted out Connie's name. It was then that Connie came and opened for her.

"Are you safe, Connie?" Lemah burst out.

"I don't know, Lemah. I *don't know*. But do me one favour…one final favour-"

"Don't talk like that, Connie!"

"I don't wish to, myself, but it's the bitter truth. Please help me and leave this house, *now*," she pleaded.

"I can't. I must help you, Connie."

"I am beyond help. So please, leave me now. My boyfriend works with the Special Security Agency. He's the one who got me the news of yesterday, so I tipped you off. I didn't know he would be at the airport himself. Now he will be here any moment, Lemah, and God help us. He will skin me alive, if I know him well. He will!" Connie broke down, and slumped onto the coffee table in front of her. Lemah dived to hold her.

"No, Lemah, don't stay here. Go!"

"Not before you've told me how I can be of help, Connie."

"I don't know!" The very despair of the situation wracked at Lemah's heart. She determined that she was going to get protection for Connie. If this SSA man came to harm her, he would find stronger hands in the house. She left Connie in the house and drove off.

That afternoon Lemah returned to Kampala. She had failed to secure the security she had intended for Connie, so she had come to report at KITANET, before proceeding to CPS, Kampala, to get police protection. She had no way but to spill the entire secret out, as far as it was safe for her to. She hoped no more danger would come of it. She decided that before she talked to her immediate boss, she would see what was going on in her office. In the office, she found Mercy in a panic. Connie's trouble had increased. Her boyfriend had been to her KITANET residence and staged a fight. Much as he had volunteered to tell her about the drama, he had not expected that it would culminate into his appearing on the KITANET screens, doing *that* to a big man. It was very dangerous to his security. So he had beaten Connie up, and when he left, it was clear that all was not well. That was the point at which Lemah got the news.

Lemah knew she had to intensify her attempts to save Connie. The poor girl had borne no ill will against anyone. She had most probably done it only to pay for the day Lemah had stood in for her to read the close-down news, though God knew she needed not pay. Now the price was getting this high. As Lemah drove to the junior quarters, she wondered what she was going to do. She owed the fame and popularity she was enjoying now to this girl's tip-off.... to Connie herself. The last thing she wanted was to fail to rescue her. She knew just what a hurt soldier could do, if soldiers were what she knew them to be.

She was late. Either too late to rescue Connie, or to be the one to rescue her. The house was locked up. No sign of life existed anywhere, inside or outside the house. The neighbours said they did not know which way she had gone, though she had been in all morning.

Lemah drove back to the station. She went straight to News Room, where she was told on inquiring, that Connie had not reported for duty at all, that morning.

"And why was I not notified?" Lemah asked, anger flushing into her system. "Thank you, anyhow." She went to her office. She was at a loss what to do.

"Mercy, do you know Connie's house number?"

"047. No news of her yet?" Mercy too was scared.

"Nope! God, I do hope she's safe."

She dialled the number. The beeper indicated that the line was clear, but nobody picked the phone. So she was not back.

She replaced the receiver. Something in her system told her something was wrong – very wrong.

Just then, Mr Nywai burst into the office, breathless and dishevelled. 'Trouble, Miss Nabasa. We've got a problem."

"Is it Connie?" She blurted out with shock.

"Yes. Her man just shot her. He is on the run."

"Where? I just rang her place now!"

"Questions later. There's nobody to help her. The girl who rang my office says everybody is shit scared, nobody will touch her. And she's not dead, yet."

Mr Nywai simply made the Audi fly to the scene of the crime. When they got to her, what was left of Connie was beyond talking to. Her pulse was still going, but all else seemed like history. They bundled her into the car, and raced into the direction of Mulago Hospital.

They were not to reach there. She died as they negotiated with the gateman to let them in. Lemah was beaten. She had not saved her unacknowledged friend… Connie, a girl who had been vulnerable all her sweet life……

Lemah was bent on doing Connie a last favour. She would get the murderer. He had to be brought to book. She drove to Connie's residence as soon as they had left the body at the morgue. Defeat Number Two. The man had delivered himself into the hands of the law at Wandegeya. He was already in custody at the Central Police Station.

Despite the defeat, Lemah still hungered to have a chat with this wicked man. She was not satisfied, yet. The following day she drove to CPS, but the man had been transferred to Makindye Barracks. He was a soldier, so he would not be tried in a civilian court. He was set for the Military Tribunal at Makindye.

The officer in charge let her have access to the prisoner, after she had identified herself. She was given two guards to take her to his cell. When she entered the cell, they remained at the door, waiting…..

When the prisoner saw her, he already knew who she was. He was taken aback at first, but he steeled himself.

"What do you want here, Lemah? I would advise you to be off right away," he said. Lemah stood a few paces away.

"I want to talk to you," she said firmly.

"You won't. I brought myself to the law, and you do not know why. You can't know why. So please leave." He was not angry, but neither was he courteous.

"I must talk to you, *Afande*……why did you do it?"

He regarded her for a long while. Finally, he spoke - still calmly, but not politely.

"That's the very question I want to put to you – why did you put people's lives at stake by such a selfish act? You develop your career at the dear expense of other people's jobs – lives even? Now see where it has landed me. You made me kill Connie. Lemah, I killed the girl I loved best the world over. So what can stop me fro-But well, no use. Yet I had to….Better than what we would all have to go through for this…. *I – killed – Connie*….! Oh Jesus!" he broke

149

down. Lemah believed him. She recalled Connie breaking down that morning. She thought about why Connie had refused to he helped, yet it was clear what she would go through. Was she offering a sacrifice? Now what was she, Lemah, to do in this case? He was right: the mistake was hers. She had killed her Connie. How terrible! Utterly terrible!

"*Afande?*"

"Please don't talk to me….at least not about this. My original intention had been to make you the third person on our list – in addition to Connie and me. Yes, I am already a dead man. I had to hand myself over. A third death would be a waste. A mean waste, in this case. Useless. Besides, what is life without Connie? I killed her, Lemah! But I am a soldier, so my case has to be handled by the army. Not the civilian courts and whoever. So I called the right people so that they could do the right thing. That's why I am here…God, no. Killing you, Lemah, would be useless. Your death would make no sense. That would be typical murder. So do me one big favour: Leave!"

She made for the door.

"Just one minute, Lemah," the man called after her. She stopped, but did not turn. "How did you manage to do all that – I mean the pictures, words and all: Did you get it all?"

"I don't want to endanger more innocent people. If I reveal that, I will be jeopardising not just the jobs, but also the lives of three people at the airport. Aren't two lives more that enough?"

"Yeah, go, Lemah. You're the last person I am talking to. When they get in here, those guys… Oh, you don't know who I mean? The MPs – Military Police. When they get here, I will not say a thing. I am already dead, and dead men don't speak. So you're the very last I am speaking to."

"Will you not defend yourself?" Lemah asked, close to tears.

"Against what? Just do this for me, Lemah. Please remember that I did not murder Connie. I could not. I killed her, and intentionally too, but I did not murder her. I know you will never understand this. Luckily, she did. That's why she did not cause a scene. Now that she's dead, I understand how much we love each other. In death, all is perfected. Even our love. Do remember that of us."

He paused awhile.

"Go now."

She walked away. This was more than Lemah could handle. The journalist in her could not, nor could the adventurer, nor the ambitious spirit in her. This was not her stuff. She was, yet again, beaten. Utterly defeated. She had been wrong about soldiers. They were people, and this particular one was more person than all the civilians she had ever met.

As she drove back to KITANET, a strong chill poured over her. Goose bumps developed all over her body and her entire frame shook. Her teeth were chattering, too. Was she falling sick?

She was just able to drive into the KITANET area, and her engine went dead. She slumped onto the steering wheel, and vomit issued from her mouth with unrestrained ease. And she was bleeding in the nose.

Mr Ssali saw her first. Without touching her, he called Mercy out. Poor Mercy, she nearly fainted. After the shock of Connie, if Lemah also followed, it would be enough to break the stoutest heart.

When Mercy got to her Boss-friend, she was a total mess.

Vomit, blood and a limp body. They dragged her out of her car, put her in order, then put her in the KITANET ambulance. She was rushed to Mulago Hospital.

D'Souza received all this news with disbelief. A newsgirl dead. Ms Nabasa, newly appointed Chief Researcher and General Programmes Producer, taken ill under mysterious circumstances. All caused by news Ms Nabasa had fished concerning guerrilla activity. What was he supposed to think?

He had asked Mr. Nywai to cover up Ms Nabasa, and to find a replacement for Connie in the Newsroom. Connie was dead; that was beyond help. And, honestly, she was good; but many are available who could equal her. Not so Lemah. Lemah was good in a way that only she could be. She was changing the shape of operations in a way that amazed D'Souza, considering her age, and the attitude society had towards women. He hoped sincerely that nothing would go wrong.

The doctors said Lemah was suffering from nothing specific. Shock, maybe, but shock could not explain the cold feeling and the vomiting. Well, they treated her, and on the following day she was discharged. All sound and fit, like a fiddle. Only her mind was not at peace. She had heard that her soldier was to face firing squad that afternoon.

Did he really have to? Could he not explain himself to the army the way he did to her? It was a situation anybody with a heart could understand. If there were others like him in the army – regular forces, or intelligence, or whatever – they sure ought to let him off. If only she could…..But no, it was too late.

She attended the occasion. Such a great throng there was to witness this man lose his life for loving a girl. For that is how Lemah looked at it. He was proving his love by dying without defence, without a struggle. This crowd that stood by, condemning him and scoffing at him, did not know a thing. If anybody was guilty of anything, it was them. They did not know love; nor did they love. They were miserably ignorant!

Lemah's hero, for that is what he had become, was brought in, accompanied on his last journey by such an escort as he could never have had in his life, at his level. He was calm and complacent, a true picture of the lover. The hero. The conqueror.

A structure had been erected, on which he was bound, and a hood put on his head. Why bother with such things as binding and blind-folding him? Lemah actually thought that in that binding, they set him free; and by putting the dark cloth over his eyes, they acknowledged his farsightedness. She admired him, true, though she did not quite understand exactly why he had KILLED, but not murdered Connie. But in her heart of hearts, she believed him about his loving her. He was dying as a manifestation of that love.

The first command to the six soldiers who were going to carry out the execution sliced her thoughts into unequal parts. Six soldiers cocked their guns.

Six soldiers!

Second order, and six soldiers took aim.

Six soldiers!

Another order and a volley of bullets fed on the flesh of a valiant lover. Bullets from six soldiers' guns, killing one man. First time, second time and third time.

TEN

NOBODY loves heat. Warmth, yes. When temperatures rise beyond what the average human being can bear, they begin to get uneasy. If they do not shift position, they will do something about the source of the heat. But sometimes the source of the heat is beyond their reach, and this is when tension develops between the Fire Department and the uncomfortable populace who want the heat controlled, or plain done away with.

The Government was facing this kind of trouble. It was undergoing what very few of us want to undergo – being reminded of our well-known responsibilities and duties. Worse for the Government, this was coming from corners they least wanted to listen to.

MESSAGE:

It is your duty to protect your people from the discomfort of both external and internal fires. Right now, a lot of people are being choked in illicitly lit fires - small fires, big fires, all manner of fires. Several of them from within. We are tired!

REACTION:

Trust us. We gonna get damp canvas and throw it over all these fires once and for all. We got the ability. We done it before, we gonna do it again. Trust us. *Trust us.*

RESULTS:

Two sides formed. "We", who later turned into "They", and The Others, who became "The Rest of Us".

And the two rubbed, from within. And heat was generated from within. And there was fire from within; but since there was no smoke, how could anyone say there was fire there?

No one. No way!

ELEVEN

....**IT** rained heavily. Torrential rain, the kind that puts everything to a standstill. Long rain, for whose end people wait in vain, so they can go to fulfil appointments delayed by hours; so they can rush and ease themselves hours after they first developed the need; so they could return home and seek warmth in more reasonable ways than a proffered cup of coffee, a borrowed jacket, or closing all ventilation on a room, then gasping for fresh air. It was that kind of rain.

Lemah just stood there, letting it wash over her. At first, it had been unbearably cold, but she had got used to it; and she just stood there....hour after hour. She saw nothing but the rain, heard nothing but the rain. She felt nothing but the rain. Those were her only three sensitive senses then. She tasted nothing, smelt nothing. Her blouse of soft silk and the jeans trousers dripped with the rain, as did her long, beautiful hair. She did not even remember that her simple Omax watch was not waterproof, and it too was full of the rainwater. But she could not see this, because the watch was not rain. It only contained some of it. She could not feel its presence on her wrist, because the wrist too felt only the rain. She was almost saturated with rain....Where she stood, a lot of water had collected, and it gushed over her, from somewhere, to somewhere else. She did not bother about whether it was clean water or not, because she did not see it. She saw only the rain. She did not even hear its licking and gurgling sounds as it flowed around her, for she heard only the rain....

Till it ceased to pour down, reduced to a drizzle, and then stopped altogether. And a strange thing happened, and she saw it: A rainbow stood across the sky, dark in its brightness, and vivid, and almost touchably close. It seemed to envelope Lemah and the structure on which the soldier-hero had been killed. It was also reflected in the puddles that had collected all about her. She sighed, and then slowly turned, to walk away from the place of death.

She was just walking away when a familiar sound made her stop in her tracks. Was she right? Yes, sure as there is day and night, it was Theo's Volvo. She did not move on, she did not go to meet him. She stayed there, rooted.

Theo confirmed his fears: something was grossly wrong.

He had been to her house, and found a note indicating that she would be at the firing squad site. Panicking, he had driven like a madman, to come and be there with and for her, should she need him. He was right.

"Lemah, what could be the matter? God of Abraham, you're drenched! Where are you coming from?" He was scared.

"I'm coming from here. At this place of death….You stare so. Did you hear of the soldier-"

"Who murdered his woman? Yes, of course!" Theo sounded angry at the fact that someone could murder his own woman!

"Don't talk so, Theo. There's a lot you do not know. I think nobody knows anything…Did you know the girl?"

"How could I? I just heard these things from the people at the station."

"You didn't know Connie, did you?"

"Not our Connie certainly? Not her!" he whimpered.

"That Connie, *our* Connie. She was killed by that soldier… But it is a difficult story. You shall know it some day, though!" Lemah leaned against a tree, exasperated.

Theo did not know what to say or do. Lemah was certainly distressed. It showed on her face. He heard it in her voice. He had known her for some time now, and he was positive. She was not anywhere close to her normal self.

157

"Has Connie been your friend – someone close?" He moved to her, but did not touch her.

"Not what you can call a friend in the conventional sense, but maybe it would have felt much better if she had been. She…I don't even know how to put this. She is…she *was* someone I had started to look at as a person; a human being. I treasured her, Theo. And she is dead!"

"It's such a shame!" Theo muttered.

"Such a pity you don't know everything, Theo. Anyway, you shall know it, someday." She rubbed her hands resignedly, like Pilate washing Jesus' blood off his soul. She stood erect, off the tree.

They did not make a move. Lemah did not budge, and Theo could not. Lemah just did not think of it, her mind was too full of lurid staff. Theo had no right to lead her on, at least not now, and certainly not in the open. She was wet. Some of the water had dripped onto the ground where she stood, but her blouse still clang onto her body with water. Her hair was mangled, and her eyes were the colour of *chilli* sauce.

Theo thought of so many things he wanted to do, but he could not bring himself to do them. Not out of cowardice, not out of the fear to hurt or wrong Lemah. The snag was that he did not understand her well enough, yet, to be able to do the right thing or, at the barest level, the appropriate thing.

Lemah spoke first, after the long silence.

"Theo, people are more than just the flesh and blood that make them appear to us. They are living beings, and that is what makes all the difference."

"Did you – oh well, life is certainly a most important aspect in determining the way we look at people."

"- or treat them," Lemah added for him.

"Yeah, I guess."

"You see, Theo, people cannot just be summed up into a one-sentence lesson. Life makes this a vain endeavour. This incident, Theo, has taught me a big lesson about life. It is more than they teach us at school."

"Don't talk so, Lemah. You sound alien; strange!"

"I am sorry. Perhaps you're right. We are all alien to Reality, one way or another. And when we attempt to accustom ourselves to it, we either make mistakes along the way – mistakes we may never remedy, or distort Reality, or plain get lost. Ah, look, I am sorry I still sound like this."

"I understand, Lemah. I think I understand. I am sorry."

"Maybe I am over reacting."

They fell silent again, but this time the cause was different. It just occurred of a sudden, simultaneously, spontaneously. Theo felt it, but was wary of showing it. Lemah too was conquered by it, but she did not want to embarrass Theo. She loved him better…

Theo realised that Lemah's face was drawing close to his, somehow. Her entire body did move, yet her face did. He could almost feel it on him, and he ceased to see anything else but her face. Like one acting on a surge of electric power, he took her in his arms, drew her to him and kissed her with all the passion on the continent that evening. She responded with full force, the way a car does when one shifts to a stronger gear, and then presses fully on the accelerator. It was an experience, by God!

When they let go of each other, Lemah walked to Theo's car, which was parked a little way off. She opened the rear door and entered, pulling the door after her. When Theo followed, it was not to talk to her. It was not necessary. He got into the Volvo, started the engine and drove to Lemah's house. There, Lemah got out like acting

159

on remote controlled power, then turned and bid Theo good night. And boy, was it a proper one!

Theo drove away. He drove, but if he did it right, it was to be credited on instinct. His mind was flooded with the evening's achievement. The hands felt only Lemah's stiff shoulders; the eyes saw her enchanting face and his entire make-up reacted to her own reaction to his passion. And the Volvo sped on, with strength, with power, with inspiration. But not with Theo's skill. If there was no other proof that he was unconscious of what he did with and to the car, his driving straight on along the road, past the turning to his house, left no doubt at all in the angels who kept guard over his life. So maybe it was by divine intervention that right in front of him, someone happened to be pushing a car, and controlling its steering, all by himself. The driver's door was open, and the man used one hand to push the car, and the other to control the steering wheel. Theo came to, then, and slowed down. He discovered that the man was none other than Lord, one of the presenters at Theo's station. He had stopped to drop a friend who had asked him for a lift, and when he attempted to start the car to drive on, it failed.

"Any trouble, man?" Theo called with astonishing gaiety.

"My starter just failed, sir. Got some, say, twenty thousand shillings on you, sir?"

"Yeah, park by the side and get this." He plunged his right hand into his hip pocket, and pulled out an amount of money he did not bother to count. He handed all of it to Lord. The young radio presenter looked at the wad of notes, re-scrutinised his boss, said an incredulous Thank You and went back to his car. He just sat in there, unable to believe or comprehend how God works his miracles. If this was not a miracle, the word existed in vain. He counted the money and realised he had just got sh300,000 from his boss.

Theo did a 3- point turn and drove to his house. When he entered his bedroom, it was 7:25p.m. He stripped, lay on his bed, face

160

upwards, and he watched Lemah's face up on the ceiling till morning. When he got up to fix himself breakfast, he knew he could now tell his confidants two things: One, that he had finally found a girlfriend. And two, that he was in love.

When Theo drove off, Lemah could see that the highway she had been travelling on had finally come to an end, and she – they - had taken an Access Road to where they wanted to end up. She had felt it in their bodily reactions as they kissed. If she had not experienced this after that Mankind lesson, she might have thought this a dream, or a product of Winged-Horse fancies. But she had been through that other bit of life, and no degree of imagination could have stretched her mind that far, that deep.

She entered her house, picked up pen and paper and sat down to write a letter to Theo. She did not have to compose the letter. It tumbled out of some new-found secret chamber of her heart. Things flowed out, the way sand flows off a tilted tipper truck. It was a letter such as only a woman who felt the way Lemah did that day could write. And when she sent it, she knew deep inside of her that a major step had been taken in their relationship.

To-date, Theo has never recovered from that letter.

TWELVE

THE fires of anarchy were spreading almost wantonly from nation to nation, all around Uganda. Like a thermostat of catastrophe, the Kenya-Uganda border kept closing and opening, with accusations and counter-accusations oscillating between the two neighbours. Professional and non-professional groups were being deported from either country. Dissidents were being claimed for from either country: Give him over for proper trial! Extradite him! You have no right to try him over there! Local *wanainchi*, on their part, rubbed hostility into each other's sore skins, whenever they got the opportunity for it.

Damn these Kenyans, all they care for is their brothel-infested city, nothing else! When they're here, we're all over ourselves with hospitality from the heart's core, but just cross into their damned land at Malaba or Busia, you may not go back there, for love or money.

And what's there in that lousy Uganda? What good is in Ugandans? They think the brain of one man is enough to do ample thinking for 18 million people! Argh, confound them, lousy Ugandans. They have failed to do a thing for their country, they are either masquerading as expatriates, or liberators in other people's homes!

Then there was heat being generated between Uganda and Congo; with accusations and counter-accusations of giving support to rebels attacking each country. Rwanda was also unhappy about one thing or another. Surely, something was amiss.

This sort of talk had ceased to surprise anyone. Even at home, friction was developing amongst the populace. Whenever officers had less work to handle and they relapsed back in their chairs, the talk turned to the spreading fires in the region. Whenever teachers chatted together after heavy meals in staff-rooms, the topic was the rumour that some people were working towards the re-existence of one African nation, with one President. In some circles they even said they knew who that President would be.

"You know this is rather sensitive, and no amount of insulated talking is going to calm anyone down."

"When it occurred here, nobody knew what was happening. History was made. The start of a regional fire."

"Then it spread to Rwanda. Even the intelligence here could not explain how it started."

"So we were told. And before we understood how things were happening so successfully in Rwanda, tongues of fire were licking at Burundi!"

"Now it is the Congo!"

"And other neighbours are on tension. Nobody knows what may crop up. Nobody knew. Everybody knows this fact, and to-date, very few can explain what, how or even why. Only when.

The spread of this regional fire intensified at a moment when Lemah's thinking was undergoing a transformation; almost a renaissance. The death of Connie and her soldier-man had opened a new chapter in her life, both as a journalist and as a social being. She no longer looked at people as objects in news items, but as full-scale beings, to whom things happen, sometimes as a consequence, and sometimes as an accident. She was teaching herself to believe that good news, like everything else good, was made. People's lives were the raw materials - in rapes, in massacres, in robberies, in wars. What this meant to Lemah was that people were used.

Used.

Where these news-worthy events occurred, they were never considered as news, but as disasters or calamities. That was life. To the radio, TV and newspaper world, it was looked at as news. That was commerce. Money. Capture the grotesque. Sell more. Very absurd!

So when Theo rang up Lemah to suggest a joint news venture between The Station and KITANET, he was shocked at her response. She was not going to engage in dehumanising ventures any more.

"What is so dehumanising in this, Lemah? All we're doing is studying and reporting about the recruitment and training of secret forces. The rumour doing the rounds-"

"See? Rumour. And private lives are involved in this. Lives we want to unearth, possibly to their detriment. Theo, I am gradually pulling out of that sort of news."

"Good word. *Gradually.* So why do you want this to be the ppoint when your new resolution takes effect? Lemah, this is something nobody else knows! Besides, I could do it alone, but radio has limitations. It will make hotter news on TV!"

"How?"

Theo was silent. He could sense Lemah's trap. "How, I asked. See? It is there in your silence. It will be hotter news because you are exposing somebody in something they did not want the world to know – yet. Pictures better than voices."

"So are you for guerrilla warfare, and coups, and colonisation… all this rot?" Theo was beginning to heat up.

"No, and nobody said as much. All I am saying is, if it is for the benefit of the person I expose, I do it. If it is for career development and money and red-hot news, I am out of it. And that is it."

Theo rested his case.

THIRTEEN

LEMAH had been in this state for over an hour. She felt heavy, pensive. All about her ceased to be what it had always been, and looked new, without anything definite that made it look this new. Her desk – the fond desk she had always sat at to pursue her dreams on wings of ambition, now looked no more than a wooden structure, bearing two telephones, files and notebooks and loose papers and pens and markers and high-lighters, and her characteristic coffee flask. She was like a drug addict… Her gaze shifted to the wall on the left of the entrance to her office. There was a large print of the KITANET logo, a mast with a disk booster with the globe floating on the booster. That was her world, the place where and by means of which she had set out to reach out for the end of the rainbow – her dreams' rainbow. She was now learning the futility of this. A rainbow is beautiful, but a sign of prohibition on anger and punishment. It is not a prosperity sign. It is visible alright, but we cannot reach out for it, you are bound to hurt yourself in the process.

On the same wall, at the extreme end, was Lemah's favourite cynicism in print:

There's somebody in this establishment who knows all that's going on.

That Person should be fired immediately!

One day D'Souza himself had entered her office, studied it like he was seeing it the first time and said: "I agree, Lemah. You should be fired!" Lemah knew only too well that from D'Souza, that was a compliment. She said a hearty thank you, and the two laughed, laughter that announces a feeling of comradeship. Would he now think her a comrade with what she was contemplating? She was not very sure.

The rest of the wall was bare. The right hand side wall had a framed picture of her mother, one of Connie in the News Room, one of the President, and a gorgeous sunset over rolling hills and lush greenery. And as she took in all these things, Lemah discovered that she had all along known nothing about her office, about her place of

165

work – in its sense as a duty, a responsibility. She did not know herself, even. She needed to re-shape a number of aspects of her life, by the grace of God.

She moved to the large window that opened to the gardens outside. The green out there looked cordial, fresh and comely. There were various shrub-shades, flowers of varying hues, and all these were locked in by a black-and-white painted pavement. That is what spoilt it, the painted pavement. It killed the natural beauty of the garden. It caught the eye, arrested it. It reminded her of the clean tiled floor and walls of a toilet….an artificial touch lying about the truth within. Here, the artificial touch killed the beauty within. Either way, what catches the eye is not the truth, and denies a studious eye the chance to know the natural truth.

This was the sort of thing she had been doing, capturing artificially-edited sketches of life and presenting them to the world. This was journalism as she had been doing it. No, she could not lie to the world any longer… The good thing about this toilet-thing is that the clean floor and walls cannot curb the filthy smell, and the pavement cannot de-colour the flowers, or kill their scent; those that have it, naturally.

Lemah's mind was made up.

"I would like to go and work on a new programme, Dr. Kitonsa."

"C'mon Lemah, you certainly know I am no longer-"

"Yeees, you're right. I certainly know that. But I also know that in every establishment, every careful person has a brain they can confide in, consult and rely on in cases of danger, and even for the sake of character development."

"Am I supposed to thank you for that flatter?" He was genuinely flattered. This was unique, from a person of Lemah's calibre.

"C'mon, be a man," she retorted, but with unmistakable playfulness. "Anyway, as I was saying, I want to go out and work out a new programme."

"So?"

"This is going to be different from the stuff I have been doing. I want to present the people in the programmes as human beings, not as figures of government neglect, or anything like that. Do you think this is news that D'Souza will love? You know him better."

"I see...Now before I answer you, I'll tell you that the best source of good and wise counsel is one's conscience. But you've come to me, so I will tell you this. News of any sort has two sides to it: the reporter and the audience. The audience may know what they want, but they are not equipped with all the reasons for wanting it. The reporter knows what to feed the audience on, and may know why it is that specific news he has fished out. And above the reporter is our D'Souza. What D'Souza wants is success. However, he can only rely on a Lemah who has been trained in how to make D'Souza succeed as a Television developer. Make him realise that he has that in you. Have I answered you?"

Lemah pushed out her right hand with such force, her mentor was taken aback. "Thank you, Dr. Kitonsa. My programme is made."

She left for Gulu after two days. She knew what she wanted, but not how to go about doing it. She had been to the UNICEF office at Kisozi House, and she had been given a covering letter. She had also got clearance from the Government Secretariat at Gossamer Towers, to get protection while she was in Devil's Land, as she called the war-infected district of Gulu. It was risky business, almost suicidal, but worth giving a try.

The bus she travelled on moved in a convoy, along with five other vehicles – two lorries, a military Land Rover and a private saloon car. Most of the people on the bus were Luo speakers, with a few who spoke rough Swahili, with one or two phrases of English or Luganda sprinkled in here and there. She had too much on her mind, so she did not feel left out, even when the very people she shared her seat with yelled animatedly across to other people. Every now and then she saw or thought of something that necessitated writing down, and she would pull out her journal, scribble down a few reminders and notes, shove it back into the bag's side-pockets, and then fall back to her scenery-gazing.

As they raced down-course along the road, through Luweero, where the National Resistance Army (NRA.) had waged much of their protracted struggle against Milton Obote, Lemah's mind raced on backward tracks, past heaps of skulls lined by the roadside, past white journalists and adventurers taking pictures – cine, slide, video and photographs, to show the world outside the Uganda version of the costs of liberation. What she did not fully understand was the difference between a rebel and a liberator. As a student at St. James Secondary School, she had been part of a group that was taken to sing for President Dr. A.M. Obote when he was officiating at the opening of a Community Water Reservoir at Bugembe Hill. All his talk had been full of rebel Museveni and his fellow dissidents, the ruthless killings in the Luweero Triangle, the patriotic UNLA soldiers fighting them…

When that regime slid into the limbo of History, the "rebels" marched into Kampala, shoved Obote's successors aside, and put on the slough of liberators. That is where Lemah's mind failed to disentangle definitions and concepts. Now they too preached against dissident activities in the North, in Kasese and God alone knew where else.

As they left Buganda behind and entered Bunyoro, the conversation trend changed. People only talked to their neighbours, and even then, it was only occasional remarking on this or that aspect of the journey. It might have been the monotony of the journey, but they were also aware that after Masindi, they would have to cross

Karuma Bridge. Everyone knew the full implications of this. If none else did, Lemah knew it with her whole self: body, mind, blood and soul. She instinctively narrowed up her small form, rubbed her big toes one against the other, clenched her fists and tightened the embrace around her travelling bag. She was not certain anymore. How could she be, under the circumstances?

The bus came to a sudden halt, as had the other vehicles. Only one of the lorries – a Jiefang carrying merchandise from the famous Kampala-based Arua Park – trailed behind the bus. The rest were ahead and now all had stopped. Lemah got panicky, just like everyone else. Then word spread that they had to choose between crossing on the ferry at Masindi Port, or cross at Karuma. A big debate raged on this, with several voices shouting several indiscernible things all at once. Lemah could only decipher the two land marks in the two alternative routes: Karuma Bridge had Masindi Port. Eventually, after many people had disembarked and mingled with others from other vehicles, they agreed that they proceed straight on via Karuma. Reason? They had four soldiers on their convoy. Besides, there had been an ambush only eight kilometres from the bridge only two days ago. Which rebel would be foolish enough as to present his head for auction by making the grotesque blunder of returning to Karuma today? The travellers knew the place was now under heavy surveillance by government troops, so it was safe. Safer, in fact.

When the vehicles were in motion again, all conversation died down. Apart from the incessant drone of the Isuzu bus engine as it flew over the hills, round the bends and down the horizon of uncertainly, Lemah heard nothing else. If she had been very attentive, she would maybe have heard the *tu-tum, tu-tum* of her heart.

They were just leaving the bridge at Karuma behind when her heart's *tu-tum, tu-tum* was torn into by a burst of machine-gun fire. This was followed by a deafening bang as the Isuzu rammed into the Land Rover, and the Jiefang crashed into the back of the Isuzu.

The rattle of gunfire that rent the air paragoned precedence. Cries filled the air. Furious bullets grazed into the bodies of the vehicles, and into the heads, shoulders, chests, thighs and legs of cornered travellers.

Probably Lemah might not have been sure if she still lived, if it had not been for the sharp shrieking of a child in the lap of a dead girl just two seats away. The gunfire had died down as suddenly as it had started, and most of the people were as dead as mutton.

Three men stepped onto the bus wreck. They were heavily armed. One of them bled profusely from an unseen wound, and he had to steady himself by holding onto the seats as he moved. Blood soaked his tattered shirt, and he had a fixed grimace on his dark, tattooed face. He went to the front of the wreck, another went to the extreme back, and the third stood by the door, then he made what must have been an order, in Luo. There was renewed whimpering from the survivors, and they started limping and crawling off the bus. Lemah stayed put. "Get off the bus, bitch!" the soldier by the door barked, pointing a gun at Lemah. She got up to walk, and fell back. It was then that she realised that both her legs had been shot into. She blacked out, as a torment of pain rushed form nowhere, and congregated in her legs.

After putting all the survivors aside, the armed men and women set the bus on fire. Then between them, they carried off their loot and the captives, as they took them to be.

When Lemah came to, she was in a dark place, amidst lots of other stiff bodies. A stale smell pervaded the atmosphere, a nauseating mixture of sweat, urine and many other evil-smelling things.

One soldier had been watching her intently, and when he recognised that she was awake, he pounced on her, threw apart her wounded legs and before she could afford to do anything in self-defence, he was inside her, tearing her apart. He tore her already damaged legs, her confidential region, and her very soul.

She cried.

She cried in pain, but also in utter frustration, at the helplessness and hopelessness she suffered. When he was done with her, she discovered that she was not yet through with the torture…she was not to be, till two other soldiers had had their go at her. They might have been more than just the three of them, but before the third rapist was fully saddled in, there was a heavy blast outside. In a flash of a moment, there was no soldier in sight. Instead, there was the report of machinegun fire in every direction. Lemah knew that the best thing to do was to stay put, for she did not know where she was. She was in unmentionable pain. She was bleeding, but had nothing to do. She wished she could faint again, or simply die. Her mind flashed on the scene of Theo holding her, kissing her like Creation Morning. No, she was not ready to die, yet. She had to hang on. Then she passed out again.

When the government troops arrived in the cave, carrying half-dead children ranging between the ages of six and fifteen, and bags, and firearms and ammunition, Lemah was still in coma. Even when she was lifted and carried out of the cave, away from the rebel camp, and away from enemy territory, she was still in coma. She was still in coma even when, together with a few other adults and ten children, six of them raped girls, she was bundled onto a canter truck the soldiers had snatched from a civilian businessman, and driven to Kampala.

The first thing she knew amidst pain she had never known, was when she was removed from the truck, transferred to a wheeled bed and rolled into the ICU.

It was only when she was in the Intensive Care Unit at Mulago Hospital that Lemah was identified. Before she was put on anaesthesia, she was asked who could be contacted, and she gave them Theo's and Dr. Kitonsa's telephone contacts.

FOURTEEN

THERE was this talk of Constitutionalism. Fitted in well
with the pattern that if one of the aspects of society changed,
everything else had to change, as of necessity. Only this time, the
change was supposed to have a basis, a background. Talk had it that
Uganda needed a constitution that the people – this time people
standing for human beings, not Power-Wielding Creatures – made
for themselves. This might have been all very well, but the same
people who were preparing to add ingredients to the baking of a
home-made constitution were already wiping sweats of panic, as they
heard reports from all winds to the effect that everywhere else, there
was fire. Internal fire, outside-brewed fire, unfathomable fire. Here,
nothing. So to put themselves in the picture, they were helping
arsonists light up fires elsewhere. So said the reports. None knew
the source of the news. None knew the truth. None knew what all
this meant.

For lack of a more appropriate source of guidance,
performing artistes ran up and down, serving rumours, piecing up
facts and extracting predictions. Then the theatres and the stadiums
rocked with the scathing fun. There were pictures. Pictures painted
dramatically, of such long arms as could stretch across regions,
sowing seeds of re-union, and even watering them.

And at home, people wondered. Would it always be like this?
Had we had our share, and nothing else was to occur? But what if
the fire in Gulu came down, and the Kasese fire spread northwards,
and the threats of fire outbreaks in Busia and Malaba came to pass;
and sparks between Arab blood and Negroid blood in Sudan flew
into the already fiery hands of northern Uganda, what then?

History had already recorded facts regarding the Tutsi return-
invasion on Rwanda, as well as the goings-on in Burundi. They had
had and were still having their share of agony, poverty and death.
The stinging question now was: If a fresh fire broke out on home
ground now, who would fan it, who would be burnt, who would
pour sand over it?

In other circles, tension mounted as voices rose on the wind, claiming that there was no war in Gulu and Kitgum, but stage-managed machinations to treat the symptoms and causes of a cancer the nation had developed over a period of thirty years. My! There was no end to the scope of possible things one would see and hear. The papers frothed with the news, telly screens blinked with it, and radios belched with it. And if one was as careful as it deemed, one would hear tit-bits of such news at drinking places, amidst clusters that formed as they awaited the kick-off of a late match; between two colleagues who strolled to a Club for a Bell Lager after a strenuous day's work; and in capacity-ful Pentecostal churches where the pastors echoed one of the most legendary leaders the continent has known, who claimed that he did not fear anyone but God. In such churches, donned in holy armour and with uplifted eyes, the pastors speak about the topics that ride on the gathering clouds over God's people, and if nobody listens, woe betide them....

FIFTEEN

IN two weeks time, Lemah could move about in a wheelchair. With an extra week of ultra-sensitive attention from the medics, immense tender loving care from Theo, unreserved attention and care from KITANET and a strong will in Lemah herself, she was on crutches, and all over the place, proving herself able, willing herself healed. It is the other people who, concerned about her state, insisted that she take it easy, as she would find the sun still rising from the East and setting in the West, whenever she got discharged. D'Souza told her that even if she were to be the last person at the station, she would still find her job. As for Theo, there was no need for words. He made it clear in all wordless terms that if anyone possessed all his time, his resources, his attention, his love and his very self, Lemah did. So why the rush?

None, except her view that while she was still in this state, there was something she could not do, something she almost rated above her own life. For if her life was not used for the likes of such assignments, what was it worth?

She talked to Dr. Kitonsa when he came over to see her. Without arousing any uncalled for suspicions, he showed her how much she meant to him. A bouquet this day, a bottle of Lucozade energy drink the next and some other small but important something thereafter. She was grateful, and lost no opportunity to show it.

So when he called in, she requested him to get her writing materials. While he was at it, she got the medical staff to believe with her that she was not in very bad shape. All she needed was constant company, and she had this in Theo. He assured her that she could count on him for that.

When all was assembled, Lemah set to writing a script for her programme. Without preparing for it, she had more than carried out research on her topic – she had had a pungent sniff and bitter taste of it. To look or ask for more would be to slap Fate in the face with her finger in his mouth. Lemah knew better than to do that.

174

It was evident that Lemah was undergoing an upgrading course, facilitated by some Supreme Being. After the practical lesson on Connie and her man, she was now going through physical pain herself. And above all she knew the horror of being raped. She knew beyond all degrees of doubt that what counted in this game was whatever made a person human, not who or what they were. It is what they saw, what they heard, what they felt, smelt and tasted…What made the big difference was not what lay at the illusive end of the rainbow, but the emotions that are aroused when a pre-teen child is forced to lie with a grown man; when one comes to after a bout of unconsciousness and sees mutilated corpses all over, and is then gang-raped; when one is made to eat bitter leaves to be able to see tomorrow, unsure whether the leaves are safe to eat or not. That is what qualified people to be news material.

It took Lemah three days to put in place a satisfactory frame-work of what she wanted shot, and three others to have the full script ready. Then she afforded a relieved smile, and an unsteady stroll out of the hospital building, and a truly passionate chat with Theo, away from the ever-watchful eye and docile ear of everyone in the ward. This was one aspect Lemah had found hard to live with, the glares and unashamed murmurs about that is the lady of KITANET, that is Lemah Nabasa, that is the News Legend of Uganda…

It was exasperating!

The last thing Lemah did before she was discharged was to get the affected children from their wards to a specially arranged area away from the sharp smell of drugs, the shrieks of children being treated and the wailing of bereaved mothers, wives and sisters. There, she had their shots taken.

It was a gruesome story. It was a story of story-telling, but the stories bore no humour, no sarcasm, nothing of the sort. They were stories of the children carrying loads thrice their weight, of starvation, barely five miles away from the homes where the children – now orphans, had lived lives of satiety. They were stories of

175

children being mutilated to death for attempting to escape form the camps where they were kept. They were stories of infections, ailments and deficiencies that went untreated, till the victims either died, got killed (since they had out-lived their usefulness) or escaped, or got rescued, as in the case of the ones she was dealing with.

As all this went on, Lemah moved up and down, organising the children, directing the story-telling, giving orders about the filming: *No, that will not do....No, dear! Okay, try another shot....one more, for safety.....Right, give me a close-up of her sweet face.....Ignore us, sweetheart....Alright, start your story afresh....from.....no, no, no, from when daddy was slaughtered.....sorry.....cut: help her first, poor thing! Next....Oookay, give that a whole pan. No, no don't crane the camera yet....Next....Next.....Thanks kids, this will do for now. Gentlemen, my sincere gratitude. You will never know how indebted I am to you all....*

It was a painful, yet rewarding new experience for Lemah.

Two days later, she was discharged with special and stern instructions to keep away form work for another fortnight. Being the sort of person she was, she looked at this order as more of a punishment than a remedy. She had all the time been itching for her office, her work, her profession.

"Keep your mind off this work, Lemah," D'Souza told her on phone when she returned to her house. "I know what it means to you. I am personally going to get interested in seeing your programme to its completion. Relax. Right?"

"Thank you, Sir. I always knew I had someone to rely on in moments of crisis, in that establishment!" She knew who most deserved that compliment, but there was no harm in making it to a man like D'Souza. If he did not deserve it by virtue of his kindness, he was hardworking enough to merit credit on any aspect of work.

True to his word, D'Souza himself saw to the editing, mixing and final recording of the tape that bore Lemah's work. And when it went on air, boy, was it a hit! People the country over wept before their screens, as many indicated in press reactions throughout the week, and calls they made to KITANET. Lemah received lots of mail in reaction to the programme, and D'Souza was bursting with pride at having employed such a jewel of a professional at his station. If he had never had cause to always have her at KITANET, now he had more than he needed to justify it. She was his kind of journalist.

Lemah did not have to know what her boss thought of her to enjoy her period of recovery. When she was discharged, she spent the first three days at her house, then Theo picked her up and took her to his house, where he had invited in two of his sisters to, if it came to it, out-do themselves to make their prospective sister-in-law comfortable.

And who would not do a thing as small as that for a girl such as Lemah? Theo's sisters assured him that they wanted him happy, and if Lemah was a principal cause of his happiness, they would cultivate it all for him.

So when she was taken over to Theo's house, Lemah lacked nothing. At one point she actually had to protest against all this doting they did on her. "It makes me live in conditions I may never be able to sustain," she pleaded.

"Oh come off it, Lemah," said Cindy, one of Theo's sisters. "There's nothing out of the ordinary we've done for you yet."

"Please don't add that *yet* word. Makes me think the worst is yet to home." They all enjoyed a women's laugh, and Lemah took her pampering like a sedative, and Cindy and Vinah outdid themselves in spoiling her.

That day, it seemed to Lemah, had been set aside for incredible love-giving, with her on the receiving end. When Theo returned, he was on Cloud 9. He hollered out her name even before he entered the room where she lived, and when he burst into it, he

177

shot straight for her bed, scooped her up in his arms, engraved vibrant kisses all over her face, and locked her up in a hug such as she would not receive from him or anyone else for a long time, yet. "O Theo!" she cried out.

"Hush! This is me, my little gift. And besides me, there is another thing tonight. Here!" He loosened the embrace, fumbled in his shirt pocket, took out a ring, a breath-taking ring, and held it up like a trophy, for her and the whole universe to see. He then elaborately removed the one on her left middle finger, the one he had put out of excitement, and put this new one, bought out of sure affection. He then unzipped his bag, removed a small gift box and, accompanying it with a rose, gave it to her, saying that the rest was up to her.

"I am panicking, Theo. Please help open this for me!" she disengaged herself from his renewed hug and sat back on the bed, where he followed her, box in hand.

"No, love, I am bound by a self-inflicted oath not to do any such thing. Open it. Just breathe in once or twice, relax and open it up."

She did. In the box was a Montblanc wrist watch, set at a date exactly a year from then, at 2:00p.m. Above was printed the magic words:

WEDDING BELLS

The way Lemah was feeling, she knew only one wise thing to do: Go to the door, open it wide and stay there until the moment passed. It was painful alright, but if she did not do it, she would never forgive herself for what it would lead to. Theo picked the message like a rehearsed cue.

"Wise girl! The way it is, I was beginning to feel like asking Cynthia and Vinah to go find accommodation elsewhere for tonight."

"I always knew I was going to marry a dummy, my God! You can only feel that way after the ring is put on under the divine supervision of a man of God."

She floated into his arms. The door was still wide open.

"Trifles, all the time," Theo said. "Who is the other's boss – the man of God, or the man's God? Right now it is God who is monitoring and licensing all this. What then would men of God do?" He tightened his arms around her, and both were silent, in that position, for real long.

They were fully engaged, and would be married in a year......

SIXTEEN

BRIDLED trouble creeps like a skin rash…. unbridled; it gallops like a viper's venom in an artery. That is the way it seemed to Lemah, the more she heard and read stories of the spread of the fires of insurgence from the northern part of the country, to other parts. It was in almost every medium of communication. *Rebels Cross To Lira! Abductee Girls Escape, Flee to Hoima! Refugee influx in Jinja rises as Gulu war worsens!* It was everywhere.

It was not the migration of the displaced Acholi to Kakira that intrigued Lemah, but the fact that even at moments such as these, neighbours asked fleeing neighbours to construct makeshift shelters beside the granary, if they wanted a place to rest in the dark of the uncertain night. In Lemah's view, displaced neighbours needed a place in the most intimate part of the home, with a blanket and lamp all to themselves. If anything, as it was in the past, the host-neighbour should, if the main house is not big enough for everybody, shift to the goat pen in the outer-yard, and let the endangered neighbour have a comfortable place where they can figure out how best to step out of their predicament. That was Lemah's idea of hospitality.

The next item was even more shocking. The Acholi community in Jinja was being held suspect for a fresh wave of armed robberies and thefts in the town. As a result, even the meagre good treatment they had been receiving was being withdrawn. Some were being asked to leave, the less fortunate were not asked, but forced… Harsh treatment was sure to achieve this.

Was there empirical proof for the accusation? Not really, but who else could do such cruel things? If their kinsman in Gulu bushes could afford to chop off his own people's noses, ears, lips and bums, what could stop them from using guns to rob people of a different tongue?

In their circles, the accused Acholi were said to wonder whether there never was any form of crime before their advent in

Jinja; but who cared a rap whether non-Acholi hit non-Acholi in the napes with iron bars at dark street corners?

Yet Lemah knew that even if she had been well and active at her place of work, she no longer believed in the type of reporting that could expose this sort of problem in a manner that society was accustomed to. That manner of reporting did not appeal to her interests and ideology anymore; it did not satisfy her heart's desires. It put the TV-watching audience before the news-making crowd, which did not remedy a single ill of society. People had had more than enough of the scenes of savagery and hostility; they no longer knew what to do by way of reaction. Vietnam, Falklands, Iraq, Somalia, Liberia, Rwanda… so even if you had the heart of St. Joan of Ark, what would you do?

Lemah's dilemma was aggravated by a fear. In an attempt to shift ground in her reporting, she was not sure of the impact it was going to have on KITANET as an establishment. Would D'Souza still appreciate her? Would the fame of the station still soar high in the skies of success? Did these things really matter, anyway? She was not sure, anymore. She needed time to sort her interests out… To draw a compromising line that linked her new-found belief to her now accustomed methods.

More items came out. Voices on the wind were talking about planning a bitter lesson for the Eastern region, should a strong enough wind blow a few granules of war that way. You see, they reasoned, easterners had no experience to base on to decide how to handle victims of war. To use and abuse an over-used lesson, experience is the best teacher, the proponents of the theory said. Maybe after tasting of war, should there be another cause for strangers to seek refuge in fiery times, those indolent easterners would know better than to make them sit in hot ash, when what they have ran away from is heat.

Was there a grain of significance in this? Maybe yes, maybe not; other regions had already had their share. The 1979 ousting of

Big Daddy Idi Amin had been cultivated in one region; the "Five-year Goal" that had ushered in hair-rising changes had concentrated in another region; and now this Cain Vs Abel battle was giving the descendants of Gipir and Labong their share of it. But was this proof that if you gave a parcel of war-lit embers to a woeful arsonist from the West, Central or Northern region, they would not run and light it in their own yard at home? Who knows, maybe experience only girds some people's loins for yet more fire instead of guarding them against such acrimonious fights! People are hard to compact into administrable capsules of lessons. One had to wait and discover for oneself…

SEVENTEEN

PLAINLY speaking, Lemah was a healed woman. Not with all the attention Theo, Cindy and Vinah bestowed upon her.....Cindy was particularly fond of Lemah, and outwardly showed it. Hardly a day passed without her going to the dear woman's room for a chat or, if Lemah was either busy or tired, to simply sit there, gazing at her, sighing at intervals and just feeling good.

One day she walked into Lemah's room with a small piece of paper which she handed to her, smiles tearing at the lips. It was all poor Lemah could do to contain her immense joy. The paper bore a poem – or an attempt at one. Simple, short, but all the same enough to say what Cindy thought and felt. It said:

Light in my soul

Agility in my limbs

Cause for waiting

To see the colour of Tomorrow:

You, sweet Lemah.

'Thank you a lot, sweetheart,' Lemah said amidst tears of joy. 'I can't thank you enough.'

"It's nothing,' Cindy said with child-like innocence. 'You caused it, and thank you for the inspiration.' She crouched her bony body closer to Lemah's, their shoulders touching.

'Don't speak so, dear. I am only a person, a simple person. All inspiration comes from God above.' Lemah was a modest woman, but she sounded very unconvincing this time, right though she was.

'Right, too, but God has ways He reaches us. In this case you were his medium. Glory to His Name.'

'Cindy, I am touched. If I had a house of my own, I would have this poem printed out, framed, and I would hang it in the most public place in the house…' She stopped short, her brow falling. Cindy was worried and amazed.

'Is anything the matter, dear?'

'Not much. Er… I just shouldn't have used the words I used. Brought back to mind an experience I am trying to forget. Sorry I am getting distressed with my weaknesses.'

'Ah, you were talking about a house. Now, I don't know if this is not gossip, but….did Theo not say you wanted to buy a house?'

'Yeah, but I have failed to find a suitable place.'

'Place as in location or-'

'No, no. A house. Location may not matter much. True, I prefer Ntinda, but any other place will do as well.' Lemah still sounded rather distant, but she was trying to fight the memory of the soldier on the stakes, with those bullets into his body, all in public.

After a short ponderous silence, Cindy asked if Lemah wanted to look at a house a former classmate of hers was selling off in Ntinda.

'Of course, Cindy. Who is he?'

'A friend. Works with the Investment Authority. You know them, they click their fingers and money comes on its knees, at their service. So he built this house in Ntinda, and I believe it would suit you.'

'Do I look to you like I would afford that kind of house?' Lemah asked, with a cheeky wink.

'If you want to hear my honest opinion, you could buy the whole of Ntinda and still be able to survive another decade without working.'

They shared a comradely laugh, then arranged to go to Cindy's Investment Authority friend in the afternoon.

The house turned out to be the perfect answer to Lemah's dreams. Yes, she would take it, but not for the initial sixty million shillings asked for. They eventually settled for forty-eight million, and Lemah would have a house to live in, to own, till death.....

It was a marvel of a house. Five bedrooms, including a master bedroom for the head of the family, should the house be occupied by a family. There was a large sitting room, with chandeliers hanging just above head-level. The dining room was attached to the sitting room, separated by an arched door. Heading from the dining room was a corridor that led to the western wing, where there was the kitchen, store, a laundry parlour and a garage. The eastern wing too had a garage, a line of WCs and a study. The kind of place Lemah needed.

True to her word, she got her little poem computer-set, framed and hung in the sitting room. Then she moved all her property into the house, settled in and started a new life.

Lemah's immediate neighbour was a middle-aged woman who lived in a bungalow across from Lemah's. She looked haggard, but her body and face showed that she once bore the kind of beauty that would make an African goddess envious. She stood on a proud, elegant and tall frame, with a neck that seemed to peer into the unknown. Her broad and long forehead, dimpled cheeks and big but rather sleepy-looking eyes gave her what Lemah's mother used to call a princess' face, and when she spoke, one got the impression that she was under the strain of very pressing difficulties. Maybe it was this one feature that gave her away most as a woman for whom not all had gone well.

She came in to see Lemah one evening, just as Lemah was settling in after an afternoon at Theo's.

'Hello! I have been awaiting this chance, all along,' Lemah said to the lady. 'I love meeting beautiful people, if only to lift my self-esteem.'

'You flatter me too much, Madam Lemah. It is-'

'You know my name?' Lemah was shocked.

'Does it surprise you? Who would not? You surprise me, you really do.' A smile of guilt made Lemah's lips tremble a bit. She shook hands with her visitor, and then settled in a sofa on the opposite side of the room, so they sat facing each other. It might have depicted her as distant, but she wanted an unbroken time of looking at this fine woman. It was a blessing to be able to behold such grace, such beauty. Especially at a time like this.

'I know you – or should I say I know your name. But you certainly don't know mine.'

'Naturally.'

'Anything natural about it? Maybe. I am Kotrida. Around here people refer to me as Miss, a title that followed me all the way from the classroom. I used to be a teacher. But you see, I am too big for such reference. I ought to be Mrs., but that's another story. My friends, however, call me Kot, which is also double-edged. My full name is Kotrida Olive Tusiime, and you see that makes KOT. Actually that is what I used to call myself at high school.'

Lemah could see that she had found someone who could lift her spirits with stories. The lady was garrulous, alright.

'I am most honoured to meet you…..I am also confident that you will not say no to a cup of tea, will you?'

'Thank you, Madam Lemah!'

'Mind if we cut out the madam and left Lemah only?'

'Oh, I see you're a most modest lady. Fine, Lemah.' Then as an afterthought, she followed her down the corridor to the kitchen with a raised 'I too used to be modest till the world taught me to accept reality as it is, hot or cold.' She laughed unexpectedly, and Lemah thought there was a hint of pain in the laughter. Strange lady, this one. 'Lemah,' she called, after a pause, 'do you know that modesty is treated by people as camouflaged pride? Haven't people told you to your face yet that you're proud? You'll be lucky if they haven't, for I am yet to meet a good person whose goodness has not been countered with accusations of pride, arrogance, wickedness, name it!' Again she laughed, this time outrightly sardonically.

Eventually, the tea was ready. Lemah served it simple, in two china cups she brought in already made from the kitchen. She put mats on the coffee table, put on the cups, and then put a meat pie for each of them on two saucers. Kotrida's simplicity and free air was winning Lemah over – they were set to be two great friends.

As they had tea, Lemah told her visitor about herself. She knew hers was a very uneventful life, very uninteresting, and she said so to Kotrida. So it took her a short time to talk bout KITANET (which her visitor already knew a lot about; what with its fame), about Dr. Kitonsa, about Theo and his sisters, and about a few safe bits of Connie's life.

'A rich life you have led, I must say,' Kotrida remarked enthusiastically.

'You call that rich? I find it so flat!' Lemah sounded genuine. She took a long last draw form her cup, put it down before her and leaned back in her seat. Her face seemed rather low, but Kotrida was not so sure.

'You've certainly not met people with flat lives, Lemah. Mine, for instance. Only reason I can bear it is because I can afford to live on past glory. Ho! Like my sister, God rest her sweet soul. She had the flattest childhood in living memory. Yes, all she did was be born, sit and watch other children play, till she went to school, and pass, pass, pass from class to class, till she graduated as a Vet. But you know vets. What can they say or do? They relate with animals all the time. Till she married a preacher, and her entire life changed. They flew out of the country every so often, till the preacher died of diabetes, seven years into their marriage. That crashed my sister, you should have seen her. Ho! And she went back to her past life, past her original self, to real despondence. When she died five years ago, she was as good as a destitute. That's what I call a flat life…..maybe not really flat…..'

She paused, as if to consider how she could proceed.

'Maybe I am poking too deep, but have you had much interaction with men, Lemah?'

'Not….well, not practically, so to speak. Just the sort of stuff you hear in the circles of feminists, and the little experience in my life, and…..er…So far he is not a bad experience, God forbid.'

'God forbid, indeed. I don't know, am I too inquisitive?'

'No, no, feel free. I love talking to you, already.' Lemah tried to sound utterly free with her loquacious new friend.

'Second question. Look, I am not interviewing you. I just needed someone to pour my bitter past to, just in case it could make my present a little sweeter. I know I sound fickle and contradictory, but you'll make your own judgement as we go along.'

'I am all ears,' Lemah prompted.

'Good,' she said, the way you would say it to a two-year-old who had said the entire English alphabet. 'Good to be listened to again.'

She sighed.

'So the second question: do you as a journalist deal with social issues too, or you're only interested in politics?'

Lemah gave it a moment's consideration, and then said that she could handle social stories as well. It was in such stories that she could have easy access to people's emotions, which to her mattered most.

Another sigh from Kotrida, heavier than the first.

'Good!'

Very long pause.

'Here is one, right before you. Lemah, I am not seeking pity, for pity irks me, but my entire being is a story, and I don't know what you can make of it. Do I sound like I am seeking publicity?' She was serious, of a sudden. A cautious seriousness.

'Not at all,' Lemah said. 'I do understand.'

'Thank you, dear. Thank you. I'll therefore make this short, so help me God. You have already seen how talkative I can be, which is something of a pity.'

'An admirable pity, in that case. You're a lot better than me who locks all my opinions up. It kills, sometimes.'

A solemn silence.

'I came from an affluent family,' Kotrida launched into the story. 'Oh, my parents were always very rich. Being a lady of information, you must know the name Tusiime. If not as a family name, at least as a business and industry word.'

'I all along wanted to ask if you are linked to the family, but feared to sound odd,' Lemah interjected.

189

'I am. Unfortunately, when I was still in school, I was all saturated with the fact, and it modeled the way I acted and behaved. You know people don't brook snobbery, so the girls always struggled – in vain, I must say – to slash me to size. The boys had no choice, for I combined wealth with beauty, two endowments which, even when separated, can still stand individually and cause boys to sell their souls to the devil to have admission to a girl's heart.

'This followed me to university. In Year One, I kept my distance, so nobody came near me. But not in Year Two. Then, a 4th Year Technology student fell dishonorably in love with me, so much that I had to caution him against sacrificing his course for me. Course? He quarrelled. Who talks courses when there's a girl of your caliber in his life? I let him be.

'Pity of pities, he had to fight hard to, in university jargon, maintain me in my class. You can bet it was an uphill task for him. His father, too, a Mr. Byanyima somewhere in Bushenyi, was a rich man; but not to our level. I was such a strain on the poor boy!

'Now I will be honest with you, dear Lemah, that dear boy's love was never reciprocated. I was in the affair purely for the fun of it, as you may know, since you are a Makerere graduate. So I did not even think of changing roles, so that I could support him. Some girls do it, you know. But to me, he had enough, having me for a girlfriend. I considered that big credit to his name, and he could not have an allowance to it, too.'

She laughed, an embarrassed laugh which forced an already engrossed Lemah to laugh along with her.

'The long and short of it is that it came to a level where he was just too broke to sustain me. He got into a nasty panic. He feared I would drop him. And by an ugly coincidence, some man was trying his chances with me, and I had fallen madly in love with him. I was in love with this man, with my whole being. This leaked to my Engineer, who became frantic. Borrowing some money, he rushed home to get help from his father. The father was out of the

190

country. He returned to Kampala, more broke than ever before, not even able to pay his debts. I'm a devil, aren't I?

'Two days after her returned form Bushenyi, I received a letter from him. I swore never to talk about the confounded contents of that blessed letter, but I'll tell you that I immediately ran to Northcote Hall, from Block E in Africa. Literally running. When I got there, his room was locked. A note stuck on the door said in very simple English that the occupant of the room had gone away, forever. I was just turning away, confused, when their emergency call was sounded. You know them, with their so-called military culture. The news was that one of their Generals had thrown himself in front of a speeding vehicle, down at the main gate, on the road to Nakulabye!'

She paused, fighting back a gush of tears. Lemah shifted and sat close to Kotrida. She put her hand on her knee.

'I understand, Kot. I can guess how it feels!'

'Thank you.' The pain was intense, it was clear.

'Well, the other man was my love. He was a working man, working with UTANEWS. He was a big man there. But, if again I may cut this short, our affair was like the one with the Engineer-General. The affection was lop-sided, only this time I did the loving. Lemah, it is terrible when you pant for someone who does not love you at all. It is terrible. You lay your heart before them, and they can do what they please with it. In most cases you do not even notice and, when you do, you do not care in the least. It is all bliss – agonising bliss.'

'Must indeed be painful,' Lemah put in, by way of sounding helpful. This was getting too deep.

'That man moved out with me for two years, and then he wanted to drop me. Just like that. Lemah, nothing like it had ever hit me. I could have run mad. I decided he should not do that and told him as much. He threatened to hurt me beyond belief if I stood in his way. It was horrifying. I wanted the bastard, Lemah… You'll excuse my language.'

'Oh, that's fine with me. I understand… I guess.'

'Thanks.' And she laughed, a half-hearted laugh. Then she spoke on, this time a little lightly.

'Well, what do I say? I let go. Then, maybe to get me off his trail, he built that house out there for me. Now, he gave me strict instructions not to let this out to anybody. He even said I should not lie to myself that he did it out of love for me. He said he did it for two reasons: he believed that I had loved him truly, and that….he….this is a bit too much, but…..well, I'll be frank, he had de-flowered me – you know what it means to men.'

Again she paused, like to observe a moment's silence for her crushed flower.

'I…….I don't know!' Lemah had wanted to say that she understood, but she thought it was becoming formulaic and monotonous.

'Yeah! That's the way it went. Then, ah! Recently, he was fired from his job. And oh, maybe I should also tell you that I have his child, the only child I have. A sweet girl, now teaching at Gayaza High School. She is the entire world to me, a product of my girlhood follies. I love her. When he dropped me like that, and considering what I had done to the boy who had loved me truly, I decided not to give myself to another man. It would be a blunder. I knew I could never have any other man, and if the man loved me, it would even be worse. One-sided love is painful. But I was telling you about how he lost his job. When it happened, they fell out with his wife. I think the money started dwindling, or something. You see – oh yeah, I had forgotten to tell you that he had quit his big post at UTANEWS, and was in private TV business. Maybe you know him?'

'What is his name?'

'Kaliisa.'

'*What* – sorry. Er....Okay. I.......I knew him so well. Mr. Kaliisa was at KITANET, where I work.'

'Why, do you – okay, maybe I understand. He's a man of rather strange character, that Kaliisa. Anyhow, when they fell out with his legal wife, which is another bitter story, he started coming back to me. Trouble is, however, a wounded heart does not mend with the gloss of a few visits and endearments whispered from no deeper than the lips. I still hurt within, Lemah. Besides, he is *married*. Not happily, but well, he has a wife. So I feel he should go away. I don't *know*. I don't know, Lemah!'

Lemah sat upright, indicating that the storm had abated.

'So is there a way you can make a story out of such a tale, for your TV?'

'Absolutely. Yes, but... Ha! With Mr. Kaliisa in it......I have to give it a moment's thought first. Oh God! What a cruel and hard-to-understand world we live in! What heartlessness we live with!'

'That is life, my dear friend!' Kotrida said, almost inaudibly.

'And such a muddle it is, too.'

'You can say that again.'

Lemah was scared. She was full of apprehensive thoughts, now that her time was drawing near. But her case was different, at least she loved Theo, and she knew Theo doted on her. Theirs was a mutual relationship. But a friend of hers had once told her something that scared her, each time she thought of it. She had said most relationships were one way, and if they are mutual, either one of the partners ends up marrying somebody else, or they die. Before, or shortly after marriage. Might there be a grain of truth in it? She wished it was not true.

'Don't think so hard on this,' Kotrida cut into her thoughts. 'It's not like my life depends on it. I just thought-'

'No, no! Not that! I was wandering on very different tracks…..alien tracks. Sorry.'

This story was certainly fascinating. Lemah wanted to take it on. It would be a good assignment to resume work with. But what about Kaliisa's name in it? She dreaded a repeat of the Connie story. Besides, it might have nasty implications for KITANET, and she wanted to be the last person to cause KITANET any problem. She had to seek Dr. Kitonsa's counsel. He had always proved useful in such contentious cases.

'Why exactly did this – what's her name – yes, Kot. What did she have in mind when she came to you?' Dr. Kitonsa asked Lemah when she consulted him.

'I must confess, I can't claim to be sure of why she talked to me. She said, and I seem to think her genuine, that she was dying to say it all to someone who could listen. But also, she ….maybe she wants another kind of relief. Relief she can only get when she watches her life, like it were happening to someone else.'

'Now I will ask you one question, and better give it some good thought before you answer me.'

'Let's hear it.' She was a trifle unsteady.

'Do you really, *really* want to do this story?'

'If it will not portend bad for KITANET – if it will not do you any damage, yes… I want to.'

'Thank you. This is my true opinion, then. You did not go out of your way to look for this, so nobody – not even your friend Kaliisa – will think you're trying to get even. Anyway, what would you be avenging?'

194

'Nothing.'

'Fine. Besides, I don't see you doing this so it looks like it is about Kaliisa. Considering this, I am for you doing your project.'

'Thank you, Doctor.'

EIGHTEEN

A STORY is told about a mother who, to teach her child not to cultivate the habit of theft, cut off the child's fingers. Cruel? Appropriate? Curative? Monstrously unmotherly? Apt?

Here's the other story. It's about a medical doctor. To him, if a patient complains of stomach trouble, it is wrong to inject the buttocks or arm. The drug should be administered where the problem is – that is where it's needed. Unprofessional? Funny? Wise?

Nobody knows.

So it came to pass that mounting pressure was closing in on the government from various circles, to deal with the smouldering, the flickering and the blazing fires in the country. Some of the pressure came from outside, from Powers with deep-seated interests in the country. Some, however, was internal pressure.

Let us go to talks with them, *Bwana! Hapana!* Talk with who – dissidents? Over *my* dead body. So? So we drop the idea of holding talks. Period.

Let's deploy heavily in all guerrilla – infested areas. We sure have a big and strong enough force to rout all of them out, don't we? Yeah, we do, but that isn't going to work. Too many soldiers on the loose will not do what you think they will do, no Sir! But you've always said we have a disciplined army; probably the most disciplined since the birth of the nation. Yes, I have always *said*…

Just bring in forces from out and hit these boys once and for all. Which rebel in this no-go country can resist America, for instance? The way I see it, we do not have a bad name with the US – what do you think? Well, I think you've got to start thinking clearly. Foreign force? America? We do not need outsiders to solve our domestic quarrels, no way. Know what that means? That after you've brought in your neighbour to help you discipline your son or daughter, he then has means of enslaving your son, or whoring your daughter. He could decide to do worse. While he is in your home solving conflicts, he notices where you keep your millet, where you hang your stick for caning your people, and where the key to the back door is kept. I know only too well what that means, my dear.

Okay. We know the trouble spots, don't we? We have the weaponry desired to curb the insurgency. Do just that. Curb it. Annihilate everybody in the area, rebel and disciple and settler alike. As they say, a bad animal comes form a bad bush. Burn the entire bush – where will the animal come from? Ah! You man......wait a bit......*wait a bit...!*

When the fire started blistering, and eventually actually roasting to death mass-citizens, nobody knew exactly whose fire it was. Every after a big fire had razed a given area, Side A would credit it on Side B; and Side B would blame it on Side A.

The wise people scratched their bald heads. Could it be possible that somebody can burn his own clothes, if only to tell the neighbours that the man he had fought with the previous day had done it? Or was it a case of one man saying: Let me beat up his children, so that in a bid to save them the pain, he grants me what I want? It was not clear.

What was clear was this, that once the fire–tongues started licking sensitive spots, a new sort of heat developed. A new form of Masonry developed, of people who lit up fires, hid them, and heated up tongs that they then used to poke at the government: See? You've failed in your primary responsibilities. How can private huts be burnt down, and you cannot even protect them? How can you still claim to have your original sting?

Well, how could they?

NINETEEN

LEMAH'S mind was made: she would do the KOT story. For one thing, it intrigued her. It fitted in well with her new philosophy of life, not about news. It was about a human being; about people, not news-figures. But even more than this, she had taken a keen liking for this child-woman, Kotrida. Her manner intrigued her. Unlike the deferential passivity of Connie and the idolising love of Mercy, here was a woman with the fire of life, with a past that poked one into getting off one's bums to contribute to the one thing that would better the poor woman's future, whatever sort of future she wanted it to be. Kotrida's nature did not call for sympathy, no. It did not even call for anger. It called for support, for a humanitarian contribution to a feeling of: Well, I had a past, and this is me, I came out of it. Lemah decided she was going to do that for Kotrida.

She resumed work at KITANET. Everybody was all over her, their excitement refusing to be hidden. The lower-cadre employees did her little favours, the big-officed bosses gave her big, gorgeous cards, and fascinating presents, congratulating her upon her recovery, and stood in her office for a five-minute chat. As for Mercy, her name said it all. She turned her entire week into one long act of mercy and kindness, so much that Lemah felt like if she did not pay for this, she owed heaven a big one. Such was her return to work.

But the nature of her work was never the same. The old fire of adventure had smouldered down in her. Big-topic thrilling news items were no longer her sort of thing. Every time the KITANET staff smelt something newsworthy, they would think: This is Lemah's thing.....This is our news!

But it would come to nothing.

Not that Lemah became negligent. She did all her work as it was stipulated in her conditions and terms of service. She did it with an even keener sense of seriousness and order, but that spirit that always launched her into innovative adventure – always wanting to add a Lemah-touch to the trend in the media, the TV trends, had ebbed away…..

The change started manifesting in her lifestyle, too. If she had been reticent before, this time she seemed locked up. Even when she was physically available, the inner Lemah was close to impossible to access. She would once in a while spare some minutes for Mercy at the end of the day, before Theo picked her from work, and in-between assignments, she would talk to her mentor, Dr. Kitonsa, on phone. And that was about all.

"You're a very changed person lately, Lemah," Mercy remarked one evening as they wound up their day.

"Is it a marked change?"

"Can be read at a distance."

"Oh! Didn't realise. Where is it most pronounced?"

"Oh Lemah! It's there…..it's… there. Your speech - or lack of it, your….the way you relate with us, even your very countenance. You're a changed woman Lemah."

"Time does not leave us the same, Mercy!" she sighed, a sigh that told of deep things between her and Time.

"Even your attitude towards work seems to have changed!"

"Seems?"

"Is that the wrong word?"

"I don't know, you know best what you want to say….what you have observed.

Have I, for instance, become negligent?"

"Oh no, no, no! Far from it. Not negligent or irresponsible. Not you."

"But-"

"I don't know. You just aren't the same, that's all."

Theo's Volvo turned into the lot.

"The King is here, I got to go, Mercy. Thanks for the evening".

"You must be mad, Lemah. What is there to thank me for?"

"You. And now, bye. Catch you tomorrow."

She moved out of the complex, passing a few junior staff in the corridor. They made rather uncomfortable attempts at courteous pleasantries, but Lemah saved them the bother by sailing through them, unaffected.

"Hi, Honey, you're early today," she called even before reaching the car. Theo sat inside, waiting.

"Sorry, love. Can I return a little later?"

"With, me in the car."

They drove off.

"Theo's or Lemah's?"

"Lemah's, naturally!" She was resolute.

So to Lemah's Theo drove.

When Theo turned into Lemah's hedge enclosure, Kotrida was just walking away, after finding a locked house. When the car

200

stopped, she turned back, unmistakable joy engraved all over her face.

"There you are, Ms Nab – Lemah! Welcome back, friend!"

"Welcome, KOT! Sorry you'd missed me! Come, meet the man who's denying me my independence…..This is Theo. Theo, meet my new friend, Kotrida.

"Pleasure," Theo muttered.

"Oh Lemah, if you ain't so lucky. About the warmest face I've seen on a man, if you'll excuse-"

"Oh, no problem in that!' Lemah said. 'After all, I too see it, and who knows, it could be one of the magic wands that drew me to him.'

'Don't listen to her,' Theo said. '*I* was drawn to her. She is the miracle of the two of us.'

'The old game,' Kotrida put in. 'Nobody wants to be the loved, but the lover and admirer. Follows the trend. I love it when young people are in love. It's a warm, catching air they exude, wouldn't you say? And the thing about love is – are we standing here forever? Is the gentleman going away immediately? I shouldn't hold you with my prattle!'

'Oh no. It's our lack of hospitality you should pardon. Do come right inside,' Lemah explained.

'Hear who claims inhospitality! You, Lemah? And I won't take it even of the gentleman-"

"Theo – Theo, Ms Kotrida.' Theo corrected.

'Er…..yes, Theo. Thanks. Sorry. I was only saying that I wouldn't even believe that you, my dear gent- er Theo, are inhospitable. Your voice reports it all.'

'Thanks.'

'Not meant even as a compliment. Typical innocent observation!' She went straight to the chair she had sat in the first time she entered Lemah's house, and installed herself there.

'I was saying, before we entered in here, that the wonderful thing about love is that it blossoms one up. Even a simple pale person, once they are loved, they change so fast, for the better, you would never recognise them a week after the bug caught them.'

'Yeah, apparently,' Theo put in.

'Apparently? You should have seen my daughter, Tophus when she fell in love with some man. God, it was all I could do to identify and recognise her as the child I begot with Mr. Kaliisa. Have you told the gent- er Theo about Mr. Kaliisa? Well, he'll get to know, by and by.'

She paused. Theo had propped his frame forward, as he intently listened to this unsorted flow, like Aristotle listening to Plato. Lemah had brought out soft drinks from her fridge, and a bottle sat before each of them, untouched. Kotrida's, because she was busy talking, Theo's because he really couldn't bring himself to break the spell of such a woman, and Lemah, because her story was developing right in front of her.

'So that is love, my dear friends. You can't be plain when in love, no. Not at all. It brightens you up, gives you confidence, and renews your countenance. That is one miracle God hid in His children.....if only it always lasted!'

'It can, if we can always sort it from other selfish intents,' Theo said, settling back in his seat and picking up his soda.

'And that is the point. Selfish intents. You hardly ever see honest young men....young people who will love a person for love's sake. You'll not see several of them, my good friends. You are so *unique*, if you'll believe me. You're a unique pair, Lemah and Theo!'

Kotrida took up her soda and having contemplated it a while, she took off the already opened lid, and sipped at it, ever so tenderly.

When Lemah thought she could now safely come in, she quickly brought up the topic of her project. For fear that Kotrida would take it up and spend another hour talking about the characters in the story – herself, Tophus and Kaliisa, she started from a point where Kotrida knew nothing.

'Today I just confirmed that I am going to do that story of ours, Kot. I was talking to my friend and office-mate, Mercy."

'Oh, you share an office! You must be kind. So kind, you're in your own class. Take Kaliisa for example, his work-mates used to tell me, he was never the type to even accommodate a secretary... his own secretary. Poor lady, she would sit in the common typing pool.'

'Do you people now have a typing pool?' Theo asked Lemah.

'No,' Kotrida responded quickly. 'This was while he was still at UTANEWS. When he quit and came to Lemah's place, I don't-'

Lemah grabbed the thread again.

'At KITANET he was no better. A despot and bigot, that's what he always was.....The other day I talked to my boss about this project. Some very kind gentleman called Dr. Kitonsa.

'Of course I know Dr. Kitonsa,' Theo said.

'Yeah, I was telling KOT here. KOT, this Dr. Kitonsa is full of support for our project. After talking to him, and after what Mercy said today-'

'Who's Mercy again? Oh, I recall; the lady you said shares your office. Yes?'

Lemah considered Kotrida a bit, and then proceeded. 'After what Mercy said, all I have to do now is sit down and draw out a skeleton of the film, write down the story, and work will commence.

'I guess I should leave you ladies to get on with this project discussion,' Theo said as he made to pull himself form his seat.

'No, I am Lemah's neighbour, I can always return later,' Kotrida said hastily. 'You two should finish with whatever you have to do – yes Lemah?''

Lemah could not resist the offer, so she agreed with the elderly woman's proposition, at which Kotrida excused herself and made a pre-mature exit.

'What's all this project stuff about, love?' Theo asked, soon as they were left alone. 'And it involves Mr. Kaliisa!'

'Well, you have it there. It is a story about Kotrida's involvement with two men – one of whom is dead, and the other is Mr. Kaliisa.'

'What about them?'

'It's a long story, and that story is the film project I want – I am working on.'

Theo noticed her change from 'I want to work on' to 'I am working on', and decided that if he knew his Lemah well, he was not going to dissuade her from doing the project. But try he would, so that he absolved himself of any form of blame, later.

'Are you sure you want to involve yourself in a Kaliisa-related story now, Lemah?'

'This is not about Kaliisa. Kaliisa is only a part of it, as you'll see, by and by. This is a story of Kotrida's response to a world of love and faith. Her lessons from her relationships with two men, one of whom loved her, and she did not love him; the other did not love her, but she loved him. That is the core of the project. The emphasis is on Kotrida, really.'

'That is as the author perceives it. Fine. But do you expect everybody – Kaliisa especially – to see it your way? Do you?'

'Making a film project of this sort is like writing. The motive determines the style and depiction. If I see Kotrida as my central focus, I am going to highlight her, so nobody whose appearance and involvement in the story is secondary can overshadow, or even equal her. That way, I do not see how Kaliisa will have ground to take offence.'

'Fine. Fine, Lemah. Just be more careful in this project. Take care of yourself, and your friends. Your Kaliisa is not the ordinary, sort of person you are used to dealing with.'

'I will be careful, love. Trust me.'

Lemah moved over to Theo and wrapped herself all over him, till his body, mind and heart perceived nothing else but her.

When Theo left her house after 9 o'clock, Lemah set to doing the write-up of her project. She was to do it in stages, each stage representing a development in Kotrida's mentality. She was going to mix live shots of her characters' lives with enacted "flashbacks" of their past, as well as still shots mixed in interview narratives with Kotrida.

She would have loved to have similar shots of sessions with Kaliisa, but she had to do with what was safe and reasonable. Theo had cautioned her to be careful. It was only reasonable that she be.

She had to collect pictures of all the people involved in the story. Would Kotrida have pictures of Kaliisa? The things she said of him did not reflect someone whose photos she would keep in her albums. What if she did not have them? Where would she get them? Yet they were vital! She would also have pictures of – O God, she realised that she did not recall the names of the dead Technology student who had loved Kotrida, nor of Kotrida's girl in Gayaza. She would –

A knock at the door cut into her work, and when the door knob know turned, Lemah just knew who her visitor was. God had in a way answered her desire: Kotrida would remind her of the names of the dead lover, and the Gayaza daughter.

'I am sorry to be budging into your work at such an hour,' Kotrida apologised, 'but it just occurred to me that the way I left, one would still have expected me back. So I just thought I could step in briefly and make a formal farewell for the night.'

'Oh, it's all very well with me, Kot. It's not anything close to my usual bed-time.'

'Oh, I know! I know how it can be with you folks in the media. You can't go to bed on the same day of your waking up; it is professional taboo. I used to see Kaliisa. He wasn't a practical journalist, yet he always had paper-work to do till after midnight.'

'That's the way it is with us, my dear. But I can't complain. It's the answer to my heart's desire,' Lemah added.

'Who would complain? As long as the heart is satisfied, the body never feels bothered. You should have seen Tophus, my daughter. She loves her teaching, Tophus does. I must say she loves me so much, yet when we compare with her work, it beats me. Just recently I went to see her. She had just had a miscarriage, and-'

'Is she married, then?'

'Not what you would call married, in the proper sense of the ritual. Who told you that young women of these days marry? As long as they find a man who will have them as they are, they just start making babies for him. You should be lucky to have a progressive young man like Theo, who wants to marry you. Don't let anything stop the two of you from marrying. Not ever.

'But I was still telling you about my daughter Tophus and her love for teaching. She had just had that miscarriage. So I went to see her, and we were there in her house. Gayaza staff houses are real teachers' houses, my girl. Self-contained, if any house ever was. And big. So we were in her house, and some two girls came by, with a problem in English Language.'

'Oh, she's into English?' Lemah asked, just for the sake of a break.

'Yes. English and Business Education, though she does not teach B.E. I hear their department was already over-staffed when she was taken on. Actually she prefers her English, so she didn't have a problem in that…..

'Now these girls came up, and that was the end of me. Tophus would not talk to me while those children were there. They moved from grammar which the children came with, to précis, to composition, and back to grammar, sounding like J.A. Bright himself, but not remembering that I was there is the house, totally neglected!

'When the girls left, I told her she did not have to kill herself for the sake of the children. You should have heard her answer. *Oh Mummy, that is my work! That is why I am paid! They are my children! It's my world!* And yet she has only one child, whom she was following up with this one who jumped out. Yet, Lemah, what is there to ask a teacher about, in English? Either you know it, or you don't! Simple. But Tophie can't hear of such reasoning. She said that in Uganda, English is not just a language, it is a subject, and all subjects have to be taught and learnt. The children we beget!'

She seemed to have out-talked herself, so, looking at the wall clock above Lemah's head, she was so shocked, that she immediately sprang to her feet.

'We have indulged in other things, and we have not even had time to amply discuss our project!' she said bashfully.

'Well, there's really not much to discuss, now. I only discovered now as I wrote out my story, that I didn't recall the names of your late boyfriend.

'Oh, Elvis! He was called Elvis. Elvis Tilsa. He told me he was popularly known as E.T. among his friends. But I have watched this ugly creature in a film by that name, E.T, I could not take up the E.T stuff. Now I really ought to be going, dear Lemah!'

As if to prove her point, Lemah's bedside clock chimed midnight. Lemah too got onto her feet, a gesture Kotrida understood well, and started to move towards the exit, to be pushed to her house.

TWENTY

THE days that followed were work-packed for Lemah. Besides her regular work in her department, she also had time set apart daily for work on her KOT Project, as she had code-named it. She held interviews with people who had known Kotrida all the way from her childhood, to the present. All the interview sessions were video-recorded. She did a lot of movement, tracing people even in places beyond Kampala. Some of the names she was given led her to news of "She/he died some years back," or "That one left Uganda, and lives in the U.S!" Then she would be back to Kotrida, to ask for an alternative name, and again she would be on her way in search of the new source of information. And the story was growing and the project was developing.

Kotrida was now a common visitor in Lemah's house and office. When Lemah was busy on regular KITANET stories, Kotrida did all the movement there was to do, contacting people. Then, the interviews would not be conducted in the informants' residences. Kotrida would only make appointments between the informant and Lemah, and the actual shooting sessions would occur later, in settings prepared by Lemah herself.

One thing Lemah avoided was letting the project get in the way of her regular office work. She knew that with her change in attitude and direction, many official and common eyes were focused on her. If she just made one mistake, it could be to her detriment. Yet even with all the care she took, she was one afternoon summoned to Mr. Nywai's office, "for a small chat," as he told her when she entered.

'I know that recovery periods are hard on a patient,' he said, picking his ground with caution. 'So' I'll not hold you for long.'

'Thank you....Though...... I wouldn't really say I am still vulnerable in any way,' Lemah said. She could smell a rat, but she would let him take his time and unravel the problem, unaided.

'How are you getting on in your office now?' He leant forward on his desk, his hands clasped in front of him, his gaze locked on Lemah's face.

'Fine. Er…nothing I would report as not moving fine.'

'Yes, I would agree with you. Yet….I don't see the best way of expressing this difference between before and now. Yes, in the past, it was never necessary for anyone to inquire into how your work was going. We all knew, and were happy.'

'And now?'

'That's the dilemma. We still are happy…" He faltered awhile, then proceeded. 'We are indeed happy, because you are doing your work. But – don't you… wouldn't you also say it has lost that self – proclamatory touch to it? Now you're like the rest of us. You have dropped to our level, of only doing what lies within the limits of our terms and conditions. The extra is gone.'

'Is this a problem?'

It now sounded like Lemah was putting the Director to task.

'Maybe problem is the wrong word here. Not a problem in the conventional sense of the word. But you see, you got us too accustomed to your old creativity, to expect less. I know it sounds irrational of us to talk so, but-'

'I guess I understand your stand. Maybe what I need to understand better is why you refer to yourself as "we"?'

'Oh, I should have explained this. Well, you know that people always talk…..And sincerely speaking, we cannot stop people from talking.'

'Naturally,' Lemah said idly.

'Naturally…..naturally!' Mr. Nywai toyed with the word, half-approvingly, half -questioningly. 'Yes, people do talk, *naturally*. And

210

naturally, when one hears people talk, one gets concerned. So I thought to me: I will talk to my friend Lemah.'

Lemah knew just how friendly this "small chat" was, but she was not going to remark on that. Instead, she asked him whether she was allowed to know who the people who talked were.

'But of course. People who matter! People above us; you and me." He made this sound as intimidating as he could. Lemah deliberately refused to press him for details. Instead, she breathed: 'I guess I understand. A lot of things come to mind with your concerned query, but the pity is that a lot of thing s have caused the change people are concerned about. However, I am grateful for your concern. I will be ready with appropriate answers for whoever may wish do desire to hear them, should they voice their desire. Else, I hope it never gets to that.'

Of course I don't think it will. You're doing what is assigned to you, which covers you professionally. As things are, nobody would have ground to charge you with irresponsibility, even if they searched for a year for an outlet. It's just that I thought I should point this out to you, as a friend.'

The word "friend" ate at Lemah's brain, but before she could phrase out a remark on its use, Mr. Nywai dismissed her, with cordial wishes "for the best". Lemah muttered a 'Thank You Sir' and stepped out of the office.

As she walked back to her office, she mused over these developments. What was behind all this? Had the directors discussed her in a meeting? This was the most probable thing, for Nywai had kept using the collective "we". Whatever the case, he or, to use their preferable collective form *they,* were right about one thing: She was attending to her duties, and even given a whole year, nobody was about to get her on a charge of neglect of duty. Not *her.*

She was just going down when she came up against Dr.Kitonsa. Immediately, her mind told her that the truth was finally here. Summoning all the good humour in her capacity, she greeted him with a succulent smile, and turned to walk to his office with him.

'Has anyone talked to you today?' Dr. Kitonsa asked her.

'Talked to me? Many people have.'

'You…..I mean on anything particular? Has nobody specifically called you for a discussion?'

She now confirmed her suspicion about a Directors' meeting discussing her work.

'Oh *that*! Well, it wasn't exactly a discussion. If I may quote Mr. Nywai's words, he called me to his office "for a small chat." And we have just concluded it now.' She looked quizzically at him.

'And?' he said, equally quizzically.

'And was going back to my office when I met you. But if by your 'And' you mean what am I going to do, I am going to keep doing my work, and avoid anything that contravenes the station's policy.'

'And about the extra effort?

'Dr. Kitonsa,-' They had now reached his office, and he opened his door and bade her a take a seat. He sat right next to her, in front of his desk, so that both of them seemed to be engaged in a chat as they waited for the boss to come.

'Yes?' he prompted.

'Dr. Kitonsa, you already know my stand on that. I have been through a lot. I have a human heart within me. Besides being a professional journalist, I am first of all a human being. And when one goes trough all the things I have been through, one learns a lesson. The outcome of my lesson is this change in direction in my work. Give me a chance. You know about this new project I am working on. If it does not work, we shall see where to turn to next.'

212

'See? It is that having to *see* that worries Management. In the past, they didn't have to rely on probability. They got it the common news way – hot and burning. Your new way is humane, but that is not what makes news in this era. News now must be hot, ugly and heart-rending. You look at me and you think: is this a new Kitonsa? No, I am the usual Kitonsa, but I am looking at it-"

'Their way?'

'*Their* way, yes. You and I understand it your way, but that is because we are using a different lens: the Human lens. The establishment is not human, it is professional. And above all, it is commercial. It is in a competitive market environment.'

'So?'

'Take care. Yes, Lemah, take care. Bye.'

He got up, opened the door for her, and after she was out, he sat back in the same chair he had been in, and fell to contemplating the new turn of events in the establishment.

Back in her office, Lemah could not settle down. She reached for her telephone and dialled…..After a few beeps, she heard *The* voice at the other end.

'Hello Theo… Yes… rather fine…..Yes. Now I have to see you this evening. No, no, no. You just have to pass by Ntinda. I'll be in, anything between seven and seven-thirty… Fine… Bye, and big love… And oh, Theo, I don't mind an apple from my man, when you come. Bye.'

She hung up and sat back, ponderous.

TWENTY – ONE

WHEN Theo's Volvo turned into Lemah's yard, there was no sign of life in the house. It was past seven, but the house was unlit. Lemah was evidently not back. He had a copy of her every key, but he decided to wait in the car. Part of his mind told him he could drive away and first make the calls he thought he could make at her house, but another part told him otherwise. What if she turned in as soon as he drove out? So he waited in the car, his mind raging with ideas and imaginations.

Two issues churned most violently in his head. What was eating at Lemah? She had sounded panicky, which was not very like her. Whatever was the matter had to be serious, which is the reason he could not drive away, even with plans to return later. Yet he had confirmed to the woman buying his car that he would call her at exactly 8 o'clock. If Lemah was not back by eight he was going to seem irresponsible and unserious to this woman, who had always held him in high regard.

It was exactly five minutes to eight o'clock when Lemah's Sedan beams hit onto Theo's Volvo. She stopped, opened the garage door, drove in, then came out to meet Theo.

Before they said anything, they entwined in a hug that drew the Breath out of Lemah. Theo knew what this meant, and he led her into the house, where he immediately asked her what was amiss.

'Things at KITANET again. Theo, I am *tired.*'

'What exactly? Tell me!'

'People – my bosses are bothered about my not doing the things I used to do. Two of them talked to me today.'

'Which means they talked about you in a Board meeting!'

'Certainly. And that bothers me quite some, Theo!'

'Right, too. It's not a common occurrence at KITANET, and the few times it happens, it is serious. Look, I don't want to sound like-'

'No, of course. You're not just scaring me. I too know what you mean, which is why I called you.'

'What do you want me to-'

'Advise me. One, I can't go back to the sort of heartless stuff I used to do, not for all the money and love in the world. Two, KITANET is my professional home right now. I am not about to quit it in the interest of principle. And Theo, *I am doing my work*. I do what my job description prescribes for me. So what should I do?"

'That's a hard one, if you consider it. For one thing, you raised the expectations of D'Souza & Co. You raised KITANET'S image, both within the thinking of the executive at the establishment, and in the eyes of the viewing public. So for you to turn away from the very things that raised the reputation of a venture such as KITANET, and expect that they will not be restless-'

'I did not expect *that*. Okay….I did not expect that they would not notice, either. I don't know. The thing now is, Theo, I want a course of *action*!' Lemah was desperate in her appeal.

'Not in a hurry. I see your predicament, but to act rashly will do us more harm. Let's sleep over it, and first thing in the morning, I will call you. Will that do for you?'

Lemah was deliberative for a moment, then she consented to Theo's proposal.

'But if they are insistent that I return to the old stuff, I *quit*! Period!'

'Lemah, stop talking quitting. Don't even begin to think of it. You may look at your popularity now and think, I will survive. But my love, even fame and popularity must work in a context. Once out of KITANET and into the open world, all you'll harvest from your admirers is praise of your past glory. Don't quit, yet!"

215

'Anyway, let me wait for what you can tell me tomorrow'…
She fell silent, lost in meditation.

'Oh, I did not even apologise for keeping you waiting! I am sorry I was late,' Lemah said, by way of lifting up their spirits.

'Actually you ought to be sorry. I have missed calling the woman who is buying my car, all because of you. Now you have to buy it from me, if this woman changes her mind.' Lemah's light mood was catching up with Theo.

'Genuinely, I am very sorry. And to imagine what held me! After I returned to my office from talking to Dr., Kitonsa, I did not do anything constructive. I could not. So I just sat there, pondering over this and that. Then one of my Ex-Enemies came in. You know Musita?'

'Certainly! Eh, Lemah!'

'He came to my office to apologise.'

'What did he do this time?'

'Not this time. It's the last case, of the day he messed up my work, only to lead me into a victory that made my day. I am told he had expected me to take some serious steps against him, which I did not. Out of guilt, he went to Mercy to request her to arbitrate between us. But I had been to Mercy, and she knew I had dropped the case. She brushed him off.'

'Nothing you've said calls for such a belated apology-'

'Easy! Easy, Theo! So when she brushed him aside, aiming at making him suffer with that suspense, the Connie case occurred, so her mind was distracted from Musita. And since then, things have been happening at such a rate, I trust he had no way of reaching any of us. So today he came.'

'He *has* the time!'

216

'Not time. You don't get it! I was promoted to a high office. I am now an administrator. That pumped fear into him. So intimidated was he, he had not settled, till he talked to me. Now we are friends.'

'Congrats!' Theo sneered.

To him, not me!'

'Well, you have a friend….And now, I have to go. Good night, love.'

Lemah was silent.

'Aren't you bidding me good night? Have we quarrelled?' He got up, moved to her and squatted before her, holding her by the wrists and looking right into her eyes.

'You do not understand. Today has been so hard!'

'I understand, Lemah.' He sighed. 'I understand!'

'Anyway, I have to grow up. Bye, love. Catch you tomorrow.'

Theo thought he caught a hint of pain or tears in her voice. He pulled her up and locked her up in an embrace, rubbing her back gently.

'You will be fine. Just don't dwell on it so much. It will all pass.'

'I hope it does, Theo. I am mixed up.'

'Don't confess it. All will be fine, darling….I love you.'

'I love you, too… *so much*!'

'Good night. I'll see you first thing in the morning. I'll not just call, I'll come over. Fine?'

'Fine.' She disengaged herself, and they moved out of the house, to the car waiting outside.

Half an hour after they moved out of the house and into the car, Theo drove away, and Lemah got back into the house. She was pensive. She made up her mind that she was not going to cook. She was just in the sort of state for letting the food burn on the cooker. No, she would eat in the morning.

Thoughts were piling up in Lemah's mind… She had always been careful not to get onto D'Souza's wrong side. Now everything pointed towards a failure in this. Dr. Kitonsa had driven her out of his office before he could be of help… She had shifted positions in her profession, expecting to have relief from heartaches. Yet the very first venture she had pursued in her new mode of journalism had been tragic. Besides being shot in both legs, she had been raped…..by three soldiers! She had been raped….By soldiers… soldiers…

She caught herself descend into a bad state of mind, so she collected herself and went into the bathroom. Stripping to the core, she sat in the tab, and then turned on both taps, hot and cold water mixing around her.

But the rape thoughts kept crowding her mind. The searing pain. The horror of it… By soldiers. Connie… Connie's soldier… Blood… Blood all about her… Screaming children… Gunfire… Fire, blood… Her own blood…

She tore through the air with screams that woke the entire neighbourhood. She screamed, shouting: *Fire! Blood! Connie! Theodore!* Etc. Etc. Etc!

A large throng gathered at both ends of the house, trying to get in. Both outer doors were locked. Kotrida, too, was there. Fighting her way to the front, she asked if anybody had a telephone in their house. Quickly, a call was made to Theo, and another to

218

KITANET. Meanwhile, more people were pouring in, including those from passing vehicles which stopped, on the drivers seeing the crowd at Lemah's house.

The screams in the house were turning into gaggles, and indiscernible muttering. But one thing was for sure: Lemah was drowning in something. She was lapping and splashing in some great quantity of water, most probably her bathtub. Something had to be done.

After due consultation, the crowd agreed that the security guards around should be asked to fire a bullet in the lock, so people could get in and save Lemah. There was a Local Defence man in the crowd, who consented to this scheme.

The crowd scattered as he cocked his rifle, and moved within proximity of the lock. Accompanied by screams from the women in the crowd, a loud report rang out form the AK-47, and the door swung open. Glass scattered about.

People rushed in, led by a flabbergasted Kotrida. She was so terrified; she was not talking at all. She just led everybody to Lemah's bathroom, assisted by the water that was already flowing out, into the corridor. At the same time, Theo's Volvo swung into the yard, and he sprinted into the house.

'What's happening?' he shook Kotrida, and then almost immediately turned to his limp and stark naked Lemah, lying in a heap on the floor. She had gulped a lot of water, and she was foaming at the mouth. She was breathing in slow, heavy puffs.

'Quick, Kotrida, get us clothes. Hurry!' Theo was literally barking at people. Even before the clothes came, he had carried Lemah and laid her in the back seat of the Volvo, then ran and met Kotrida half way. They threw the clothes on her body, he pushed Kotrida into the car, and off they sped.

In less than five minutes, the Volvo was heading into Mulago Hospital. When the gatemen saw no sign of the car stopping, they threw the gates open and jumped aside, just in time to avoid what could have been the accident of the year.

Theo drove right down to the causality department. They carried the limp Lemah out, and put her on a wheeled bed that Theo did not wait to be given. Lemah was wheeled away, as Kotrida stayed behind to give the particulars of the patient, and the details of her disease….as far a she could tell.

At exactly twelve midnight, Lemah was admitted.

TWENTY – TWO

BY sunrise the following morning, Lemah was still in coma.

All the time, Theo was seated right by her side, and Kotrida was in the lobby, waiting. Every time a doctor came in, Theo would stand up and watch every step of the treatment; and every time a doctor moved out of Lemah's private room, Kotrida would shoot up and inquire about the progress of the patient.

The first signs of consciousness in Lemah were seen at 8:48am. She rolled her head weakly to one side. Immediately, Theo dialled 102 on the room phone, and in the next instant, the doctor rushed in with a couple of nurses in his wake.

'Anything serious?' he inquired breathlessly.

'She moved! She – her head rolled to one side,' Theo rushed through the words.

The doctor set to working. In ten minutes, Lemah's eyes were open, and more parts of her body were more alive now. Her eyes seemed distant, and she could not recognise anyone, not even Theo.

From then on, there was a constant watch by nurses in the room. Every so often, they would administer a sedative. Every so often, they took her temperature. Every so often, her progress was recorded in a file that lay at the foot of her bed.

By 10 o'clock, Lemah could whisper things in ears that were put close to her. She could also move her hands. However, she was undergoing something new. Spasms were pulling in her hands, and on her groin, and in the left breast. Again doctors got to fresh work. The spasms became more pronounced, till it was decided that a neurologist be called in.

Calls were made and, in next to no time, a lady doctor came up. The rest moved out and waited outside the room. All the time, Theo did not budge from the room.

221

The neurologist prescribed a session with a psycho-therapist. Unfortunately, Lemah was still too weak to get into any such session. So it was decided that she be put on special treatment, till such a time as when she would be able to talk to a doctor.

By late afternoon, the attending nurses withdrew, with stern instructions to Theo to call them in at the slightest negative change. He was also told not to engage her in talk, till further instructions.

'Do not listen to them,' Lemah muttered to him as they were left alone in the room.

'What?' Theo put his ear next to her head.

'Ignore their panic', she said again. 'I am fine now; I don't need to be treated like an invalid.'

'No, Lemah, you need to rest. You're weaker than you realise.'

'Okay… And thanks for coming to help.'

She drifted into sleep.

That evening, a delegation from KITANET came in to see Lemah. Among them were Dr. Kitonsa and Mercy, Lemah's Personal Secretary. Lemah was asleep when they came in.

'What exactly happened?' Mercy asked Theo, alone aside.

'Hysteria, but it was followed by a serious fever. She had a lot on her mind. But she's pulling through.' Theo was genuinely optimistic.

'Poor sweetheart,' Mercy said. 'God help her!'

'She's really recovering,' Theo reassured her.

But he did not know what Mercy meant. What Mercy had in mind was more to do with Lemah the journalist, than Lemah the patient.

After picking ample information from Theo and the doctors, the KITANET delegation left. They gave Theo financial support, and promised to be back.

Lemah was taken to see a psycho-therapist the following morning. He was a thick-set man slightly past his middle age, with keen eyes and an interested attitude. Perfectly suited to his trade. He spoke with a tender voice, peering with an unseen lens into the being of whoever he talked to. He told Theo and Lemah's doctor to wait outside.

'I am glad to get the chance to talk with you, Ms Nabasa,' he said to Lemah when the door had been shut on the two of them.

'Really it is a bigger honour for me,' Lemah said. 'It's not everyday that one talks to people of your calibre – a savant in every degree.'

'Many would not agree with you, on the contrary.' He was studying her mind. 'Many hate to have to deal with shrinks, as they call us.'

'Not me!'

'Good, then – very good!' He was looking for the slightest gap through which to enter into her case.

'Well….Er… how do you feel now, Lemah?'

'Much better, thanks. Actually I am now well.'

'*Well?*' He did not sound unbelieving, yet Lemah's reaction was an act of self – defence.

'Yes! Don't you *believe* it?'

'I do. Er…I do. It's just not easy, under normal circumstances, to have lots of water drained out of one this day, and the next day they're feeling perfect. Sure hand of God.'

'Yeah.'

'Just what happened – slipped?'

'Can't quite say… I had things on my mind, and I was just recovering from… from… not so long ago I was shot in the legs by rebels-'

'Oh dear!' The doctor had heard this before.

'I am now fine, really. But when a number of things went wrong day before yesterday, and I was all by myself, I guess my mind became over loaded, and I closed.'

'You -?'

'I passed out. Sorry!' she smiled to herself, in spite of herself.

'Ah, fine with me. Comes in handy, what with your profession.'

'You know my profession, then?'

'Oh please! Who wouldn't? Just say, was there anything particularly hard on your mind or heart, or plainly harsh times at your place of work?'

'Mmm…..Nothing serious, really. High expectations from bosses, shift in interests… the like.'

'That's all?'

'That's all.' Then as a well-thought-about afterthought, she added: 'And maybe memories of things I saw in the rebels' camp in

Acholi. I was taken captive in a bus – ambush by rebels…
Traumatic, to use your word.'

'My word?'

'You as a psychiatrist, not as the individual.'

'Is that how you view this – as a talk between a patient and a
psychiatrist?'

Lemah laughed uneasily.

'Not really!'

In all they said between them, Lemah was careful not to
mention the word rape, though it had indeed been the main cause of
her hysteria. She had for all the time since the actual rape been
repressing her reactions to it, so nobody would talk about it. She
feared the reactions and talk of the public. But most of all, she feared
what Theo would do. She knew that all else put aside, Theo was a
human being and, what is more, a man. Human like any other, man
like the rest. She would not risk.

At the end of the chat, the therapist advised against Lemah
spending time alone. He also advised against working full day.
Otherwise, he did not have much to say about her condition.

The spasms came back no more.

On the fifth day after she was admitted, Lemah was
discharged. And in all the days she had been at Mulago, only Dr.
Kitonsa and Mercy had returned to visit her in hospital, of all the
KITANET staff. These things bothered Lemah – not so much
because she was itching to be visited, but because it was an
unpleasant indicator of her relationships with, especially, her bosses.

From hospital, Lemah was driven to Theo's house for two
days of intensive doting on by Theo, before she plucked herself off
and went to her own house. Cindy and Vinah had left Theo's house.

'Lemah,' Theo cautioned, 'the doctors advised you not to live alone. Who are you going to live with?'

'I'll find a way, Theo, but I have to be back to my own house. I'll get a maid.'

'Maid? *Maid?* Lemah, this is your life we're talking about. Not work or chores or whatever. *Your* life. A maid will not rescue your life.'

'So what should I do?'

'We shall find a way,' Theo said determinedly, and they drove back home – Theo, Kotrida and Lemah.

TWENTY – THREE

LEMAH was being overwhelmed by events. She was also wary of doing anything that would endanger her health, yet there was a lot to do. She was bent on doing the KOT-Project, despite protests from Theo, who insisted that there was no serious motive in the woman's story that Lemah insisted on following up. Theo's argument was that if she dropped the project, it would also save her lots of other likely bothers – bothers she may lack the capacity to curb, otherwise.

She had agreed to live in Theo's house, till she could make it on her own again. She did not take another leave, though Theo insisted that she does. She said she would rather work half-day, which she did not do, even then. That was Lemah.

Calls flooded Theo's home number. *I want Lemah....tell her it's Betty, Kot's friend.*

May I please speak to Ms Nabasa of KITANET? It's about her project.

Please give me Lemah. Tell her Aidah has some extra information for her...

And Theo would hand the receiver over to Lemah, and move to another part of the house, as Lemah conducted her business with her agents and sources.

'Why do you always have to move away when I am talking to these people?' she pinned him one day.

'Do I always have to listen?' He was curt.

'Strange that you should answer my question with another question.' She was hurt.

'It's allowed. That's the only reason we can talk of 'counter-questions,' my dear!'

227

'I see!'

'See what?'

'Nothing.'

'See? See Lemah? You know deep within yourself that things are eating at your mind. You know you ought to be taking a rest. You know, or you should know, even better than anyone else, that at this rate, you're bound to affect your relations with others, because your strains are too much for you to contain. Why don't you-'

'Theo, you are *deluded*. Simple.'

'Deluded? Me, Theo, deluded? If I am anything, I am concerned – about *you*. Actually, a little more concerned than I can justify.'

'Why do you torture yourself, then? I don't need to be sympathised with. I am not sick. Why kill yourself?'

Theo had never known this Lemah. She was brand-new to him.

'Lemah, please resp- er….let's drop this. If I may answer your question boldly, I always move away whenever you talk to your clients, because I can't contribute to your deals, and I am not interested in them, either. I don't support them in the least. If you are answered, I beg to go and attend to my other cares.'

'Your *other* cares, eh? Other cares. Which is the first? Me? I am a burden to you, eh? But-'

She would have gone on and on, but the phone rang. She went to pick it, and Theo went out. Lemah was hurt and angry. Very angry.

'Hello?' she said coldly into the phone.

'Hello Lemah! This is Matilda – you left a message at my office.'

'Oh Mattie! How are you? How can I get to you?'

'Don't bother, I can come over!'

Lemah considered that for a while. Was she ready to conduct an interview right under Theo's roof? But the defiant spirit in her took control, and she directed Matilda to the house.

After she had hung up, she went outside and informed Theo that somebody was coming over.

'Okay with me – I don't have to lay a red carpet for them, I suppose?' And he proceeded with his work.

'No need to be sarcastic or bitter, love,' Lemah said as she turned on her heel and walked back to the house.

Hardly ten minutes later, she heard the garage doors open, and Theo drove his car out. He did not even bother to close the doors, a thing he had never done before. Lemah convinced herself that she was not that bothered. A strange conviction!

Matilda arrived soon afterwards. The door bell rang, and Lemah admitted her in. She was a mound of a woman, this Matilda. Voluminous, tall and firm. Lemah could hardly hide her astonishment at what she saw.

'Come right in, Mattie. How are you? Really kind of you to have offered to come over.'

'No pain, really. I am fine, Lemah. And how are you feeling now?'

'Oh, a lot better. Actually I am fully recovered. Will you have a cold drink, or would you prefer tea?'

'Nothing, if you don't mind. I am off sugars, so I can't have either.'

'I can fix you sugarless juice.'

'I am okay, Lemah. I am okay.'

'Fine. Now, I will not hold you long. Straight to business.'

'Don't rush over anything on my account, dear Lemah,' Matilda offered. 'I am in no thick hurry.'

'Thanks Mattie. Unfortunately, because of the nature of our space – and the time, we could not arrange to have our chat covered. So I will just take a few stills, and record our conversation on an audio cassette. Is that fine with you, dear?'

'Absolutely. Do anything that will suit the purpose of your work.'

'Good! My kind of lady,' Lemah complimented, in spite of herself. 'Now, you are going to take the lead in this. You will tell me all you know in the line of your friend's social life, particularly centring on her relationship with the late Tilsa Elvis, and Mr. Kaliisa.'

Matilda gave a short bi-directional laugh, then settled back in her seat.

'I see. Now where do we start? I first knew Kot at University, as I trust she has told you.'

'She did, yes.'

'Yes. We were on the same block in Year One, and her roomie was my O.G.'

'Roomie – oh, room-mate! Yes?'

'So we get to know, and like each other. We liked each other so much, when we got to our second year; we applied for the same

230

room, and got it. Luckily, Rita our friend – my O.G. got private sponsorship to India for a Commerce degree. She had been admitted for plain Arts here.

'Anyhow, Rita went to India, which left just Kot and I, for a while. Kot was not the outgoing type. You see, she is rather complex. She is naturally outgoing, but those days money and beauty had reached her here.' Matilda indicated the top of her neck.

'Yeah, I can see the markings of what must have been a smashing face on her. If she looks like that now-'

'Yes,' Matlida took up the thread again. 'And money. You know she is a Tusiime. Did you know the Tusiimes? That was a name of money. So it was not easy to associate with Kot, my dear.'

'I can imagine,' Lemah agreed.

'I am telling you, my dear! Then… Then came our Elvis. Elvis was in his Fourth Year at University, the year we did our Year 2. He was a good boy, I must say. He had character. So somehow, he got into Kot's life, and with time, into her heart. Everybody was shocked to see a boy in Kot's life. And a boy like Elvis, all the way from Technology! There was no direct link between a Library Science student and an Engineer. But somehow it happened. You see, Kot did Library Science, though she went into teaching.

The recorder snapped 'OFF,' and the story was cut.

'Please hold on, as I change the tape,' Lemah said. She fixed the recorder, pressed 'PLAY' and 'RECORD' down, and bid Matilda proceed.

'I was saying that Elvis and Kot became an issue at University. But you know Makerere! I guess it was the same even in your time, yeah? Money plays a big part in relationships. Regardless of Kot being a Tusiime, Elvis still had to maintain her, if you know what I mean. Makerere language, you know. He strained his pockets, and his friends' pockets, and he even had to dig into his father's pockets.

'At one point, Kot discovered that she was heavy.'

'What sort of heavy?' Lemah asked, not knowing this bit of the story. As far as she was concerned, Kotrida had been innocent, till Kaliisa de-flowered her.

'Heavy. In the family way.' Matilda answered, the way she would explain that people walk on their feet, not with their buttocks.

'Meaning pregnant?' Lemah's incredulity was just rising higher.

'Why do you find it hard to believe that Kot could conceive? Don't you know that she has a daughter – Tophus?'

'I know. I actually know Tophus; I've talked to her lately.'

'So? Did Kot tell you that Elvis was impotent?'

'Well, nothing, really. Please proceed.'

'Anyway, somehow, Kot conceived, and aborted.'

'Aborted?' Lemah's consternation was reaching its highest limit.

'Yep! And she did not tell anyone, not even the author of the pregnancy.'

'O my sweet Lord!'

'Yes, Lemah! I would never have known, if she had not been my roomie. But you know, an abortion is not anything like eating ice cream. I got to know. And I too refused to talk about it, up to now, as we sit here talking.'

'Goodness!' It all made sense to Lemah now.

Kotrida was still deceived that nobody knew about the abortion, so she could afford to edit it out of her life story, and lie that Kaliisa had deflowered her.

'Well?' She prompted her informer.

'She gradually lost interest in Elvis. You see, she had never quite loved him. It was one-sided love, all the time it lasted. The abortion aftermath just worsened it.

'Somehow, Elvis thought she was pulling out because of his empty pockets. He grew restless. His friends could no longer support him. He went to get some money from his dad – the dad was out of the country. When he returned to the University, he committed suicide. I guess you know that bit of the story.'

'Poor boy!' Lemah said tearfully.

'Yeah. He didn't deserve to die, and for a girl who wasn't even interested in him, but only in having fun with a boy – *any boy*.

'Oh, I'd forgotten! Just before Elvis died, your Mr. Kaliisa came into the picture. Employed, handsome like Al Pacino. He swept our Kot off her feet.'

'How did they meet?' Lemah asked.

'How can anyone tell how a man and a woman meet the first time? It is like we cannot explain the exact moment we fall asleep.'

'Well, sometimes it's easy – a meeting at a party, a business association, a chance meeting in a friend's house-'

'Yes, Lemah, but for Makerere girls, it's different. You will hear of affairs there that will draw the very breath out of you. So it was for Kot and Mr. Kaliisa.

'Now, I knew this Kaliisa. He had been to school with my big brother. They even graduated together. I was a child, but I can still recall the grandeur of Kaliisa's graduation party, and the boasting in his speech. Lemah, I warned Kot against moving out with Kaliisa!'

'And in popular fashion, she refused!' Lemah put in.

'You have it!'

'It follows!'

'When Elvis died, it was only to cement the affair between Kot and Kaliisa. They went places together. Every weekend they were either in Entebbe, or in Mbarara, or Mbale, or Mombasa, or Nairobi, or Kigali. I tell you, those two had fun!'

'I can imagine!' Lemah interjected.

'Till, to cut a very long tale short, Kaliisa got his fill, and gave Kot the boot. That was the year after we completed our studies at Makerere. Kot was even contemplating moving in with Kaliisa.'

'What a shame!'

'That's Kaliisa for you, my dear.'

'Such a brute!' Lemah offered.

'Though I wouldn't really call him a brute.'   Matilda said. 'You see, life is the most unpredictable thing we all ever go through.'

'Why?' Lemah was suspicious.

'I told you my brother was Kaliisa's friend, of sorts. After University, I was employed in their joint business. They were operating an Electronics shop in town. Dealing in TVs, radios, electronic cookers and ovens, name it. They had money. In the process, the three of us – David my brother, Mr. Kaliisa and I got so close. Before I could tell East from West, I had Kaliisa's child in me.'

Matilda laughed an unnecessary and embarrassed laugh. Lemah would have wanted to relieve the moment by accompanying her visitor in the laughter, but she could not bring herself to laugh. This was like a Greek farce. It was just the limit.

'Well?' she prompted again.

'I did not want to lose my name, so between the three of us, we arranged a quick marriage, and Kaliisa finally got his first legal wife – and I was to be the last, to-date.'

'Are you still-'

'No, no. We split, and very badly. I was fed up, and he was getting too broke to want me around him. We parted paths. Besides, Kot and I were, very strangely, still friends, and I was finding it hard to keep the two attached to my life. When we talked it over with Kaliisa, we parted.'

'And Tophus?' Lemah asked.

'Yes, Tophus. Kot got Tophus as a parting reminder from Kaliisa, it seems. They parted before she realised that she was pregnant. Two months later, she wrote to me that she had Kaliisa's child in her tummy!'

'Life!' Lemah was saturated with bewilderment at everything she had heard.

'Such is life, my friend. I guess you know the rest of the story. After Kaliisa discovered that Kot had his child in her – the pregnancy was in its advanced stages then – he rewarded her with a house, the one she lives in up to now, here in Ntinda. I hear you're neighbours?'

'Yes.'

'That's the house. Now wonder of wonders, when we split a handful of months ago, Mr. Kaliisa started going back to Kot.'

'She told me.'

235

'Aha! That is as far as it went.'

Lemah stopped the machine after Matilda sat back, to indicate an end to her tale.

'Thank you so much, Mattie. And, I think I like you. I feel it in my plasma.'

Matilda laughed heartily.

'Thanks, too. I have liked talking to you. You make it so easy, despite your station.'

'Which station? Mattie, I am an ordinary, plain woman,' Lemah protested.

'In which case, I need to find out about being ordinary and plain,' Matilda said, and at the same time announced her departure.

'Oh please stay on, Mattie, we haven't even had time for less official talk!'

'This wasn't official, really. Well, for you it is work, but I find it personal enough. And, there will be lots of other opportunities, you wait. Will you always be here?'

'I guess not, but if we keep in touch, you'll know. If not from me, at least from Kot.'

Matilda left.

.

TWENTY – FOUR

THE following season was fiery. There were more serious fires in the country than ever before. The northern fire burned with fresh vigour. The fire in the South-West, too, was getting more vigour from winds which blew in from neighbouring Rwanda and Zaire. What was worse, other major fires had developed out of friction between Uganda and Sudan, Uganda and Kenya, and Uganda and Zaire.

People grew restless. Internally, people wanted the Government to totally put out all fires. Sit at a round table. Offer a general amnesty. Or if you can, crush all rebels. *If you can.*

Externally, as some giants gave with one hand, they directed with the other. So it was said. Rumour on the wind had it that the country was under directives to discipline certain neighbours, and to make peace with others.

In the midst of all this, business was booming in the country. Gold from Zaire. Milk and other foodstuffs to Rwanda. Untaxed fuel from here to there. And the fires raged on…

And in the midst of all this, KITANET was looking on, blaming their downward descent on Lemah's irrational change in attitude. D'Souza himself was disturbed. After tasting of high success, it was not exciting at all to be so plain; nobody noticed their presence any more. He had personally talked to Lemah, and she had promised to reconsider herself: She had not.

She had spent a lot of time making this Kotrida nonsense of a film, which had been as effective as cold ash. Not worth a second thought, except as plain entertainment. And even then, it would only entertain someone with sexist thinking. He, D'Souza, was a businessman, not an activist. He would have to act, somehow!

He was still thus deliberating in his office, when sudden alarms tore into the air, followed by the ringing of his desk phone. He dived for it, only to be told that there was a fire at the main complex. He shot out of his office.

237

There was wild activity all about. The women were screaming and wringing their hands. Two vehicles were turning out of the yard, and out of the main gate. Mr. Kaliisa had been spotted in the vicinity hardly half an hour back. Somebody had to get to him and find out something….At the same time; the Police had to get here. They had thought of ringing them, but later agreed that if it was the Uganda Police they were dealing with, somebody had to drive over, in addition to the telephone call. A call had also been made to the Fire Department.

It was a big fire. It was disastrous fire. Computers, furniture, studio equipment, books, name it. All got burnt. D'Souza practically wept. Yes, wept like a spanked child.

Lemah was at the station. When the fire broke out, she did not know what to do. She had seen Kaliisa around. Instinct spoke to her heart: ESCAPE!

She did not use her car. She stealthily stole away, and ran all the way to the nearest Bus Stop, where she boarded a taxi to her house. She was panicking, and barely keeping the tears back.

At KITANET, the fire engine arrived a whole half hour after the fire broke out. Very little could be done – the entire first two floors were destroyed, save for the bare concrete walls that stood, smouldering with smoke! D'Souza was livid!

After the fire had been put out, and all the salvaged property and equipment assembled out, the Police got into action, asking questions and recording statements – in ink and on tape. The car which had tried to chase after Kaliisa had returned; its occupants crestfallen - defeated. They only mentioned that Kaliisa was Prime Suspect. The Police took note.

Meanwhile, journalists were all over the place, writing notes, taking pictures and interviewing KITANET staff. They called radio stations all over Kampala, and the news spread countrywide, of the burning down of the KITANET establishment. D'Souza was in uncontrollable tears!'

When Lemah got to her house, she sure confirmed her suspicions. In his own handwriting, Kaliisa had told her never to meddle in his life again. He added: *"Show this to police. They will surely arrest me and lock me up. I will be in a prison I can get out of, after sometime. But YOU WILL BE IRRETRIEVABLE. Take care."*

Lemah was terrified. Theo had warned her. Now they were not seeing eye-to-eye. Where was she to go?

But Theo was there. He raced into her yard, and he had hardly parked the car when he jumped out. 'Are you safe, Lemah?' he gasped.

'I don't know, Theo. I must disappear.'

'Do not! In fact, you should not have left the station at all. I was there just now, and they had already noticed your absence. You don't know what damage that will do to you!'

'What do I do now, Theo?'

'Get into the car. We drive back to KITANET, *Now!*'

They did. When they got to the station, it was still swarming with people. D'Souza had gone back to the office, with Dr. Kitonsa and some police officers. He had left directions that if Lemah came by, she should be told to wait for him.

When she came up, Mercy rushed over to her. She burst into tears, and threw herself into Lemah's arms.

'Lemah, it's horrid! It's *horrid!* And D'Souza himself wants to see you. He said to tell you to wait here. He's down in his office, talking to the law, with Dr. Kitonsa.

'Have you talked to Dr. Kitonsa at all?' Lemah asked.

'He saw me move up to him and he waved me away. I gave up the attempt.'

'O my God!'

D'Souza, Dr. Kitonsa and the two Police officers walked out of the office. D'Souza saw Lemah, and seeing off the Policemen, he sent Dr. Kitonsa to summon Lemah. 'Please keep calm,' Dr. Kitonsa said to her. 'You'll probably lose your job, but that's all. Keep calm, and say nothing rash. Good luck.'

'Theo, I'll be back presently,' Lemah said as she strode up to D'Souza's office. A few journalists recognised her and ran after her, but she out-paced them and took cover in the building.

In D'Souza's office, she found him standing, waiting for her. He did not wait for her to say anything, or to sit down. He just told her to hand in all KITANET property, except the car, and call it quits.

'I do appreciate that you did your best for us. I loved you, Lemah. But your sudden turn of attitude, and this insistence on poking into Kaliisa's life, is very detrimental. Sorry, but bye. Now go!'

She did.

When she got to Theo's car, the pressmen still swarming around her, she told him to drive off. Then she remembered her car. Calling to Mercy, she gave her the keys and requested her to drive it car to her house in Ntinda.

Without consulting with Lemah, Theo drove out of town. From Nakasero, he drove to Kampala Road, and then turned left. The traffic was light, so he raced down the road, and did not obey the road lights at the Entebbe Road turning. He swung right, and could have rammed into the back of an omnibus taxi at the Queen's Way round-about, had not the taxi-man swerved sharply. Theo was already away, heading towards Gaba.

Lemah said nothing all the way. Ordinarily, if Theo or anybody else drove recklessly, she would fasten the seat belt and grip the sides of the seat. Not this time. She just sat there, kaleidoscopic images racing throughout her cloudy mind.

They had been in the habit of going to Nanga Hotel, a modern manifestation of the country's new look. When Theo turned into the parking lot, he did not stop to pay for the safety of the car, as he always did. He instead drove round to the gardens, parked there, then literally drew Lemah out, and into one of the grass-thatched *manyatas*. The couples in neighbouring huts were doing their best not to show that they noticed something out of the ordinary, but even if they hadn't bothered, neither Theo nor Lemah would have noticed, or cared one way or the other.

The first thing she said was in answer to Theo's question: 'Why did you do it, Lemah?'

'Do what – do you imagine I lit that fire?'

'Hell, no!' Theo barked, then checked himself, and attempted to put control in his voice. 'Lemah, everybody told you NOT to do that film. I did – but well, let's leave me out of it, for there are worthier people to talk about-'

'Who? Who else advised against it except you? I asked Dr. Kitonsa-'

'Roast your Doctor Kitonsa!' Theo lost all control of the shouting again. 'And what has he done for you, under the circumstances? Where is he now? Answer me: WHERE?'

'Theo, much as I appreciate your concern, I also want you to appreciate that I am an adult, not a child. I am a person, not a puppet or a dummy.'

'Oh really?'

That stung her, and an urge developed in her to slap him, but when she raised her hand, she instead let it reach to the button for the fan on the roof of the hut.

'Hopeless!'

'Who, me?' Theo asked, laughing sardonically. 'Am I hopeless now? Strange. Well, thanks.'

'Sorry. Theo, I am in a bad way. You know it. So why should you choose this to be the moment and place to crucify me?'

'Because if you do not learn your lesson *now*, you may never, and that will be bad for us both.' Theo's voice was firm, and his tone uncompromising.

'Learn? I have learnt. Theo, I have more than learnt. For your information, I am regretting a lot of things now. More things than is safe to say out now.'

'Oh is that it? Pity!' He had an edge of ridicule in his tone now.

'You may misunderstand me, if you choose to. All I am saying is, I am being forced to learn, all too suddenly, that I have wasted a lot of time, and a lot of chances. That's all!'

'Fine. Now tell me this one: What are you going to do next? You made your mistakes, wasted your time and chances, what now?'

Lemah blew up.

'Damn you, Theo, I told you I D-O-N-T KNOW! Fine? I don't know. Okay, you are here, Mr. Superman, save me. Indomitable, Invincible, Infallible Mr. Superman: Save me. Why do you shut yourself to reason all the way?'

'Now what have I-'

242

'I don't care anymore, Theo. I don't care. Clear? Give me up. You can throw me out the window now, and I wouldn't care a rat's arse about it. I have been through a lot, Theo! More than you know!'

Images that had been slouching in corners of her mind now took on flesh and became real in her head. Connie was there, as was her soldier. The bush bus was there, crossing Karuma bridge. The gunfire, the pain in the legs… the capture….the rape! She was hysterical now. She threw caution to the winds.

'Drop me! What do I lose? What do *you* gain? Nothing! I now have to pay for the sins of the past. I am paying for the ghosts in silence. What do I lose? If you have been through the worst, the worse and bad seem only like Kindergarten, after University. Have you ever been raped? Have you? Answer me, Mr. Superman. Do you know the pain and horror of rape? You don't! You don't!' She was screaming.

Theo stood up, picked her up by the hand and led her back to the car. He rolled up the windows and closed the sky-light, but he knew the noise would still be heard, if anybody passed by. Luckily, nobody did.

'I have paid dearly, so leave me. Right? Dearly. You, you with you unschooled mentality and attitude, know nothing! So leave me alone, PIG!'

She stopped suddenly, and broke down into uncontrollable tears. She cried like a child, yielding to the giant sobs that stopped short of rocking her in her seat. Theo did not touch or talk to her. He was thinking…

Close to an hour later, she was still crying, though now in a subsided manner. She was more conscious of what was happening, and what had happened. Actually, she was now weeping over a broken secret. The game was up.

Again, Theo did not consult with Lemah. He put the car in ignition, turned round and drove back the way he had come, and did not stop till he reached Ntinda, at Lemah's house. Still silent, he helped her out of the car and into the house, which he opened with his copy of the key.

After he had led her to her bed, and made drinking chocolate, and put salt bread on a plate for her, he whispered an inaudible good night, and went away.

Silent.

TWENTY – FIVE

*KALIISA **was arrested
the day after he
committed two deadly
offences: He set fire to
the KITANET complex,
and strangled Kotrida.
Her body was
discovered in her house,
after midnight, on the
day of the KITANET fire.
Her house had been
open all that time, with
the lights on from the
time Uganda Electricity
Board switched on the
Ntinda line, after the
day's load shedding.
That was at 9 o'clock in
the night. When even
after midnight the door
remained open, and the
lights were still on,
neighbours got
concerned, and gathered
the Local Council
leaders around. They
went for a Policeman at
the local station and got
into the house.
Kotrida's body was
found lying in the door
to her bedroom.***

The Police mounted a search for Kaliisa. He was not at his house, but his youngest daughter mentioned something about Aunt Matilda. Now this Aunt Matilda was the child's mother, but because all the people in the area were called uncle if they were male, and auntie if they were female, whenever Matilda went to visit her children at Kaliisa's, they called her Aunt Matilda. And that evening, before the children went to bed, Matilda called her biggest girl and told her to carry some essential supplies to her house, for Daddy.

Kaliisa was arrested at 6 am. the following day, as Matilda attempted to drive him out of town. He was driven straight to Kampala Central Police Station, from where he was taken to Luzira Maximum Security Prison.

The news of Kotrida's death hit Lemah like a marble slab on her scalp. She was already drained from weeping overnight, but tears still rolled down her cheeks. The Police had taken away Kotrida's body. The most painful part of it was, she was too involved in this, she could not move around. If the Police wanted her, they would find her in her house.

She wished for some human company. Subconsciously, she wished Theo would call her, or plain come by. He did neither. She thought of Mercy… No, she would not involve the poor girl in her endless woes.

The Police did come. She was still in her bed, half-weeping, half -thinking. A knock at the door shook her to alertness. When she opened the door, a plainclothes officer showed her his card, and requested to be let in.

'Come in, officer. I knew you would come,' she said. In her mind, this was like a TV serialised story. She was involved in a maze of events, involving deaths, fires and deeper, deeper tragedies that only her soul felt.

'Nothing serious, though,' the officer reassured her. We only want to hear your side of the story.'

'About?'

'About everything, your work time with Kaliisa, your project about Kotrida – do you know that she is dead?'

'Of course! She is my neighbour, and a friend.'

'Was,' the officer corrected.

'Oh yes, was. A neighbour called in very early and told me.
I've also heard about Kaliisa's arrest. Voices from beyond the walls.'

The man was writing.

'Well, what do you know?'

Lemah told him everything, leaving out no detail.
Occasionally, he told her to pause, as he found the best way to phrase
her information, or to say something again, or ask for clarification.
When he was satisfied, he said he was grateful, and if they needed to
hear from her again, they would get in touch. 'No need to fear, we
know you're innocent. It's just that a lot of these happenings stem
from your work.'

After seeing off the officer, Lemah was too lost to go back to
her bed. She sat on the carpet in the sitting room, and let life sweep
over her. This was too much for one soul, too fast.

Theo did not call, and he did not come over, that whole day.
Neither did anyone else come by. The Police rang her to ask a few
more details about her KOT-Project, and for the rest of the day, she
just sat there, in her house, on her carpet, lost.

It was eight o'clock in the night when Lemah got up. She
had been asleep for over an hour. Hunger ate at her inside like a
tribe of goblins in her tummy. Still in her night gown from the
previous night, she went to the kitchen. Theo had left her tap
running. Luckily, there was no stopper in the sink, otherwise the
whole kitchen would be flooded. She turned off the tap, then made
herself a quick, light meal of cheese omelette, salt bread and coffee.
She made her coffee so strong, it looked like used oil and reeked like
a drug. She had the meal there in the kitchen, still in her night gown.
Then she went and took a bath, dressed up, and drove out.

She went straight to Theo's house. He was away. She opened the house and entered. There was no sign of his having been in, in the recent past. She would wait, she decided.

After waiting for an eternal quarter of an hour, she decided to call his office at The Station. The phone was disconnected. It was then that she realised that he was intentionally hiding from her. But why? Because they had quarrelled? True, it was the first time they quarrelled that violently, but did he think she was an angel? Oh, it was the revelation about her rape. She had told him about the rape, and it had taken him purely by storm. All that time, she had never mentioned it to him, poor boy!

Having waited in vain, she decided to write to him. She rummaged in his study and found paper and ink, and she wrote him a letter:

Your House.

My dearest Theo,

I know you're hiding from me. I wish you would know how much I want you with me. But that aside, I implore you: Do talk to me. Tell me exactly what hurt you most. I think I know, but can't be sure. I'll make up, I promise. Please come back to me, I need you. What with the death of Kot (I know you hate the name) and the Police coming, and calling, etc, it's hard on me. I am waiting.

Love you,

L.N.

She put it on the table in the sitting room; put his torch which he used every night on it, and drove away, back to Ntinda.

She was just opening the door of her house, after locking up her car in the garage, when her phone rang. The Police again! She thought. But it was not them, it was Theo.

'I have seen your note, thanks. Now in very few words of plain language, tell me: how do you make up for rape? How?'

'Which rape, Theo?'

Lemah surprised even herself with the question, because she knew that they both knew what Theo was talking about.

'Which rape? Fine, I'll-'

'No, Theo, I get you. But-'

'No, just tell me. They raped you. SOLDIERS raped you. You know as well as I do that you cannot be the first any of them slept with. This is an era of AIDS. Well? How are you going to redress that?' He sounded so cold, so determined.

'Theo-' she began, then stopped, lost.

'Yes dear? I am waiting for an explanation about how you plan to make up for the time I've lost, banking on you as the woman I would marry. All the hopes... all the-'

'Theo, what do you mean? You talk as if it's all over!'

'As if? Lemah, get real. You have messed the entire universe up – for you and for me. Then in an irate tantrum, you suddenly throw it in my face that three soldiers raped you. For all that time, you kept it away from me. What else don't I know? How much more are you holding away?'

'Nothing Theo! Absolutely nothing! I promise.'

'Promise nothing. What would you say? What signs would I have? We decided between us to keep ourselves pure till marriage, and God knows, I would never have known that anything went wrong. Till the day we marry! But you were deceiving yourself, because I would never take to church a girl I have not been tested with for HIV. Not Theo.'

249

'Theo, let's take the test, then!'

'And what would it do – restore your virginity? Mend you up?'

'You don't have to be vulgar, Theo. I am guilty, and it's now for you to decide-'

'I already have: what we have shared, we have shared. From now on, let's just be plain, platonic friends! He hung up.

Lemah broke down. Her whole world was shattered. She wept bitterly, till she fell asleep….

….And she was walking, out in an endless field of white flowers. They were beautiful flowers, uniformly reaching up to her knees. The sky was clear, and the sun bright, but not hot. A soft breeze blew around her, bringing with it a sweet scent from the entire field of flowers. Then all of a sudden, she stopped. She had heard a voice. A rather familiar voice. Or was she deceived? It came again, this time clearly. It called out to her. Connie's voice. But where did it come from? It seemed to sound from no particular direction, as if it called from within her, yet from so far away. It called again… but no, this time it was another voice… It was Kot calling. Calling out in desperate fear. Then both were calling. From all over. Then Theo joined them, his voice cold, yet commanding. He too called out to her. She grew frantic. In her panic, she started to run. But the flowers entangled her and she fell. By now, the voices had turned into gun-shots, ringing all about her. Then a voice commanded her: Come here, you bitch! She tried to stand, but fell back. And a shadow came over her, and she was defenceless…..defenceless, as shadow after shadow took their turn at her. She was sore. When they were done, and gone, her eyes opened. The atmosphere was still. So still, she could hear the silence from light years away. The field of white flowers now looked like one endless sheet of white. Then from very high up in the sky, she saw a thin rainbow form. It was so distant, yet so distinct. Then it seemed bigger…..and bigger…..

It was coming down. Oh God, rainbows don't come down! Panic gripped her. But the lower it came, the more gorgeous it seemed, and the calmer she became. Till it stopped just above her, and she got onto it and started walking. She walked away from the old world, from herself, up to the unknown. And she went up, and up, and up, **unendingly.**

BOB G. KISIKI

January 2001,

MUKONO.

ABOUT THE AUTHOR

Bob G. Kisiki

Bob G. Kisiki is a Senior Sub-Editor with Sunday Vision, a member of Uganda's premier media house, The Vision Group, where he has worked since 2004. He has taught Literature in English and English Language, both at high school and at Makerere University in Kampala, Uganda.
Kisiki is married to Susan, and they have three children.
He has also authored The Kind Gang (Fountain Publishers), a novel for young adults, poetry in Echoes Across the Valley (EAEP, Nairobi) and short stories in various anthologies and journals.

.